MR. CROOK LIFTS THE MASK

MR. CROOK
LIFTS THE MASK

by Anthony Gilbert

Random House: New York

MR. CROOK LIFTS THE MASK

1

The weather that Thursday night was as temperamental as a prima donna. At one instant the moon shone brilliantly, painting houses and trees with a silver brush; the next, it vanished behind a cloud and the passers-by on the far-distant earth were obscured in shadow. There was no wind, but the forecast said rain to come.

May Forbes, forty-nine, unwed and envying no one, came down the sixty-two steps of her apartment, a small carefully covered basket in her hand, two sixpences concealed in her fabric glove. She turned away from the town and headed in the direction of a wild piece of land known as Broomstick Common. Rumor said there had once been a coven of witches there, and though no one had ever set eyes on a witch, they'd undoubtedly left their cats behind. Cats of every sort and color, wild as young tigers, thin as the proverbial rails. May might have paraphrased Captain Cuttle—cats are my passion. She would dearly have liked to keep a cat herself, but those sixty-two stairs, no balcony, a bed-sitter with a cooking stove on the landing and all sanitary facilities shared with the tenants on the floor below made that impossible. For one thing, it wouldn't be hygienic, even with a cat-tray, and for another—and this was the argument that weighed with her—it wouldn't be fair to the cat.

May worked at Robinson's Drapery Store in Wells Street. Ten years hence, when she was approaching pension age, she'd find a corner in the country with a patch of garden, and then she could really keep a cat.

Until then, life was full of interest.

Across the street old Mrs. Politi, the immensely fat, self-styled widow of a Soho restaurateur, pulled back her curtain to watch her go. When Signor Politi disappeared after the war—the ribald said she'd overlaid him, poor fellow, and put him out with the rest of the trash for the dust collectors—and the Council slapped a compulsory purchase order on the premises, Mrs. Politi took over an old ragshop and filled it with crockery and glass that she picked up from sales, bazaars and street markets. The shop was really like a huge cave with a little counter at one end and some shelves against the wall, but all the cheap stuff was grouped on the floor.

May had met her when she bought a pile of cracked saucers at a penny apiece.

"For my cats," she explained.

"You have cats—here?"

"On the Common. They live quite wild there and of course no one feeds them. I suppose sometimes they pick up things from the rubbish tip, because it's astonishing what people will throw out, but they're more than half starved."

"So you feed them?" Mrs. Politi didn't attempt to hide her scorn. "You think they grateful?"

"I don't expect them to be grateful," retorted May. "And if you think they're fierce, just ask yourself what kind of an example the human race has been showing them for the past thirty years."

"So now cats eat off plates like Christians," Mrs. Politi jeered.

May was too polite to ask who else would be likely to eat off cracked and chipped china. It amazed her to think there was a market for such flotsam and jetsam; half the goods were labeled Cracked or Damaged, even the simpering china shepherdesses were minus their hands, and the great funereal urns looked as if some giant had bitten pieces out of the rim.

Mrs. Politi followed her line of thought. "Nothing you can't sell if it's cheap enough," she declared. "Like those women pay a pound for a hat started at six pounds, they don't stop to ask when can they wear such a hat, it is a bargain. So, they see a nice bowl—real class—ten shillings. They don't stop to ask what use to them. A bargain, see?"

"I suppose there are a lot of fools going about," May conceded.

"You one of them," Mrs. Politi retorted. "Toil and moil for those old maids when any of the big shops in the High Street pay you half as much again."

"I'm an old maid myself," said May. "And I couldn't bear to work at one of the big shops, all branches of something bigger still, no—no individuality. With the Misses Robinsons . . ." She paused.

"You someone? Ho, yes. Someone to be trampled on, taken advantage of."

"Miss Alice and Miss Phyllis don't trample. It's like— it's almost like having a family of my own. I haven't anyone, you know, except a niece married in America, and she only sends a card at Christmas. I don't suppose she tells anyone her aunt works in a shop."

"And when the shop close down?" Mrs. Politi had asked that question only tonight, when May looked in on her way back from work in case there were any scraps to go in her cat basket. A frugally run household of one didn't leave much over, though Miss Phyllis was very good about giving her bits now and again, anything her precious pigeons wouldn't eat. And every evening she stopped at Mr. Liverseed, the fishmonger, to exchange a few coppers for bones and fish heads and sometimes fish even he wouldn't dare try to sell.

"All this fuss about a lot of blasted cats!" said Mr. Liverseed reprovingly. "And half the people in the world not having enough to eat."

"You convince me that these scraps will go to Biafra if my pussies don't get them," retorted May, spiritedly, "and of course I'll waive their claim. But you and I both know they won't. They go into the offal bucket . . ."

5

It was no wonder she was an old maid, thought Mr. Liverseed, sourly. No man likes a woman who knows all the answers. But since he liked his coppers as much as Mrs. Politi did, he wrapped up the rather smelly parcel and took his payment.

It was after calling at his shop that May rang Mrs. Politi's bell. Tonight Mrs. Politi surprised her by giving her a quite sizable piece of rabbit. True, the rabbit was a bit "high," but cats who live on commons and haunt rubbish tips can't be choosers, and even human beings sometimes liked their food, game for instance, in a state that May, down to earth as always, frankly considered rotten.

Mrs. Politi asked after Miss Alice, the older of the two sisters, who had recently had a stroke.

"She's getting along quite well," declared May, undaunted. "It was only a little stroke."

"One little stroke followed by one bigger stroke," said Mrs. Politi. (When Arthur Crook met her a little later on, he said, "There's one won't give even the Angel Gabriel best, and if he knows his onions he won't waste time trying." But at that stage May had never heard of Mr. Crook, and if anyone had told her she was going to meet him that very night, she would hardly have believed him.)

"She doesn't step out quite the way she did," May began, and Mrs. Politi said, "That one don't step no further than her coffin one fine day and that soon."

"Miss Phyllis and I manage quite well." May refused to admit that trade was on the decrease; they were still covering expenses, and it's natural for tides to ebb and flow. "And her nephew . . ."

"That nephew!" Mrs. Politi nodded sagely. "He never come in twenty years, why he come now?"

"Because Miss Phyllis wrote and told him about her sister. And he hadn't visited here for twenty years and more because his work's in Canada. She said she'd never have known him. But he's been awfully good, helping with the accounts, he's even taken Miss Alice out for a few rides, which is a great treat for her. She's always enjoyed her little walks . . ."

Mrs. Politi threw up her hands. "Oh, May, you too simple to live. Young men don't come half over the world because an old lady they wouldn't recognize have a stroke. You think him an eagle, soaring" (she rolled her *r*'s in a way that aroused May's admiration) "in the blue, so close to heaven. I tell you, he a vulture. One day soon you find the boards up and you out of work."

"Then Miss Phyllis and I will have to set up a little stall on the pavement, won't we?" said May. "Or we might get a corner in the market."

Mrs. Politi would have shrugged her shoulders if her neck hadn't been so short her head was sunk between them.

"You go to your cats!" she cried. "They fit company for you. And when they tear you limb from limb, maybe you remember what I say."

May bustled off, a little cottage-loaf of a woman, rosy as an apple—must have been pretty as a girl, Mrs. Politi thought.

May had calmly accepted a difficult not to say curmudgeonly male parent as her duty and thought how fortunate she was to have her own home. And after he died and left her with nothing she had fallen on her feet once more and got this job with the Misses Robinson. Like a new home, and in a small shop you soon got acquainted with the regulars. And then she'd always been clever with her hands; she did repairs, lining, lengthening and shortening skirts, according to the fashion, replacing zippers, taking in coats when their owners shrank with the years and, where possible, letting them out when the reverse process happened. A full, pleasant life, with Wednesday half-day closing. On Wednesdays she and Mrs. Politi generally went to the local cinema, and afterwards to the Pilgrim's Progress for a drink and so to a trattoria where Mrs. P. talked to the proprietor in his native tongue, and they got special service. Saturday was choir practice for the chapel, and Sunday nights, of course, it was chapel itself. But the other four evenings she trotted along to the Common, bringing whatever she'd been able to salvage for her beloved cats.

She stopped at the top of the main road to get the

carton of milk—she always brought two sixpences in case the first proved to be a rejected coin, or the machine was out of order and took the money but didn't yield the milk, then she crossed the main street, walked down beyond the library, the chemist, the tobacconist, crossed another road and it was like finding yourself in a different world. For some years now local councillors had been suggesting the site should be drained and used for building, to be opposed by other councillors who pointed out that such a course would involve considerable expense, that there was no other place to dispose of moribund cars and, most of all, that the far end of the site overlooked the canal, which was as neglected as the rest of it. Even lovers and tramps didn't come here much, it was too uncomfortable. The dumped cars had been stripped of everything usable, and no one cared about them any more except some of the local children and they were never in evidence after dark. Even romantic May didn't pretend she could recognize individual cats. Mostly they were streaks of darkness flying from shadow to shadow. "Probably they rats eat your food," Mrs. Politi had suggested, but May said she'd never seen any rats there. Of course, there might be water rats in the canal, but they were rather pretty things, with blunt noses and rounded furry ears. "You!" cried her friend once, stung to annoyance. "You argue with the Lord God Himself and you see where that get you."

But one cat in particular she had come to know, a little white creature, light as a snowflake and so small she seemed scarcely larger than a kitten, yet this same cat had recently littered and there were five little bunches of fur who would one day, if they were enabled to grow up, join the population on the Common. May was certain that that thin form couldn't possibly provide adequate sustenance for the family, and she had started to bring an extra allowance of milk for the mother, and put down twice as much fish and meat as before. She came very carefully through the bushes, slipped out and set her saucers and vanished again like a shadow. The moon that had hitherto been very bright now moved languidly behind a cloud, but she thought that all to the good. She knew no wild cat would emerge so long as she was in sight, and for her own

8

comfort she must be assured that the provender did go to the little white cat, and not to some fabulous monster envisaged by Mrs. Politi. Scarcely daring to breathe, she waited. And sure enough, after a minute or two one slender white paw appeared as the little cat fastidiously made her way toward the milk. How gracefully animals move, May reflected. Perhaps it's having four legs all more or less the same length. The cat ate some of the meat, then carefully collected what was left and retreated with it to her lair.

May backed cautiously away and around the edge of the rubbish tip. It was the source of one of Mrs. Politi's grimmer jokes. Come the Last Trump, it won't be just the sea that gives up its dead, she prophesied. The tips will give some big shocks, too. May tried to forget that as she scurried past, depositing her saucers in accustomed places, but tonight she had, as Crook would have put it, her eyes on sticks looking for a particular cat seen only twice previously, but instantly winning her heart. His appearance—she took for granted it was a male—was undeniably striking. He was black with patches of deep amber. She had gone to the public library the following day to consult a book on cats and decided he was a Burmese with just a touch of the tar brush, which, of course, set him beyond the pale. All the same, his smallness and solitariness haunted her. He might be hunted away by the resident cats or even, if Mrs. Politi was right, be attacked by a rat. Looking for him by the light of the tiny torch she always carried, she progressed further into the wasteland than she had hitherto done, and was reluctantly about to abandon the search when suddenly, coinciding with the return of the moon, he shot out from a clump of plant known to botanists as Fat Hen and went charging toward the canal.

Fencing this canal from the Common was a paling marked in large insolent words: KEEP OUT THIS MEANS YOU. Rumor said there was an unexploded bomb on the towpath, others that the paling was simply to prevent a large mortality rate among the children who played there. May saw the little cat streak into the bushes, then emerge and vanish through a weak place in the paling. Her first thought was, He probably doesn't know there's a canal there, he could fall in, probably he can't swim, even if he could, he might be attacked by water rats for trespass. While these crazy thoughts blew like cobwebs through her brain, she was herself hurrying along the side of the paling, looking for a weak spot. It was asking too much of human nature to expect the children wouldn't have broken through somewhere, and sure enough, there was a place where the fencing was so dilapidated that even her plump form could squeeze through.

The canal looked sinister and deserted in the fading light. It saddened May, who remembered that once canals were part of the life line of England, loud with traffic and gay with flags. This canal was more like a graveyard, with nettles growing along the edge. May imagined all kinds of rubbish being dumped there, possibly even dead animals. She shivered and turned back toward the gap. It was hopeless to try and catch the kitten. She would put down the saucer and hope it would find it on its return.

She had just squeezed cautiously through the paling when she heard a sound that brought her to an abrupt halt. Someone or something was coming through the wasteland from the direction of the road. She was so accustomed to the notion that no one but herself used this place after dark that she was instantly apprehensive. All of Mrs. Politi's warnings rushed through her mind. "One of these dark nights, May, you wake and find your throat cut and no one more surprised than you" was a familiar one.

The newcomer clearly was not on foot. It was a car that was nosing its way over the rough ground, bumping from one uneven surface to another. At first she thought it was some owner come to discard a useless model, but a moment later she knew that wasn't so. No driver herself, she yet could tell that this was no wreck approaching her direction in the darkness. Fortunately, there was a good deal of wild growth and bushes where she stood, and she concealed herself, crouching down, in the hope that she would escape notice.

Why should anyone come here on such a night, if it wasn't to discard an aged car? Besides, the site for old cars was some distance away. She knew, of course, that various amorous activities took place in the backs of cars, though it had always seemed to her a most uncomfortable arrangement, but again— why come so far when there was virtually no likelihood of interruption much nearer the road? There was, of course, the possibility that the car's owner had brought rubbish to dispose of in the tip, but her earlier objections held here, too. Nobody bringing something bulky would want to carry it so far when the tip was readily available further along the upper road.

While she thought all this, her heart racing and pounding, the car came to a standstill a little distance away. The door opened and someone alighted. She dared not put on her little torch for fear of revealing her whereabouts, and common sense told her that no man with honest intentions would be skulking down here at such a time. She found that by parting some of the twigs of her concealing bush she could just make out a shape, a man undoubtedly. She saw him walk around the side of the car and open the boot. Perhaps, she thought in her romantic way, he is a bank robber. Banks were being robbed nearly every day and surely the spoils must be concealed somewhere. She believed that a large part of the train robbery notes were still hidden in some place whose whereabouts the police had not been able to uncover. Or if not banknotes, then jewelry, or rather massive silverware, even crates of furs. It was improbable the police would think of looking here and the children who played on the site didn't come to this part, they frolicked over the skeleton cars and ventured, illegally, through the palings and along the canal bank.

May was of a law-abiding temperament, she knew it was every citizen's duty to assist the police in every possible way. All the same, like most people, she had an illogical disinclination to tangle with them, even on the right side of the law, if it could be avoided. She wondered if, while X. was digging a pit to conceal his treasure, she could edge out unheard and unperceived.

While she was still considering these possibilities, the unknown had extracted a spade from the boot and had turned on the headlights. It was fortunate for her that she was outside their aura. The ground under these shrubs and stunted trees was sandy, which she supposed was why this place had been chosen.

Very cautiously she moved a few steps. These brought her close to the rear of the car, so that she caught a glimpse of the contents of the boot. Something large, ungainly and rolled in a rug had been thrust therein. Her heart almost stopped beating, then began again with such violence it seemed to her it must be audible through the length and breadth of the Common. Because surely if you were hiding stolen treasure you would wrap it in a mackintosh sheet (to preserve it from damage from damp). A rug suggested hideous possibilities.

She moved away more quickly, and her speed was her undoing. She liked to say of herself that she had been born under a lucky star, but now her luck deserted her. Her foot caught in a trailing bramble, she slipped, the torch fell from her hand, and as it did so its minute beam streamed out—like a fallen shooting star, she reflected, scrabbling quickly, finding it and pressing the button so that once more darkness reigned. But it was too much even for an optimist to hope that it had not been noticed. The sound of the spade delving and flinging the sandy earth came to a dead stop.

"Who's there?" called a voice.

She lay still as death—an unfortunate comparison, really. The man moved a step or so in her direction.

"Who are you?" the voice demanded.

May remembered a favorite saying of her tiresome platitudinous old Dad. *"L'audace, l'audace et toujours l'audace."* Which, translated into English, meant roughly, "Grasp your nettle boldly and then you'll rarely find it stings." May thought that might be true but she had never made the experiment. Arthur Crook's more down to earth version was: Be bloody, bold and resolute. May could dispense with the blood, but boldness and resolution were clearly called for here. She straightened herself, pushed aside the undergrowth and said, "Oh, have you seen a little cat, a Burmese, at least mostly a Burmese? It came this way and I'm so afraid it may be lost.

But I don't suppose you have seen it, have you? It's so young and all these wild cats about, and then the canal . . ."

She caught a fleeting glimpse of the man. He wore a black mask, resembling those worn in harlequinades in her far, far distant youth, and over that one of those woolen contraptions known as a balaclava helmet.

"You mean you're here on account of a blasted cat?" The man's voice, which had a muffled quality, was incredulous.

"I didn't mean to come so far," acknowledged May, boldly standing her ground. "But it ran off; I think it must have got frightened. There are some wild cats here . . ." Just in time she bit off a reference to the mother and her brood, thinking this might be just the kind of man who'd think it fun to stamp on the heads of a family of newborn kits. "Well, if you haven't got a garden it's dull for any animal, kept indoors most of the day." ("The situation provides the man" had been another of her father's platitudes, and how right dear Father was, as always, May reflected.) "So whenever it's fine we come down here, it's the nearest open space and usually I don't let him out of my sight. But he ran off suddenly and squeezed through the palings, and I don't like the idea of him so near the canal, cats can't swim, you know. And the fact is," she wound up breathlessly, "I've rather lost my way. We've never come this far before."

"What way's that?" the man asked.

"Do you know St. Leonard's Road?" It was more than a mile from her own flat, but it isn't only the lady lapwing that can practice deception in the interests of its young.

"You've come a long way," said the man suspiciously.

"The worst of it is you can't put a cat—a kitten really —on a lead as you can a dog. Of course, they say they're wonderful at finding their way back—cats, I mean." (Oh Father, help me, she prayed, and she wasn't addressing her Heavenly Father at that.)

"If I do see him," said the man slowly, "I might bring him back for you. What's your number in St. Leonard's Road."

"Oh, you'd never be able to catch him," said May quickly. "He's very timid, half wild really."

"You're not supposed to go through those palings," the man said.

There was a thoughtful, even a leisurely note in his voice that froze her blood. (Like Arthur Crook, she found clichés very satisfying.) He seemed to be considering what was the best thing to do with her.

"Naturally I know that," she said quickly, answering his rebuke. "But you can't expect Tom Jones—that's my kitten—to realize that. And he's so young . . ."

"You take my tip," said the man, "you go back to St. Leonard's Road, toot sweet. If the authorities knew you'd been trespassing you could find yourself in a lot of trouble."

"I'm sure you're right," she acknowledged meekly. "I'm sure it's going to pelt and I haven't brought an umbrella."

"What's your name, in case the kitten does surface?" the man demanded.

She made herself sound surprised. "Miss Jones, of course. That's why he's Tom Jones. I live at number four. Mind you, I have to be very discreet. My landlady doesn't really allow animals, but with him being so small, and I'm very careful he doesn't harm the furniture or carpets . . ." (If Father had heard her prayer, he was playing up like a trump.) "I can't understand that, can you? Not liking animals, I mean, when so often they're nicer than human beings."

"The proper place for animals is a zoo," said the man roughly. "Now then, missus, you get off home . . ."

"It's Miss Jones," she corrected him. "Oh dear, this is the strangest conversation I've ever held. It's like talking to a ghost. I can't even see you. I suppose if I keep going I shall eventually come to the road, and of course from there I know my way."

"Luckier than some of us you do," the man said. He suddenly switched on his torch, keeping the light low, and she stumbled away, hardly able to believe her good fortune. To-morrow would be time enough to wonder if she should say anything to the police. But I don't even know where the place is, she reminded herself. And there was a text in the Bible, "Sufficient unto the day is the evil thereof."

It had been, on the whole, the sort of day you wouldn't want to live through again. It wasn't only this last terrifying encounter. Although she had stood up so bravely to Mrs. Politi, she had known her first real stab of fear long before she set out for the Common. That morning young Mr. Hardy—he was the old ladies' nephew, son of the only Robinson sister who had married—had approached her, while Miss Phyllis was searching for a particular kind of vest in the little stock room, to say, "I'm glad to have a chance of a word with you, Miss Forbes. It's my Aunt Alice, I'm very much concerned about her."

She had looked surprised. "You don't have to worry, Mr. Hardy. Miss Phyllis and I . . ."

"That's not quite what I meant. But it must be obvious to you both that she isn't going to be able to carry on here much longer, and when she breaks down—I'm sorry to seem brutal but it's best to be plain—she's going to be a whole-time job for someone. And that someone will be my Aunt Phyllis. So—what's going to happen to the shop? You couldn't carry on single-handed, you know, even if there wasn't an economic factor."

"I believe in crossing bridges when you come to them," May had said.

"I've had a word with my aunt's doctor, and in his opinion she should give up work immediately, and husband her strength."

"Then she'd better change her doctor," was May's spirited reply. It was fantastic as well as impertinent, twenty years of virtual silence and then this sudden appearance and attempt to change all their lives overnight. "What value will Miss Alice's life have if she can't work? It seems to me you need training for being idle just as much as for a profession. And being alive means more than just not being dead."

"So you'd have her run herself into the ground," the young man said.

"It's where we shall all end," May pointed out.

And he groaned. "You're as bad as my mother. She never sat if she could stand, and she never walked if she could run. You've missed your vocation, I used to tell her. You should have been a marathon contestant, probably got a gold medal."

May didn't think this was quite the way to talk of your dead mother, but she passed it over. "I think at her age Miss Alice should be allowed to choose what she wants. Retirement may be all right for rich, healthy people, who can travel and play golf, or whatever it is rich retired people do to ameliorate their boredom, but my father's doctor used to say that more men broke up during the first five years of retirement than at any other age. Miss Alice wouldn't thank you for tying her into a chair and putting it in the window and telling her to watch the world go by. She's been a part of that world too long."

"There's your own future to consider," young Mr. Hardy argued.

"If they gave up the shop, what would they live on?" May demanded intelligently.

"If they strike while the iron's hot they'd get a good price for the site. If they invested that, with Aunt Alice due for her pension while Aunt Phyllis will be in a couple of years, they'd have enough to live on in some quiet hotel or boarding house."

"They may not like the idea of living in a boarding house after they've had their own home for so long." They lived very cozily in rooms above the shop, and despite her stroke Miss Alice could still manage the stairs, if she took them slowly. Being a shop, there were what house agents call sanitary facilities on the same floor behind the stockroom, so she only had to do the stairs once a day.

"They'd get used to it," said the young man.

"I daresay you can get used to a coffin," May agreed. "But that doesn't mean you want to settle down in one until you must."

"I was talking to a chap in the Golden Fleece last night," Mr. Hardy went on. "He tells me the Council is proba-

bly going to requisition that site and the sites of a number of
other shops around it for their building program."

"They can't do that," exclaimed May. "It's people's
living."

"They'd make just the same reply if you asked them.
And the place is spreading rapidly. You'll find it won't be possible to meet increased rates and rising costs of living out of a
few pairs of stockings and papers of pins. The fact is people
nowadays don't want to go to the village shop, they like the
big stores where there's more choice and you find all the
novelties. You must face facts, Miss Forbes. My aunts' contemporaries are a dying race . . ."

"We're all a dying race," declared May.

"But some of us die sooner than others. Oh, don't mis-
understand me, I know you have their interests at heart, but I
feel some responsibility for them, too. I can't stay over here
much longer, I've got my own interests in Canada, and I'd like
to know their future was assured. If they wait till they get a
compulsory purchase order the price will drop considerably.
They'd do much better for themselves to bow out gracefully
now. And from what they say about you," he added more
kindly, "I'm sure you'd have no difficulty getting employment."

"I shall be all right," May assured him. "The Lord
looks after his own."

"Plenty of people have said that, and look where they
are now. I had hoped you'd support me when I put the project
to my Aunt Phyllis . . ."

"You're talking as if Miss Alice was a moron. She's as
sharp as ever. It's not that I don't appreciate what you're
trying to do," she had added more graciously, "but change is
difficult when you get older."

But though she had defended the sisters both to this
young man and to Mrs. Politi, she knew there was good sense
in his arguments. She also had heard rumors of the Council's
plans but she had chosen to discount them. But supposing they
were genuine . . . Maybe I should urge them to take the best
possible price, May reflected. It would be a blow to her, of

course. It wasn't that she doubted her ability to earn a living—if the worse came to the worst you could always take a pail and brush and go around charging goodness knows how much an hour doing the jobs more delicate-minded people didn't want to do for themselves. And she liked doing housework. But that rather dark, rather cluttered shop had become a second home to her.

Am I letting myself be prejudiced in my own interest? she wondered.

So concerned had she been as she stumbled along, turning over these facts in her mind, that she found she had reached the main road before she expected. Her knowledge of the neighborhood where she had lived for so many years was limited to a mile or so from her home, and this part of the road was completely strange to her. She looked hopefully for a bus stop but there was none in sight. She had taken so many turns and twists, avoiding bad places, declivities and solid obstacles of shrubs, that the bump of locality, never very large, now betrayed her completely, and she set off resolutely in the wrong direction.

The road seemed very quiet; no one was about. The moon seemed to have decided to pack up for the night an ominous wind had arisen, bringing with it the promise of rain. When she had walked a little further she found a bus stop, but it was only a Request sign carrying no timetable, so she couldn't tell when the next bus was due. At this hour of the evening they probably only ran at long intervals. There was no one waiting, which seemed to indicate no bus could be expected at present, and while she hesitated, the first lances of rain began to fall. She decided her best plan would be to walk to a compulsory bus stop, where she might find both a timetable and a shelter.

She had gone a short distance when the night's unnatural quiet was broken by the sound of a car in the distance, traveling in the direction whence she had come. Perhaps, she thought hopefully, I could thumb a lift, and she had actually slowed her footsteps when second and wiser thoughts prevailed. In the films she and Mrs. Politi preferred, the heroine was constantly accosting strangers in cars, with deplorable results, but no one, simply no one, could have designs on a woman of nearly fifty who wasn't even carrying a handbag.

And I certainly don't have any state secrets on microfilm, she reminded herself.

And then the terrifying thought assailed her—she wondered it hadn't presented itself immediately—that if she didn't have state secrets, she had a certain piece of knowledge that could be dangerous if not actually fatal to the unknown man. She, and presumably only she, knew about the mysterious car on the Common. She had privately congratulated herself on the skill with which she had extricated herself from a very awkward situation (and that was putting it mildly). But suppose X. had deliberately let her get away because he had a job to accomplish and didn't want any witnesses, and now, the job done, he intended to wipe out the only person who could testify to his presence—the thoughts whirled through her head like snowflakes. The newspapers were full of accounts of road accidents, many of which involved hit-and-run drivers. The road ahead seemed empty, nobody who didn't have to be out would be abroad on such a night; a big car would make nothing of bowling over a solitary pedestrian and dashing on.

He doesn't know my name, I don't know his, she reflected feverishly, moving at a pace of which she hadn't believed herself capable. Don't they say the most successful murders are those where there's no obvious tie-up?

She wasn't carrying anything that might identify her, so that even after she was found, it might be quite some time before anybody could put a name to her. She felt her breath coming quick and fast; soon she'd have to stop. If there'd been a ditch she might have lain down in that, but there was none, not even a tree. Not that she could have climbed a tree, true, but surely if you hid behind one the driver might think twice before smashing himself up. She turned on shaking legs around a corner to find herself face to face with a gaily lighted public house called the Mettlesome Horse, with a swinging inn-sign of a horse prancing on its hind legs, though what that had to do with beer and spirits she couldn't imagine. Without pausing for further reflection, she rushed at the swinging door and pushed it open.

Mr. Forbes had been a teetotaler—"Wine is a mocker, strong drink is raging," he would declaim from nonconformist pulpits—and May had never entered a public house until after his death and then only in the company of stronger characters, like Mrs. Politi, in whose shadow she thankfully concealed herself.

There seemed to be a good many cars standing in the inn's forecourt—a large dark one, a low blue number, an aged but dignified yellow Rolls (it was one of the few makes of car she could recognize, only a duke or a pop star would dare drive anything so conspicuous) and the usual gaggle of minis and small cars with 1000 and 1100 scrawled on the boot. Obviously quite a popular place, she reflected, and one where a woman on her own should be able to hide for a short time. Another cliché popped into her mind—there's safety in numbers. All she had to do was wait here, if necessary till closing time, though one hoped it wouldn't come to that, and then spill out with all the rest. There were bound to be a few people going home by bus, particularly in these days of breathalizers, and of these a proportion would be going in the same direction.

But no sooner was she inside than she began to wish herself back in the anonymous dark. For some inexplicable reason she felt as conspicuous as if she were wearing no clothes. The bar was pretty full. All the seats at the counter were occupied and so far as she could see, all the tables. There wasn't a single other woman by herself; there weren't even any female doubles. All the women present were with husbands or what were nowadays called boy friends, and they came every conceivable shape and size.

Out of the crowd a voice said, not violently but very definitely, "For Pete's sake, shut the bleeding door." She hadn't realized she was still holding it open, but she dropped it like a hot brick. The diversion had caused several people to look in her direction who wouldn't otherwise have noticed her. She tried to appear calm, searching the crowd with her gaze as if she expected to recognize someone, but naturally she didn't. She saw one woman lean over to her husband and murmur something with a knowledgeable grin, and she felt the blood pouring into her cheeks. Just when she felt ready to drop dead with embarrassment, she noticed a small table in a darkish corner that no one seemed to want, and she made for it, as though it were the Rock of Ages sticking up out of a boiling sea.

She had abandoned her notion of staying here, unnoticed, until she could leave in a crowd. She'd just wait a little to get her bearings. If she was right and the driver of the car was after her blood, he'd come in, and he'd be bound to order something to drink, and while it was being brought she could make herself scarce. Her ears were strained for the sound of wheels, and after a minute she heard a car draw up, a door slammed and the pub door opened. A man and a girl came in together. They were quite young and she knew at once had nothing to do with the mystery man from the Common. For one thing he was much too short. The two threaded their way over to the bar; the man hadn't even looked around the room. She drew a deep breath. Another five minutes, she thought, and then she'd make her bid for escape . . .

She was aware of someone standing beside her table and she looked up to see a young man with more hair on his face than a Dandie Dinmont and wearing a dubious white coat.

"Want to order?" he asked insolently.

She stiffened her spine. "I'm—waiting for someone," she explained. Well, so she was, waiting for the driver of the bus.

"P'raps he's got held up," suggested the young man in the same tone. "Better have something to while away the time."

"I'd prefer to wait," said May.

"This isn't a railway station," the youth pointed out. "We only provide seats for patrons."

"I'll wait another five minutes," May said firmly. "The truth is, I'm feeling a little faint."

The young man breathed exasperation. "It's not a hospital either. That's about a mile up the road. If you ring them they might send an ambulance. Or there's a hire car firm . . . phone's on the stairs." He nodded his hairy head in its direction.

"I shall be quite all right if I can wait a few minutes," May insisted. Oh, go away, go away and leave me in peace, screamed her heart, but they couldn't have been on the same wave length because the young man didn't seem to hear a thing.

"If you're feeling faint you should take a drop of brandy."

For the first time since her entry she realized that her sole capital was the spare sixpence she had brought for an emergency in case the milk-vending machine let her down. You couldn't even get a cup of coffee with that. Come to think of it, it very likely wasn't enough to get her home, now that all the fares had been raised.

"I don't care for brandy."

Oh, help me, help me, she prayed, though this time she couldn't have told you whom she was addressing. Certainly not Father, who would have turned in his grave, if there'd been enough left of him for any action so energetic, to think of his daughter sitting on her lonesome in a public house. But someone must have heard, because her desperate prayer was answered immediately in the most unexpected fashion.

2

Mr. Arthur Crook, a legal beagle from London—or, as he liked to call it, the Smoke—and owner of the yellow car that had attracted May's attention, had been sitting at the bar for some time, reflecting that if he were Prime Minister he'd make it a capital offense to serve hogwash under the glorious name of beer. He noticed May the instant she entered, and his heart had warmed to her on sight. Just my cup of tea, he thought. These no-longer-young biddies, looking as though butter wouldn't melt in their mouths, had, in the past, furnished him with some of his most satisfying cases. He saw at a glance that she was frightened to death, and not only by the company in which she now found herself, though he wouldn't have blamed her if that had been the sole reason. A rumty-too lot he called them, in his sturdy Edwardian way. The voice of the young barman, that he didn't attempt to lower—playing for laughs, thought the outraged Mr. Crook, I'll soon have him laughing on the wrong side of his face—swept through the bar. Mr. Crook set down his glass and marched across the room.

"Well, fancy seeing you here, Rosie," he said, dumping himself in the spare chair. "A bit off your normal beat, aren't you?"

The young man sniggered.

"And you can wipe that smile off what you call a face," Mr. Crook went on, raising his voice slightly, "unless you want to find yourself plastered against the wall like a blowfly." He turned to May. "What'll it be, Rosie?"

"Lady doesn't like brandy," the young man said and smirked.

"Then you shouldn't be trying to sell it to her. On paper at least, this is still a free country." About half the people in the bar were looking at them now. Not that Mr. Crook minded; he was more surprised when they didn't stare. "O.K., Sugar, you leave it to me," he added blithely.

He gave an order that May couldn't comprehend. When she went out with Mrs. Politi she generally had a glass of sweet sherry or on occasion a small port.

"And I'll have a double Scotch," Mr. Crook continued. "And any water that's needed I'll add myself."

"You can't talk to me like that, chum," said the young man, suddenly recovering his spirit.

"You must have got cloth ears," was Mr. Crook's imperturbable if discourteous retort. "Didn't you hear me say just now it's a free country? And we'd like those drinks before the bar closes."

The young man hesitated, then decided that discretion was the better part of valor and beetled off in the direction of the bar.

"Sometimes I think we've jumped into 1984 when the pig is king," Mr. Crook continued affably to his companion. "Though why we should insult the pigs I couldn't tell you. Had shock, have you, Sugar? Well, that shows you ain't dead yet, and that's more than can be said for some of the folk I've met hereabouts."

May looked at him, wholly fascinated. It wasn't simply gratitude that he'd got her out of a nasty situation, it didn't even occur to her it might be a case of jumping out of the frying pan into the fire, she didn't think that angels come in strange disguises—another of dear father's clichés—she was simply fascinated, there was no other word for it. If he'd been Sir Lancelot and St. George for Merrie England rolled into one, she couldn't have been more enchanted. And yet all she saw was a round brown barrel of a man with popping bright eyes and red hair and brows that wouldn't have shamed a fox.

"I'm very grateful," she panted. "The fact is—I'd forgotten I hadn't any money except my bus fare—and I lost the road . . ."

"I'd be glad to lose practically any road I've been on in these parts," agreed Mr. Crook buoyantly. "You should have called the boss. No innkeeper wants trouble in his bar, he's got his license to consider. Must be hard up for help if that's the best he can muster, but maybe it's his brother's son and . . . Well, well, look who's here."

The landlord himself brought the drinks. "I'm sorry about that, Mr. Crook," he said, and May wasn't the only person present who was startled to realize her companion had been recognized. "My lad didn't understand the lady was with you."

"All this free education," grumbled Mr. Crook, putting some coins on the extended tray, "and that's all there is to show for it. Where did we meet?" Crook added affably, "it's not often I forget a face."

"Well, one of my patrons recognized your car, Mr. Crook. Quite a landmark, I understand."

"At this rate," suggested Mr. Crook agreeably, "I'll find myself getting buried—no, interred, you don't get buried in abbeys, do you?—in Westminster Abbey, and then there'll be a rattling of bones to wake the dead."

The landlord grinned and went away. May was watching with an admiration that bordered on soppiness. And this is happening to me, she thought, forgetting for the moment the other things that had happened that evening that were responsible for her being here at all.

"See how it is, Rosie," said Mr. Crook. "More people know Tom Fool than Tom Fool knows. You can drink that stuff with confidence," he added. "It'll be what they serve to the family, not the swill they consider's good enough for customers."

"I don't know what came over me," May confessed.

"Only—there was no sign of a bus, and there was this car . . ."

"Like I said, you've had a shock." He felt in his pocket and produced an oversized business card. "Do as a marker for your prayer book if you don't need it for any other purpose," he offered encouragingly. "Who was that chap who was always waiting for someone or something to turn up?"

"Mr. Micawber," said May. "And my name's Forbes, May Forbes." She looked at the card he'd given her. It said *Arthur G. Crook* and bore two addresses and *Your Trouble, Our Business. And We Never Close.* It didn't occur to her at the moment that he might be a lawyer, she put him down as a music-hall comedian, a busker, or perhaps someone who went out to entertain parties, though there was no mention of conjuring on the card.

"Angels come in strange disguises— What's the matter?"

"My father used to say that."

"In my case, it was my Mum. And, of course, the converse is equally true. According to her, my Dad looked like Sir Galahad and your own particular guardian angel rolled into one, but if ever there was a case of appearances being deceptive . . ." He shook his big red head. "I've been wondering all evening what in tarnation I was doing in this dump, and now I know. You're my answer to prayer."

"I was just thinking the same about you," said May.

"What was it?" Crook inquired curiously. "You came in as though all the bears in the Himalayas were after you."

May picked up her glass. "What is this?"

"Called black velvet," said Crook. "Good for the nerves."

"What a lovely name for a drink! I do feel such a fool," she confided. "I think I just panicked. I was feeding the cats on the Common and—usually there's no one there, but tonight there was this man . . ."

"Which man?"

"The one who frightened me."

Suddenly she felt more foolish than before. One was constantly hearing of middle-aged spinsters suspecting quite innocent strangers of raping intentions or some sadistic treatment; the local paper had had just such a case only a week or two before, and it had turned out to be a case of sex frustration. Apparently the poor creature had secretly wanted to be raped, at least that was what the doctors said. She had a vision of herself in court, faced by a contemptuous jury who would doubtless write her off as a hysteric, if they didn't use even more direct language. And probably it was a dog, she decided, the idea having just come to her. A big dog. If people don't have gardens and the dog doesn't actually die at the vet's, it's a problem to know what to do with the body. You can't treat it just as rubbish, not someone who's been your friend. She couldn't imagine why she hadn't thought of that before. It didn't precisely explain the mask and the balaclava, but she was a slow-witted creature, she reminded herself, the right explanation for that would probably strike her when she was going to bed or even making her early morning cup of tea. She felt she'd made herself quite ridiculous enough for one evening.

"It was so unexpected," she added quickly. "I didn't expect a voice then."

"Like I said," Mr. Crook pointed out, "it's a free country. Any reason why you shouldn't have been there? Or, come to that, why he should?"

"Well, I don't know. I went for the cats." She explained about the cats. "And I was afraid of the kitten getting drowned." She explained about the kitten.

"And this chap was on his owney-oh?"

"Well, I don't know, do I? He just asked what I was doing there."

"Any business of his?"

"I didn't think of that."

"Ask him what he was doing there?"

"That wasn't any business of mine."

"Sauce for the goose," suggested Mr. Crook, wondering what she was concealing and why. She didn't look the sort that hung about hoping to collect insults and thereby win a little publicity. Anyway, in that case she wouldn't have made a beeline for the Mettlesome Horse. Still, let patience have her perfect work, and usually she achieved a bonanza. He didn't say as much to May, who wouldn't have understood what he was talking about if he had. "So you behaved like Little Miss Muffett, who was frightened away?"

"It's not a very nice neighborhood," May pointed out apologetically. "And it was quite dark—and Mrs. Politi always says there may be rats there. I always say of course not, but she could be right."

"Rats with human faces," Mr. Crook acknowledged. "Now, you hold on to that card and if ever you find a use for it don't hesitate to ring. You can even reverse the charges, if it's more convenient. You're what I've been waiting for all evening."

"But you didn't know I was coming," May protested.

"The wicked didn't know the flood was coming, but it caught them just the same," Mr. Crook reminded her. "I wouldn't mind betting my Sunday morning titfer that chap wasn't there for any good reason, and I hope I'm a good citizen . . ." His guardian angel might have taken this unwinking, but the authorities would have seen it as a rather considerable poke in the bread basket. "And remember, if I was drinking slops because you were on the way, you came in, whether you know it or not, because I was here. And I never did hold with this ships-that-pass-in-the-night mularkey, there's something round the corner, and the odds are you and me are going to trail it together. And if your suspicions should be aroused, remember, before you go into your Joan of Arc act, it's always as well to get a legal opinion. It's my experience that most people who've lived blameless lives don't know their own rights, and it's not every rozzer thinks it's his job to explain them."

Recalling this conversation later, it surprised him a little to realize how certain he was that this was going to turn into a matter for the police.

Mrs. Politi had closed her shop a long time ago; for a while she had sat in her doorway on an upright wooden chair, an ordinary enough proceeding in her native land but one looked askance at by her prim suburban neighbors. "I don't go to the world no more," Mrs. Politi would explain. "The world, she come to me."

Pulling back the curtain of her bedroom she saw that there was no light across the road in the top-floor room where May lived. "I always warn her she get eaten by those hungry cats," she muttered, "and no one but herself to thank." Presently, however, she saw a big yellow car roll majestically down the street and stop a few doors away. The door opened and May got out. Mrs. Politi couldn't believe her eyes. Mind you, she didn't suspect the worst. The car itself was of a vintage that commanded respect. Crook's enemies, who were legion, said it dated back to the time when a man walked in front of these new-fangled monsters waving a red flag, and the maximum speed was five miles an hour. "You try it," Mr. Crook told one of them once, "you won't have time to pull out your stop watch before you're under the wheels."

Mrs. Politi gasped with delight. Who'd have thought it of her, the demure little spinster, always yapping about her cats and collecting bits of food, and all the time . . . She a deep one, thought Mrs. Politi. Like a well. But no well had ever been dug that she couldn't plumb in due course. She looked forward to getting the whole story out of her friend— and I will do it or I am a Dutchman, she assured herself, utilizing a phrase from the country of her adoption. And everyone knew her parents had come from Turin and she had never set foot in Holland in her life.

The next evening she waited impatiently for May's ring at the bell. She always rang, though often there was nothing for her. It was a warm, even a sultry evening, and Mrs. Politi brought out her chair and eagerly watched the street. Later, she thought, there might be rain. When half-past seven, May's normal time of call, had gone by and there was no sign of her, Mrs. Politi began to feel a little anxious. You could set your clock by May. At a quarter to eight she hadn't arrived, then the Protestant church clock sounded the hour. Mrs. Politi lifted her eyes, not to the hills but to the top window almost opposite, and saw through a crack in the curtains that a light was burning. She heaved herself out of her chair and waddled over the street.

When May heard the bell she peered cautiously out of her window. Mrs. Politi's bulk was unmistakable. May could no more have suspected her of being last night's mystery man in disguise than she could have suspected a circus elephant. She came hastening down the stairs.

"Come in, Lilli, come in," she said warmly, almost pulling her friend across the threshold. "What's wrong?"

"You should tell me," retorted Mrs. Politi, staring with dismay at the steep flight of steps facing her. "May, you are not ill. You went to work this morning as usual. That I see with my own eyes. So—tonight I collect food for your worthless cats . . ."

"Oh, don't, Lilli. Call them worthless, I mean. The fact is, I'm not going to the Common tonight."

"Then you *are* ill?"

"No, not exactly. I do feel rather tired, though."

"Too tired to feed your adored cats? That I cannot believe. May, you are concealing something."

By this time they were in May's neat bed-sitter. This was furnished in a quite unexceptional manner, the only striking features being a large photograph of an uncommonly dogmatic old man, Papa Forbes—deceased, and regretted by no one except his daughter—and a plethora of cats. A chowder of cats. Lilli couldn't recall where she had heard the expression. Wherever the eye turned, it lighted on a cat—in china, bronze, plaster—old birthday cards, even the towels bore representations of cats.

"You will turn into a cat yourself one of these days," Lilli warned her.

"If you must know," May acknowledged reluctantly—she had spent all her defiance keeping the truth from Mr. Crook, who, she suspected, might be a good deal more ardent if she had so much as mentioned her suspicions, "a man spoke to me."

Lilli Politi put back her head and laughed. It was a

lovely laugh, girlish and gay and very surprising to come from that stout old woman.

"So—a man spoke you? He was perhaps the one who brought you home?"

May didn't stop to wonder how her friend knew about Mr. Crook, any more than she would wonder on the Last Day how the Recording Angel knew so much about activities of which she'd never spoken to anyone. She answered with complete candor. "Oh no, Lilli. He—he came to my assistance, there wasn't a bus and of course I hadn't any money, only sixpence, you know I never take any money with me—and it was just starting to rain and he offered me a lift. I had gone further across the Common than I meant and took the wrong road."

Lilli raised her thick brows. "The girl who took the wrong turning," she intoned. "May, you a slyboots. Did you ask this man who he was?"

"He wasn't going to abduct me," cried May, with a sudden return of her old spirit. "It was—it was his good deed for the day. I was a bit shaken, I admit it."

"And that is all you have to say?"

"Everything," said May firmly. If she hadn't confided in Mr. Crook she certainly wasn't going to give any details to Lilli Politi. She was a good neighbor, and she really did care for May, which was surprising, seeing she thought her a fool and declared that fools were anathema, but once she mounted the steed of her imagination, Pegasus wasn't in it with her.

Lilli, however, was not disposed to let her off so easily. "What did he say to you, this man on the Common."

"I don't think he was alone," cried May. "He just wanted me out of the picture. He didn't try and assault me, if that's what you're thinking. I told him I'd lost a kitten and he said if he found it he'd bring it back."

"You told him your address?"

"Yes, but not the right one. Oh, Lilli, it was such a sweet little cat, mostly Burmese, I think."

"Burmese, Chinese, Celanese, they are all one to me," Lilli declared. "Have you told the police?"

"The police? I've got nothing to tell them. I told you, he didn't try and attack me in any way. And if I did tell them, they'd say I had only myself to blame wandering about on the Common after dark. You don't seem to be able to make people understand about dumb animals."

"I have heard," said Lilli, "that the giraffe can make no sound. If that is true, it is the only dumb animal I know. But I see you do not wish to confide in your old friend."

"I've told you," May insisted. "I had a bit of a shock and I decided to give it a rest for a few days. After all, the scraps I take can't really make a lot of difference. It's just that one likes to feel one's doing what one can."

Lilli didn't pursue the subject any further, she could see she would learn no more tonight. But one day, probably quite soon, May would feel the need for a confidante. She could not, however, forbear to put one final question.

"What were they doing, these two—trespassers?"

She watched, eyes alight with mischief, to see how May would cope with that one. But May flummoxed her completely when she said, "If you really must know, Lilli, they were burying a pet dog."

She had told herself this so often that eventually she might have come to believe it, only before that happened, the balloon went up. In fact, while she tried to fend off Lilli's inquiries, it was already on its perilous flight.

Reuben Gold (Ben for short) was the son of a local jeweler and pawnbroker, Solly Gold, who had a corner shop in Dorset Street. From the front he looked like any other jeweler and watchmaker, but around the corner the notorious three brass balls flaunted themselves. He did a good pawnbroking business, though he seldom spoke of it, for he was known to give a fair price, and his reputation with the police was high enough for them to know that if he were offered stolen goods he would report it at once. He was a short, hard-working man, who kept his nose clean, cooperated with authority, made a fair but not an exorbitant profit on all his transactions, and thanked his stars that he was now a citizen of a country where he need not conceal either his religious or his national origins.

Ben was nine years old, the child of his father's middle age and the only son. Two daughters had already made advantageous marriages and quitted the home roof. On the Friday following May's perilous adventure, Ben and two school friends were playing on Broomstick Common among the wrecked cars, giving themselves the names of famous racing drivers and making all the appropriate noises for a Monte Carlo rally. A few other lads were doing much the same. Of the wild cats, there was no sign, they never came out till after dark, and in any case Ben had brought the family dog with him. This dog's name was Who, not after the famous doctor, but because even an expert might be forgiven for not being sure about his parentage.

"Who did your mother meet after dark?" someone had demanded, when Solly brought him back from the dogs' home, he being then about a year old.

"A dog is a dog, no?" Solly said. Ben had wanted a dog; Solly thought Who would be a companion for his wife, Leah, while he was at the shop and the boy at school; Leah, who had no particular feelings either way, wanted whatever her menfolk wanted. Who was certainly no beauty, but Solly declared that a dog of such fearsome and unusual aspect would frighten off any child-stealer. (There had been one or two cases of children being approached by a nameless man during the past year or two, and one child had actually been criminally assaulted.)

"He's got a heart like butter," Ben scoffed. "He wouldn't only let the burglar in, he'd show him where everything was hidden."

"You talk too much, my son," Solly reproved him. "Do I want a dog that will bite strangers, bring the police about my ears? So long as he looks that he would attack, that is all I ask."

Even Ben couldn't argue that Who didn't look a real villain, with his cropped ears and huge teeth. He had some Alsatian blood in him, everyone agreed about that. Solly, who had heard of pure-bred dogs becoming hysterical and attacking even their owners, had no fault to find with his appearance, and he paid no attention to Ben's witticism that he was a sheep in wolf's clothing. On this evening he snuffed about contentedly enough while the boys played, then suddenly, to their dismay, he began to move toward the palings through which venturesome May Forbes had squeezed herself.

"Who, come back. Come back, sir," Ben ordered. Solly had exacted a promise from his son that come what might, he would never go into that forbidden area. But now the normally obedient Who paid no attention, and nose to ground, looking remarkably like a wolf, he followed a trail the boys couldn't detect.

"Oh, look," cried Frank Vines, one of the three, "he's gone over the fence."

"He can't," cried Ben. "He's such a fool he'll probably fall into the canal."

"He can swim, you idiot."

"That won't help him if he comes back stinking of canal water, and shaking it all over Mumma's carpet."

He began to run alongside the fence, calling to the dog. To his relief, after a minute or so he saw Who had stopped, then he sailed back over the fence and went into the wood.

"Perhaps he'll find buried treasure for you," suggested the third boy.

Who, when they came up to him, had his nose to the ground and was pawing among stones and clods of earth. Ben caught his collar, but he might as well have tried to shift the Rock of Gibraltar.

"Oh come on," Ben adjured him. It was Friday night, when the family kept the Jewish family feast and there would be trouble indeed if he were back late. Leah would light the candles in a ceremony that had been enacted for centuries; even Ben, accustomed as he was to heathen companions to whom God was an expletive rather than a Divine Being, would have felt the bottom had dropped out of his world if his parents had abandoned the practice.

"Come and help me to pull him," he yelled.

Frank, whose father had a butcher's shop in the High Street, said, "He's probably a police dog in disguise. Perhaps some of the train robbers' loot is hidden here."

"How would Who smell that? Dogs don't understand about money."

The third boy, Jim, a small pale creature who looked as if he'd grown up in a dark cupboard, said acutely, "Well, he's found something, I suppose you could call it treasure, though it's not exactly buried."

Stooping, he picked up a small gleaming object that the dog must have unearthed in his frantic pawing.

The other two clustered around him. "What is it?"

"It's a ring, any fool can see that."

"Probably came from Woollie's," said Frank scornfully. "No one would leave a real ring here."

Ben took the ring gently from his friend's palm. "No," he said after a moment. "This didn't come from Woollie's. It's what they call an antique. I know, my father's told me."

"Then perhaps it comes from Woollie's antique department." Both boys yelped with laughter. Only Ben remained grave.

The ring was quite charming, an antique gold setting with three minute flowers whose petals were made of colored stones.

"They're only chips," said Ben knowledgeably, "but they aren't glass. I'd like to show this to my father."

"Perhaps he'll be able to tell you what it's doing here," jeered Frank.

"Perhaps it's part of a hoard," contributed Jim. "I say, Who is excited, isn't he?"

"I expect he wants his share of the treasure." Frank looked at the eager dog, the great excavating paws. "He looks ready to dig his way through to Australia."

"Give him a chance," Jim urged.

"I can't. I've got to go back. Come *on*." Ben tugged furiously at the big dog's collar.

"We might get some spades," Frank began, but to the

surprise of both boys, Ben exclaimed, "No. Leave it. If there is anything there it's nothing to do with us."

"How about the ring? We found that."

"I found it," insisted Jim.

"No, you didn't. Who found it. Anyway, if it's valuable it doesn't belong to any of us. Only—he doesn't dig for nothing. My father stopped him doing that when he started digging in our yard."

"It's probably only a dead cat," said Frank carelessly.

"Since when did cats wear rings?" Jim riposted.

"Then some chap and his girl were walking here and she dropped the ring . . ."

"Without noticing?"

"Perhaps it was loose."

"We ought to mark the place," Frank suggested. "There must be a stick or something."

Ben stepped backward on something that cracked under his tread. "It's a saucer," he discovered. "What on earth's that doing here?"

"It'll do to mark the spot. There can't be many saucers lying about."

"Perhaps the witches had a tea party," suggested Frank, who considered himself the wit of the party.

Ben had managed to prise the dog away from the mysterious spot. Now he began to make his way back as speedily as possible.

"Perhaps someone's offered a reward," Jim put in resourcefully.

"If there was a reward there'd be a notice outside the Copper Shop."

"Perhaps there is. Have you looked?" But of course they hadn't.

Solly Gold had a glass screwed into his eye and was examining a watch when the three boys and the dog came bursting in. He flapped a hand at them to enjoin silence. After a minute he removed the glass and inquired formally, "And what can I do for you, gentlemen?"

Jim giggled and exchanged glances with Frank. Ben said, "It's this ring, Dad. We found it near the canal, at least Who unearthed it. They think it's Woollie's, but it isn't, is it?"

Mr. Gold took the ring and let it lie for an instant in the palm of his hand. "The canal, you say? I thought that was Council property."

"This side of the fence, Dad. Who went over the paling and we had to get him back, and then he started digging and Jim saw this ring. And we thought it queer because nobody really goes down that way."

"Because of the bomb," Frank explained.

"I daresay there never was a bomb there," said Jim.

"So you know better than the police. So clever boys are nowadays. When I was your age I knew nothing, we believed what our elders told us. But you were right to bring me the ring. I know it well. It was an unredeemed pledge. But in such a place—why? why?"

"We could hardly drag Who away," Ben assured him eagerly. "He was digging like mad."

"As if he thought there was buried treasure," added Jim.

"A dog has not enough sense to be interested in buried treasure," Solly assured him soberly. He turned to his son. "My son, could you find this place again if you should be asked?"

"There was a saucer there, I don't know what it was doing."

"A saucer. Then perhaps—there is a little lady who goes to feed the cats—perhaps she . . . but why down by the canal? No, that is very strange."

"Is it really valuable, Mr. Gold?" demanded Frank.

"Valuable!" Solly shrugged. "A relative word. I know what the young man who bought it paid for it. I made him a reduction because then he may return for the other ring, the ring for the wedding." He could never resist an opportunity to instruct the boy he regarded as his heir. "It is good business to come down a little on your price with an eye to the future. Remember that, my son. Make an exorbitant charge and you have money in the bank, but next time your customer goes elsewhere."

"It's a gamble really, isn't it?" suggested Frank intelligently.

"It is a knowledge of human nature." Solly always answered questons courteously even when they were put to him by young hobbledehoys like Frank Vines. One day Frank might be a man of substance, then he might give some of his custom to Ben. Look ahead, that was Solly's motto. Life is the present and the future. The past is over and done with, so waste no time on that.

"Do you think we ought to take it to the station, Dad?" Ben inquired.

Solly could never quite accustom himself to the title of Dad. He had called his own father Papa all his life, but he felt that being himself a Jew by birth and British only by adoption meant that Ben would have enough to differentiate him without his insisting on the old-style title.

"You forget what day it is, my son? It is Friday night." And Ben nodded. "Go back, now. Explain to your Mama that I may be a few minutes late. Leave the ring with me. If there should be a reward you will be told, rest assured of that."

"Coo, what do you bet there is buried treasure there?" Frank cried as the three of them turned away. "I don't know about you chaps but I'm going back to have a dekko."

"Me too," agreed Jim enthusiastically. "Too bad Ben can't come. Ben's got to go back to his Mumma."

Ben shrugged his shoulders in a very good imitation of his father. "You couldn't be expected to understand," he said. "What do goys know? And anyway, had you thought that perhaps the one that left the ring there may have thought of looking for it, and he might be—well, might be a bit annoyed if he knew you'd taken it? My father will give it to the police —well, report it, anyhow."

"You're only saying that because you can't come with us" jeered Frank, but when Ben and the dog had gone their

ways, Jim murmured uncertainly, "Suppose there really is a
bomb down there and we step on it?"

"The bomb's the other side of the palings—remem-
ber?" But Frank's step had also slowed a little. If Solly really
intended to talk to the police they might come haring down
and be none too pleased to find their job had been taken over
by the public. Mr. Vines was always on at his son about the
importance of staying on the right side of the boys in blue.

"We could go to the Common anyway, there's no law
against that." So off they went, thanking their stars that Friday
night was the same as every other night of the week in their
households, except that, being pay night, their dads had an
extra session at the Case Is Altered.

3

Mr. Gold put up his shutters promptly on the stroke of six and went along to the police station. The first officer he saw took the matter pretty lightly. Some girl had lost a ring, he conceded. What of it?

"I think," said Mr. Gold, "if I wore your uniform I would ask if anyone had lost a girl."

After that the station sergeant surfaced. They all knew Solly by reputation at least; he was a reliable member of the community, he wouldn't be trying to make monkeys out of them, and the sergeant thought he wouldn't be much pleased if someone reversed the process and tried to make a monkey out of him.

"I am telling you what my son told me. Ben is a truthful boy. And he had witnesses, two of them. One is the son of Mr. Vines, the other I do not know. Moreover, they all agreed that the dog wished to continue digging and must be pulled away by force. Now, the dog was not interested in the ring—you would agree there?"

"If you say so, Mr. Gold."

"I say more," Solly continued. "I have seen that ring before today. I sold it to a young man . . ."

"You can't give us his name."

40

"A young man who paid cash. With cash you do not ask for a name."

"You'd know him again?"

"There are some faces a man does not forget."

"This lad of yours, will he be able to find the place again?"

"There is a broken saucer nearby. In any case, the dog would know." He looked through the station window. Clouds were coming up fast. "There is no hurry," he suggested softly. "If there is treasure underground it can wait till the morning. If you are afraid of trespassers, you can set a man to watch."

"I can't turn out a squad of men to dig a bit of deserted ground because a tuppenny-ha'penny ring was picked up there," Spence exploded when Solly was gone. "Most likely the girl was larking and dropped it out of her pocket or something. We'll be the laughingstock of the force if we start digging and all we find's a dead dog."

"News to me, Sarge, that dogs wear rings."

The sergeant scowled. The young rookies these days didn't know where to draw the line.

"A lady's ring, isn't it? You know, Solly Gold might have something . . ."

"Mr. Gold to you," the sergeant snapped.

"He said he might start asking about a missing girl."

"Get cracking on the records," Spence said. "Anyone local been reported missing?"

"Well, not that I remember. All the same . . ."

But no one had reported a missing girl. Nor had there been any inquiry for a lost ring answering the description.

"You can't do much about missing persons, not if they're over eighteen," Spence said rather gloomily. "Unless there are particular circumstances, sickness, lunacy or of course some suggestion of a criminal record. The Sally Army's the best bet for that."

"We don't know any girl is missing yet."

"The ring could belong to whoever put that saucer there. It's hardly the kind of place where you'd look for one."

41

"Funny no one's inquired about it, then."

A police constable, one of those hard-working men who always seem to be behind the door when promotion's handed around, murmured, "I might ask Nance."

"Who's she?"

"My wife, Sarge. I don't know how it is—I always tell her she's a loss to the force. I don't know if it's a sixth sense or what, but there are occasions when she seems to know about a crime before it's been committed."

"You want to watch your tongue, Hunter," the sergeant advised him. "You mean she might have heard about a missing girl before we did?"

"That's what I'm saying. It's like the bush telegraph. Don't ask me how she does it, but if there is a local girl missing and her family don't choose to come to us, you could do worse than talk to Nance. There's the ring, too."

"You think she'll be able to tell us who that belonged to?"

"I don't know about that, but she'll recognize it all right. It used to be in Solly Gold's side window. We were walking past one evening not so long ago when it caught her eye. Now that's a good-class thing, she told me. You'd never think of buying me anything like that. I ask you, Sarge, on a police constable's pay. He was asking something like fifty quid for it, though I daresay he came down a bit when it came to the crunch. And here's something else I remember. About a week ago she came back and said, 'You've missed the boat, George. You won't be able to buy me that ring, after all, because it's sold. Someone's pipped you on the post.' Well, I said it didn't mean because it had gone out of the window, Solly still hadn't got it. He's always changing his stock. But she said no, she'd gone in and asked him."

"You've taken your time remembering all this, haven't you?" suggested Sergeant Spence ungraciously. "Anyway, we know it was sold and to a young man Solly thinks he'd know again. But it stands to reason he wouldn't be buying it for himself. Have a word with your wife, Hunter, by all means, but

42

make it clear to her that we've no knowledge that anyone's missing, and we haven't been asked to make inquiries."

Nancy Hunter sniffed when she heard her husband's story. "Some girls don't know their luck," she said. "If all she was going to do was lose it down by the canal, it might as well have stayed in the window. Canal." She thought. "That's a funny place to go courting."

"Haven't heard of anyone doing a flit, I suppose?" her husband suggested.

"I thought you were supposed to be the policeman, not me." She considered for a minute. Then she said, "That Linda Myers walked out of the house a day or two ago, at least that's what Brenda Myers says."

"Linda Myers? That's Tom Myers' girl."

"Mind you," continued Nance, paying about as much attention to her husband as she usually did, "I reckon Tom was crazy expecting a girl like Linda to settle down with a new wife barely ten years older than her. And since Peter was born it's been a regular Fifth of November in that household, fireworks day and night. At least, that's what I hear."

"Linda's never been in trouble," reflected George Hunter thoughtfully.

"She may not have been in trouble, but she's the kind that makes it all her days. If you ask me, Brenda Myers doesn't want to know."

"Doesn't want to know what?"

"What's happened to her. She's always fancied herself, you know. Lolita number two, that's Miss Linda. And always on with the new love before she's off with the old."

"What you mean is the two didn't get on."

"And that's the understatement of the year. It's no wonder you haven't got your stripes yet, George. If you ask me, Linda hoped she'd drive Brenda round the bend or make her get out or something. She'd been number one in Tom Myers' house ever since her mother died when the kid was thirteen, and then suddenly she finds herself sitting at the side of the table and expected to baby-sit. If it was my kid I'd sooner have a gorilla for a sitter."

"When did she light out?" George was accustomed to winnowing chaff from grain where Nance was concerned. A less patient man wouldn't have bothered, but he knew that when you'd sifted the chaff, you often got quite a nice little harvest.

"I told you, about a couple of days ago. Walked out in just what she stood up in, from what Brenda says. Mind you, there was some talk a while back about her going with a married man, but you can't believe all you hear."

"You hear such a lot," suggested George, "maybe you know who she is going with just now."

"I'd need to be a computer to keep tabs on all her conquests." Nance sniffed again. "Mind you, I'm not bringing any accusations. Let's say she gets bored a bit quicker than most or needs more attention. I did hear she was going around with a foreigner." Meaning, as George readily understood, a stranger to the district.

"How did you hear about Linda going AWOL?" he asked.

"I was in the post office, and Brenda was sounding off about it. She'd arranged to go to a bingo session or something with a friend and had asked Linda if she'd look after the kid."

"More likely told than asked," George Hunter murmured.

"Anyway, the girl said, 'He's not my kid,' and there was a real up-and-a-downer. Linda said if Brenda wanted a baby-sitter she could do what everyone else did and get one in, but you know that's not so easy, and some of these girls . . . Bessie Bates did that and she said something made her come back early and there was this girl shacked up with her boy friend on the sofa and the poor kid yelling its head off. Anyhow, Linda said she'd had enough, she had her own life, and thank-you and good-bye. And that was the last Brenda saw of her."

George Hunter looked considerably more troubled than his wife. "When was this?"

"Bingo clubs are Thursdays, and Brenda didn't mention it till this morning, so I suppose yesterday was the day Linda walked out."

"But—doesn't Mrs. Myers know where she's gone?"

"I shouldn't think Linda was much of a hand with a pen. And she is eighteen, there's not much Brenda can do about it. In fact, she said it was something to have peace in the house, and she was going to make the most of it while it lasted."

"But Tom Myers?"

"He's a traveler, as if you didn't know. Only gets back at weekends. That's one of the reasons he wanted Linda to stay at home, company for his wife—that's what he thought. It's a funny thing how some men never learn. Two wives and a daughter, and he knows no more about women than the day he was born."

"The overstatement of the year," suggested her husband. "I suppose you don't happen to know if it was Linda wearing that ring you fancied?"

"Well, but you said it was found by the canal. Linda 'ud never go there. We know the type of girl who goes down to the canal with a fellow, and the type of fellow. Linda may be a bit wild, but she's not that daft. She may be young," added Nance shrewdly, "but she knows how many beans make five."

"That's where the ring was found," said her husband, "and no one's put in an inquiry for it, and it wasn't bought at any five-and-ten store, as we both know. And to date no one's been reported missing. You know such a lot, Nance, you don't happen to know who she was going around with just lately. Besides this foreigner no one else seems to know about," he added quickly.

"That girl changes her boy friends more often than you change your shirts," Nance told him. "Has it occurred to you to ask Brenda Myers? She may not know where the girl is, but she'd recognize the ring. It's not the sort you'd easily forget."

"We don't want to alarm her unnecessarily," said George. He looked disturbed.

"I wouldn't say Brenda Myers scares easy," was Nance's cool retort.

"There's nothing more we can do tonight," Sergeant Spence decided when he had received his subordinate's report. "We'll get on to Mrs. Myers in the morning, and see if she recognizes the ring. We can't put out a search for the girl officially without a bit more evidence that someone could have harmed her. She's a right to change her address without informing her stepmother, but I'll tell you this." He paused weightily. "I wouldn't care to be in Brenda Myers' shoes when Tom comes home, not if anything has gone wrong. Tom Myers will do his nut, and we've trouble enough in the manor without that."

Brenda Myers, interviewed next morning, proved uncooperative. It was clear she was not unduly worried by her stepdaughter's absence.

"I don't know why you wanted to get me up here, Saturday and all," she scolded. "Tom 'ull be back after dinner and he likes to find everything just so. It's not as if it was the first time her ladyship's gone off in a huff, and for the same reason, because I suggested she might give a hand in the house. Well, it's her home too, isn't it?"

"What happened the last time?"

"She stayed away a couple of nights, then walked in as cool as you please. 'I've been staying with Sophie,' she said. 'Didn't she mind you using her toothbrush?' I asked, because she hadn't taken a stitch with her. 'And fancy any friend of yours not having a phone'—to let me know, see? 'Oh,' she said, 'I phoned but there wasn't any answer.' You don't have to believe her, but what authority have I got? The fact is, that girl's done nothing but make trouble ever since we were married, always nestling up to her father and saying do you remember, Daddy, when Mummy was alive we did this and that? Making out she misses her so. As if Tom wants to keep on being reminded. She only does it to spite me, of course."

Sergeant Spence sighed. Another one-eyed witness, he reflected, the sort that can never see more than one point of view, and that her own.

"So you're not really worried, Mrs. Myers?" he suggested.

"You can take my word, that girl will be back by three o'clock. Tom gets home then and she won't let him find her gone. And she'll have the same story—she tried to phone and there was no reply."

The sergeant was a persistent man. In his job you learn to be. "You don't know any way you could get in touch with this Sophie?" he urged.

"Let me tell you something," said Brenda. She lighted a cigarette defiantly, but he noticed her hands weren't quite steady. "I don't even know for certain there is any such person as Sophie. Oh, Linda says so, but you'd need to be round the bend to believe everything that girl tells you."

"She's never rung up and asked for Linda?"

"Miss Linda doesn't give me the chance of finding out anything about her affairs. If she telephones, it's when I'm out of the way, though from the size of the bills she doesn't lose many opportunities. But I'll tell you this, Sergeant. The only time I came in and found her on the phone she hung up sharpish and then said, 'That was Sophie.' Well, you know how you can get a sort of echo from the other end of the line, and if that was Sophie she's more like a man than any girl's got a right to be."

"Letters?"

"If she gets them they don't come to the house, and I'd say they don't go to the post office either. That Maggie Ryan would talk the hindleg off a goat before breakfast. Anyway, I don't suppose she gets any. If she can sign her own name it's all she can do. It's the phone these days."

"This young chap who gave her the ring—could it have been him on the line?"

"Seeing I don't know his name, it could have been anyone."

"Mr. Gold remembers him buying the ring. Not anyone he recognized, so likely he wasn't local."

"Linda did talk about some London chap—wait a minute, she put a name to him—Chris, she said. I didn't think, but that girl wouldn't step out of her way to know another girl. I never set eyes on him myself, and even the ring—well, she said she'd earned it and not the way I might think. To tell you the truth, Sergeant, I didn't think much about it. I mean, I don't think she picked it, she'd go for something more showy. Besides, she talks so big about how she's going to give all of us a surprise one of these days, to hear her you'd suppose she was going to marry a lord."

"Not many lords round these parts," offered Spence doggedly.

"Oh, Churchford lads aren't good enough for her. If she had her way she wouldn't even let on that her Dad was on the road. My father's a traveler, I've heard her say like—who was it?—Mungo Park?"

"Marco Polo," murmured the sergeant, offering his tidbit of culture-vulture.

"Silly, really, seeing everybody knows about Tom. I suppose she thinks a lord wouldn't fancy a workingman for his father-in-law. Funny thing is, Linda's so daft I sometimes think she believes her own stories. Where did you say you found the ring?"

When she heard it was by the canal she looked incredulous. "Even Linda couldn't be that mad. I tell you, Mr. Spence, if anything's happened to that girl Tom 'ull kill me. Are you sure, Mr. Spence, the boys weren't having you on— about finding it down by the canal, I mean? You know what kids are."

"I don't think Ben Gold would try and pull anything like that over his father."

"What were they doing down by the canal?"

"Walking Mr. Gold's dog. It was the dog really that dug up the ring."

Her breath whistled in her throat. "You didn't say it was dug up."

"Well, the dog scratched about a bit, and then one of the boys noticed the ring, and Ben took it back to show his father, and he recognized it and brought it to us."

"Perhaps Linda gave it back to this fellow and he was so riled he threw it out," Brenda suggested, but there was no conviction in her voice, and the sergeant didn't even pretend to consider the possibility. During this past minute her composure, which had been stiffened by a sort of scornful rage, left her; she was white as paper. Hurriedly the sergeant dispatched one of the constables for a cup of tea. "And don't forget the sugar," he added. "Sit down, Mrs. Myers." For she had come to her feet. "It's been a bit of a shock, but we don't know that anything's happened to the girl."

"You try telling Tom that," Brenda said in a wraith of a voice. "I've always been afraid of that girl getting herself into trouble in the back of a car, say, but the canal!"

The tea came and she sat stirring it absently, around and around until it began to slop into the saucer.

"This Mr. Polly Linda works for," Spence urged. "He's the hairdresser at Crisps Corner."

"They don't call them that any more. Beautician, Linda says. She did work for a bit for old Miss Robinson, though what use she was to them, don't ask me. I could have told them she wouldn't stick that long. A lot of old pussies going in for packets of hairpins and cheap lines of handkerchiefs. Still, Miss Alice seemed to take to her. She must do quite well at Polly's, she always seems to have enough to buy a new dress or a handbag. I don't doubt she could wind him round her little finger, as she does her father. Oh, I don't deny," continued Brenda grudgingly, "she's got a taking way with her. She did want to go in for modeling, have a London flat, you know, but her father put his foot down there." She sighed. "The truth is he knows nothing about her. You'd have thought a man who'd been married twice would have learned something about women, but not Tom."

When pressed to amplify that, however, she simply shook her head. The police went off on another tack.

"Wouldn't Mr. Polly wonder if she didn't turn up on Friday? It's usually a pretty busy day."

"She'll have covered herself, somehow, you may be sure of that. Anyway, these young girls, no sense of responsibility, change their jobs as often as they change their hair-dos. What happens now?"

"We can't do much until she's been reported missing, and even then only if there's some suspicion of foul play. It's not a crime to walk out on your job or leave home."

"You just wait till her father gets back," said Brenda grimly. "He won't thank me for sicking the police on to her if she's simply gone off for a lark, and, like I said, I wouldn't be surprised to find her on the doorstep when I get back. She knows which side her bread's buttered, and she'll have a story as pat as you please."

"What do you make of that?" the sergeant asked a colleague when Brenda had departed to take her place in the Saturday queues at the supermarket.

"Frightened to death of Tom Myers, couldn't care less about Linda. Wouldn't really surprise me if the girl had planted the ring . . ."

"Don't know how you ever got taken on the force," said the sergeant brutally. "One thing, you'll never make it in the brains department. Plant the ring indeed! It could have stayed there a month without anyone finding it. All the same," he brooded, "I'm sorry for Mrs. Myers when Tom gets back, if the girl's still missing."

The constable, quite unmoved by his superior's remarks, commented brusquely, "Wouldn't surprise me if we were a bit sorry, too."

Tom Myers came storming up to the station within twenty minutes of his return to Churchford. He demanded to see the ring, which he instantly identified.

"I couldn't be mistaken, my daughter showed it to me. She got it from a young chap called Chris. No, I don't know his other name, but according to her he should be coming over tomorrow to meet the family."

"Did you assume it was an engagement ring, Mr. Myers?"

"Don't ask me. The present generation doesn't seem interested in engagements. But from what my girl said, it did sound serious. Mind you, she's had small presents before, like all girls, a charm bracelet, a brooch, but nothing like this. The young chap didn't get that for half a dollar. Well, what have you done about finding her, I mean? My wife says she walked out on Thursday."

When he heard they were waiting for him, he blew up.

"Your daughter's not been classified as a missing person, Mr. Myers; she's over eighteen, and the ring was only brought in last night. We don't even know she was wearing it at the time she left Churchford."

"You don't know my daughter. If she didn't want to go on wearing it she wouldn't throw it away. You could raise a few pounds on that. And what's it doing down by the canal? Let me tell you this. My girl wouldn't let me come back and find her gone, not without a note or a phone call or something, and there's been nothing. She didn't take any luggage with her, all her muck's on her dressing table, even her wig, though they call 'em hairpieces nowadays. All the girls seem to have 'em, don't ask me why, even that's in its box. How many more suspicious circumstances do you want before you can get to work? And let me tell you this, if they're not enough for you, they're a damn sight too many for me. If you won't get on with the job, I'll call in a couple of pals and we'll take some spades and go down and dig on the canal bank ourselves."

He means it, too, the sergeant thought. He was a man who'd confronted plenty of violent no-gooders, but not many had chilled his blood like this pale desperate father facing him across a table—"like a hand grenade when the pin's loose," he described him later. They didn't like the situation themselves, and if it should prove they were barking up the wrong tree, at least that should calm Tom. At all events they could see for themselves if there'd been more digging there than the dog would account for. It was odd what a difference Tom's visit had made. There wasn't one man setting out on that Saturday afternoon who didn't feel his blood chill a bit at the prospect before him.

They borrowed Solly's dog, Who. Tom suggested that. "He knows where he found the ring," he insisted. "There's been enough mucking time wasted as it is."

"The boys said they could identify the place by a cracked saucer," one of the policemen said.

Tom turned on him like the wrath of God. "I said get Solly's dog. This is my girl we're talking about. What do I care if your faces are red?"

So they agreed. After all, there could be more than one saucer and they didn't want to spend half the afternoon trailing through the muck and brambles of Broomstick Common looking for the right one.

"And keep the crowds away," added Tom Myers fiercely. "This isn't a peep-show."

They piled into the police van, the officers with their spades, Tom Myers, the dog and last of all Solly, because the dog wouldn't go without him. One of the policemen muttered that he wasn't a police dog, wasn't even trained. Solly, overhearing this, said, "He made it possible for the boy to find the ring. And I tell you this. We buy him a ball and presently the ball is lost. So he must have a piece of wood instead. Then we find him sitting by a cupboard in the hall, hour after hour sitting— like a cat watching a mousehole. At last we look, and there is the ball in the pocket of an old coat. I had forgotten. That dog is no fool."

The bush telegraph had been busy already with Linda's name, and when the van drew up as near the canal as was possible a small crowd was standing about, muttering, speculating.

Tom Myers turned, his face white and tense. "Haven't any of you people got homes to go to?" he demanded. And to the police, "Get those ghouls out."

"Stand back, please," said the senior sergeant. But they didn't move until Who suddenly turned and showed his tremendous fangs, and throwing up his head, let out a roar that made someone exclaim indignantly, "That dog's a menace."

"Too true he's a menace," Tom agreed. "Say the word and we'll let him off the leash. Well, you've come here for sport, haven't you?"

"We'll deal with them, sir," the sergeant promised, but though they withdrew they didn't go far. The Common was public property, wasn't it?

When they reached the palings Who was shown something belonging to the missing girl, and was then taken off the leash. As he had done two nights before, he leaped forward like a great black cloud, with the men in pursuit.

"There's the saucer," exclaimed one of them. It was a large pale blue affair, cracked across the middle. There was no time to stop and speculate as to how *that* got there, for the dog was digging furiously. Solly had some difficulty in prising him away, but once he had got the leash on the collar he beat a quick retreat. They'd done what was demanded of them, and Solly believed in keeping his nose clean and out of other men's affairs. Besides, he was a father himself; and he knew Who would never have made that furious assault on the earth for nothing.

The presence of Tom embarrassed all the others, but they could hardly ask him to go, and in any case he wouldn't have listened.

So the hideous job began.

She hadn't been buried very deep. If whoever was responsible had dug the regulation six feet the dog mightn't have found her. No one, seeing her for the first time, would have guessed she'd passed for a real beauty, so light, so vivid, great violet eyes and shining, shining hair. The youngest of the constables turned aside, retching. One of his superiors caught his arm.

"None of that, my lad. You're a copper, and don't you forget it. This may be the first time you've ever seen anything like this, but it's not likely it'll be the last." But he spoke without rancor, remembering his own first experience, when he'd been one of a party to find the body of a small boy, assaulted, strangled and concealed in a ditch. The young policeman was sheet-white, but he stood his ground after that. Tom Myers stared at the body with the awful expression of a man who has learned that what seemed too bad to contemplate is after all the truth.

"You identify her, sir?" the sergeant said.

"Do you have to ask that?" Tom muttered between clenched teeth.

"Yes, sir. We have to ask."

"That's my daughter. Was my daughter, rather." He still seemed unable to accept the appalling truth. This—this thing, with blackened face and starting eyes, nothing here of the reputed peace or beauty of death—he couldn't yet equate it with his reckless darling.

Two of the men had gone back to the van for the stretcher they had brought with them against just this emergency. They lifted her out of the unhallowed grave and covered her quickly.

"Get ahead, Bevan," the sergeant said to one of his men. "Clear that lot off from round the van. We don't want another murder on our hands."

"Now get back," said the policeman to a crowd that seemed mysteriously to have doubled. News that the stretcher had been sent for had brought their interest to boiling point. "You've had your fun, haven't you? Just think—we've got the father here—suppose it was one of your kids?"

"If she was mine she wouldn't be in this situation," declared one hardy soul.

"That's what you think." Bevan's voice was suddenly so fierce they all recoiled. "You don't know. That's one of the Creator's jokes. You just don't know."

They retreated then, though he suspected they were only watching from behind clumps of shrubs and trees. But when the dreadful little procession came crashing through the undergrowth he decided it wouldn't have mattered either way. Tom walked like a man in catalepsy, seeing nothing but that swollen unknown face.

"Where are you taking her?" he asked presently.

"It'll have to be the mortuary, Mr. Myers."

"For all the ghouls to come and gape at?"

"No one'll be allowed in who can't show he's got a good reason. And we'd like you to come along with us now, we shan't keep you long. We must just have your formal evidence of identification. Better than you having to come back later . . ."

P.C. Hunt was on duty when they got back. "Nip round to Mrs. Myers and let her know what's happened," the sergeant said. "It's not going to break her heart, but she'd better be warned. Tom Myers has had as much as he can take, she's going to have a lot of responsibility during the next twenty-four hours."

"You would have to pick on me," Hunt muttered.

"You're a married man, aren't you? I can't send one of the lads. The best thing would be for Tom to get as drunk as an owl tonight, only he's not that sort. And if ever you say I told you that I'll call you a liar on the Book."

They brought Tom a cup of tea that he said he didn't want, but was surprised to find he had drunk almost before he'd finished speaking. Superintendent Boscombe of the local C.I.D. had a word with him—he began to think they'd never be done. The official reassurances that they'd get the chap, never fear, ran off him like water from a duck's back. At present he was wholly possessed by grief. There would be a time for vengeance, but that would be later. Even the thought of his wife and baby son was no comfort to him now. He had some ado to absolve Brenda from blame. If she had won the girl's confidence—he wrenched his mind away from that tack. It wasn't that simple. He answered questions like an automaton, said that if he heard from Chris he'd be in touch, agreed to attend the inquest, and refused the offer of a car home.

"Better keep an eye on him when he starts coming round," said Boscombe sagely. "Still waters run deep—no one ever said a truer word."

4

The inquiry shifted to the Polly household. Mr. and Mrs. Polly were just back from the cinema when the police arrived. It wasn't Spence any longer, the job had been passed to the local C.I.D. As the press had it, the police were treating the case as one of foul play, though play seemed an inappropriate word in the circumstances.

"Linda Myers?" asked Mr. Polly. He was a dapper fellow, dark, trim, as neat as a new sixpence. Mrs. P. was more solid, but well dressed in a rather unenterprising way. Like a wall she was, it 'ud support you and never collapse, but on the other hand it 'ud never let you through, and if you tried to scale it the odds were you'd find spikes on the top. The police officer found himself wondering if Polly had ever tried to get through and sample the world on the other side of the wall. Mrs. Polly brought the detective-inspector into the room she called the lounge. Like Mr. Polly, it hadn't got a hair out of place. No kids, the man registered, though they could be married and gone into the world. Mr. Polly was forty if he was a day and his spouse could give him a few years.

"I last saw Linda on Thursday about four-thirty," Mr. Polly said. "She asked if she could get off a little early—we don't close till half-past five—she said she had a date. She had no late appointment that evening and she said she'd make up the time next week."

"She didn't drop any hint as to where she might be going?"

Mr. Polly showed fine teeth that owed nothing to the National Health. "I didn't ask her. You have to give the young folk some leeway these days, and in a sense you could say she has me over a barrel."

"What sense would that be, sir?"

"She could get a job at Agnew's any day of the week, and we both know it. We're a very conservative establishment, running with a small staff, and nowadays, you have to face it, the bulk of the money's in the hands of the young people. Since Agnew started up in the High Street a couple of years ago, the competition's got very fierce. My wife—" the officer had contrived to get rid of Mrs. Polly during this conversation —"she says it's all young men with beards wanting permanent waves and girls in mini-skirts, but that's where the money is. My two chief assistants, Miss Reith and Miss Buxton, have been with me for some years, but what I wanted was someone contemporary. And Linda is certainly that. She has the makings of a very good little hairdresser if she can only stay the course."

The door was jolted open and Mrs. Polly came in carrying a tray. "I'm sure you'd like a cup of coffee," she told the inspector graciously. "And seeing that Mr. Polly can't tell you anything I don't know, I take it there's no objection to me joining you."

"What do you think of the girl, Mrs. Polly?" the inspector asked.

"A regular little flibbertigibbet, a here-today-and-gone-tomorrow sort of a girl. Oh, I daresay she winds my husband round her finger as she does everyone else, one has to admit she has looks, but no stability. Never count on that one, I tell my husband."

"Were you surprised when she didn't turn up yesterday morning?" the inspector asked.

"Her father telephoned to say she had a chill . . ."

"Her father? Are you sure, Mr. Polly?"

Mr. Polly looked flustered. "That's who he said he was."

"Mr. Myers wasn't even in the district. He doesn't get back till after midday on Saturdays."

Mr. Polly looked more flustered than ever. "I'm only telling you what the chap said. I took the call myself."

"And of course you didn't recognize the voice."

"He said he was Mr. Myers. Look, Inspector, what's all this about? Has Linda got into some sort of trouble?"

"You mean you hadn't heard? why, the place is buzzing with it."

And he told them about the find on Broomstick Common.

Mrs. Polly was the first to speak. "I can't pretend to be surprised. No, Fred, it's the truth. That girl was asking for trouble, and now she's got it."

"I can't take it in," said Mr. Polly in dazed tones. "She was like—oh, like a beam of sunlight. Even some of our older customers couldn't resist her. She had such coaxing ways. She'd make them try out new styles they'd never dreamed of. 'If you don't like it I'll take it all down and do it again for free,' she'd say. You couldn't help being attracted by her. You'd hardly think anyone would dare—put out a light like that, I mean."

"I never knew you were such a poet, Fred," said Mrs. Polly dryly. "Oh, I admit the girl was a good little actress, but then she had plenty of practice."

Mr. Polly turned a pale, outraged face upon her. "Don't talk about her like that," he said hoarsely. "She's dead, isn't she? But why, Inspector?"

"We don't know that yet, sir. It could even have been a sort of accident, only that's not the way a court's going to look at it."

"Murder under extreme provocation," suggested Mrs. Polly.

"It's a funny thing," said Crowthorne reflectively.

"The public's going to think worse of this chap for burying her than for strangling her. Murder can be a matter of impulse or, as the lady says, of accident; it's even possible to get it reduced to manslaughter if you can show there's no premeditation, but burying the body, that's something you do deliberately."

"If she was stupid enough to go down to the canal," Mrs. Polly began, but her husband said, "We don't know she did go down there, do we, Inspector? You only know you found the body there. And she wasn't a wicked girl, she liked to feel she could—well, you said it yourself, Laura—she liked to think she could wind people round her little finger. I don't think she got much change out of that stepmother of hers . . ."

"If any sympathy's going, mine's with Brenda Myers," said Mrs. Polly frankly. "I always told Fred that girl would play her games once too often."

"What did you mean by that, Mrs. Polly?"

"The way she used to play one man off against another. She didn't even bother to get off with the old love before she was on with the new."

"Then you might be able to tell us the names of some of her admirers. That would be of great assistance."

Mrs. Polly shrugged her expensively covered shoulders. "I wouldn't even know their names. I only know that she always seemed to be around with a new man—there was that chap said to have come from London, she was running around with him for a while . . ."

"You don't know his name?"

"Tall, fair fellow. I'd have thought he was a cut above Linda. Not that Tom Myers isn't a very respectable sort of man; I daresay it's not his fault the girl ran so wild."

"Laura, can't you take it in you're talking about a girl who's been murdered?" Mr. Polly's voice sounded anguished. "I daresay she made trouble for herself, but no one deserves that sort of comeback."

"She never mentioned anyone called Chris, I suppose?"

Mr. Polly frowned. "I don't recall—but then I didn't see such a lot of her. Why don't you have a word with Miss Reith or Miss Buxton." He hesitated. "Perhaps I should say that Miss Buxton isn't altogether unprejudiced. She and Linda never really got on. Miss Reith was different. She was more tolerant. 'She's only young,' she'd say, 'and she'll have responsibilities soon enough.'" He supplied the addresses of both his assistants. There was a girl who helped with the shampooing, and he gave her name, too, but he didn't think she and Linda saw much of each other. This girl had only been with them for a fortnight. "Agnew snaps up the young ones, it's better money for them there," he explained.

"Friday's the day she'd draw her salary, isn't it, Mr. Polly?"

"That's right."

"You didn't think it odd her not coming in to collect?"

"I told you, I had this telephone call."

"Oh yes. From someone calling himself Mr. Myers. Can you remember if it was long distance?"

"Now I come to think of it, it was a call box. It didn't strike me at the time."

"No question of your sending her salary round?"

Mr. Polly looked a little sheepish. "As a matter of fact, she'd subbed most of it during the week. She'd wanted to buy something and she'd put down a deposit and she wanted it specially, she said, for a date she had on Thursday."

"Do you generally allow your assistants to sub on their wages?"

"Miss Buxton and Miss Reith wouldn't dream of asking. Well, they're middle-aged women, they budget. I did think it was some proof of the relations between her and her stepmother that she couldn't ask Brenda Myers to lend her the cash."

"Probably asked her once too often," suggested Mrs. Polly waspishly. "I know the type—take, take all the way."

"It's the way she was born," said Mr. Polly. "Some people are like that. It's second nature to them to put out their hands and expect whatever they want to be put into them. Just as there's the other sort that do the giving automatically. Why, even clients who'd never have tipped Miss Buxton or Miss Reith more than a shilling or eighteen pence at most, would part with half-a-crown to Linda."

"I don't want to speak evil of the dead," said Mrs. Polly, "but she was a little golddigger. I'm sorry, of course, that she's come to this terrible end, and I hope you find the man who did it. I suppose she wasn't in trouble?" she added abruptly.

"Isn't getting yourself murdered trouble enough?" her husband demanded, his voice as harsh as the north wind. "And she simply lived for the day. 'Yesterday's gone and we don't know about tomorrow,' she used to say." He stopped there, as though it was being borne in on him more finally than ever that tomorrow would no longer be her concern.

"He protested a lot, didn't he?" said Inspector Crowthorne to Sergeant Bailey, who had accompanied him. "In his favor in a way. He wouldn't have dared be so partisan if there'd been anything between them."

"I don't think Linda Myers would ever have looked at a man like that," said the sergeant, "Polly's forty if he's a day, and if he even looked across the road at another woman Mrs. Polly would have his head on a charger for breakfast. The whole place knows that."

"I shall have to get up a bit earlier in the morning and learn what everyone else seems to know," the inspector murmured. "Let's see Miss Buxton and Miss Reith and get their reactions. Women are always the best witnesses where another woman's concerned; I mean, they see things a man wouldn't even notice or understand if he did."

The bush telegraph had been at work all right. Miss Buxton had heard the news and had immediately telephoned Miss Reith. Crowthorne found them together in Miss Buxton's flat, which reminded him of the Polly establishment, a place for everything and everything in its place (particularly Mr.

Polly). Miss Buxton expressed genteel shock, but the inspector saw that to her illogical female mind, justice had in some way been done. (Crook, who saw her later, said, "The girl might have been a jackdaw strung up by a farmer as an awful warning, for all the feeling she showed.")

"I can't tell you anything," said Miss Buxton firmly, taking the lead as Mrs. Polly had done. "Neither of us knows anything, do we, Margaret? No, of course we don't, all we know is rumor, and rumor isn't proof, and proof is what the police want, isn't that right, Inspector?"

"I couldn't have put it better myself," Crowthorne agreed.

"Still, you might know the name of someone she'd been going round with," put in Sergeant Bailey. "She could have confided in you—I mean, her and her stepmother . . ."

Miss Buxton laughed harshly. "I don't see Linda confiding in Brenda Myers. Why, it was war to the knife between them. Brenda was as jealous as could be of that girl—well, we all know she was the apple of Tom Myers' eye; yes, we do, Margaret, you know how startled we all were when he got married again, and only a man would have been crazy enough to suppose those two would settle down together. Why, I believe Linda would have made a play for the boss himself, if she hadn't known it was a waste of time. Poor Mr. Polly, he's like one of those birds with a label tied on its leg . . ."

"Oh, Audrey, don't," Miss Reith besought her. "I know you didn't always approve of Linda, but she's dead, and in this dreadful way. I do hope you find out who did it, Inspector, and if I could help you in any way, I would, but Linda hardly spoke to us. I suppose to her we were as old as the hills . . ."

"Speak for yourself, Margaret," Miss Buxton snapped. "And she stayed because she knew she could do just what she liked there. Don't tell me Agnew's would have let her keep her own hours, well, more or less, ten minutes late in the morning, an extra quarter of an hour for lunch, and did you ever know her stay five minutes after we closed to help to clear things up or take a late appointment? And we all know how she favored her friends, saying she'd just trimmed a neck when you and I know she had given a full cut, and not charging for a shampoo and telling the boss she'd just damped the hair, which, of course, you have to do before you can set it. Why, with my own eyes I've seen her put on a special application, which is three-and-six extra, but there was never any mention of it on the bill."

"That's not the kind of thing the sergeant wants to know," insisted Margaret Reith. "He wants to know if we can help with any suggestion of someone who might have killed her, and of course we don't know. To die in such a dreadful way . . ."

"How she'd enjoy all the fuss if she knew about it," commented Miss Buxton viciously.

"You didn't like her, did you, miss?" suggested the sergeant.

"I don't like cheats, and she was one. And all that showing off! I remember saying to her once, 'When you have your own salon, and I suppose that's what you're looking forward to,' and she laughed and said, 'Come the day, I'll be giving the orders. It 'ud be nice to have all that power. Don't you ever wish it could be you telling the others . . .' I said, of course, I was perfectly satisfied with my job, and so I am, Inspector. Mr. Polly's a most considerate employer, and of course Linda took advantage of it. I'm sure Mr. Polly knew she wouldn't stop long anyway, which is why he didn't really bother. She'd never stop long anywhere, that girl. She was with Robinson's at one time, but it didn't last."

"We should all enjoy power if we had the chance," said Margaret Reith simply. "And she was very young."

"She knew how to get round you all right." Audrey nodded. "And she wasn't so irresistible that she didn't get herself murdered in the end."

"You have to have something to get yourself murdered," Miss Reith said.

They both agreed that the girl had left early on Thursday evening, though neither had actually seen her go.

Miss Buxton said someone came in without an appointment for a trim . . . "and we generally manage to fit them in if they're regular customers, because it doesn't take long and Linda was quite clever at that kind of thing, and I could see from the book she had no appointment that evening, and then I realized she'd disappeared. Mr. Polly said she had asked if she could go a little early and as we weren't expecting anyone else he'd agreed. Just out of hairdressing school," fumed Miss Buxton, "and she got practically the same rates as experienced assistants like Miss Reith and myself. Have you any idea who's responsible, Sergeant?"

"If we knew that, miss, we shouldn't be asking questions, should we?"

"There was this one called Chris," Miss Buxton meditated, and the sergeant's attention sharpened at once. "No, I don't know his other name. I was admiring that ring she had, and she said, 'Yes, Chris has good taste, hasn't he? Though I earned it, and not the way you might think.' "

But when it came to giving a description of the mysterious Chris the sergeant got very little help. "I saw her once or twice with a tall, fair man, late twenties, I'd say," Miss Buxton allowed. "She liked them tall; she was quite a little thing herself, which was an advantage in its way, because she could make even short men feel big."

"So where does that get us?" demanded the inspector sourly. "A tall, fair chap called Chris. Well, that ties up with what Solly Gold tells us, but it doesn't give us much of a lead. Of course, if Myers is right and this chap is coming to see him tomorrow . . ." But neither he nor the sergeant believed that one.

"Girl may simply have said it to keep her father calm," the sergeant said.

"Oh, and the autopsy has just come in," the inspector added. "Girl was pregnant—no suggestion from the stepmother?"

"Not a word, and if she'd known she'd have told. She couldn't hope to keep a thing like that hidden."

"Could be a motive," Crowthorne hazarded, "though in this permissive day and age it's not a very good reason for committing murder."

"Unless it's a married man," countered the sergeant shrewdly. "One who didn't want to lose his status and didn't fancy paying out blackmail."

"It doesn't have to be a premeditated crime, of course. Well, I think we might call it a day."

The telephone rang and it was Solly Gold, ringing to say he'd just remembered something. Several weeks earlier he had seen some rather pleasing blue cups and saucers in Mrs. Politi's self-styled antique store, and had gone in to inquire how many were available. He had wanted three but she only had two, though she had a number of additional saucers. She said she always bought the odd saucers because it was surprising how easy it was to sell them. People bought them to stand under flowerpots or for makeshift soap dishes or ashtrays. He had been reminded of the occasion this evening when his wife served tea in the cups. He was certain that the cracked blue saucer his son had noticed near the impromptu grave was one of those from Mrs. Politi's store. He had heard that there was a little elderly lady who often went out during the week feeding the wild cats on the Common, so it seemed possible that she was responsible for the saucer being where it was.

"If it had been there for long it would be encrusted," said Mr. Gold earnestly. "So much rain, so much mud. But the saucer was clean, licked clean, my Reuben say. So perhaps the little lady heard something—no, I have no information, it is just an idea. Her name is Miss Forbes, and she works at Robinson's." He couldn't supply her address, but there wouldn't be any difficulty about obtaining that. She was, he pointed out, no client of his, but she must have a kind heart to go all that distance for cats that didn't even belong to her.

Too late to do anything about that tonight, the authorities decided. It was 10:30 P.M., and the rain was coming down in sheets. Tomorrow they'd contact Miss Forbes, though they didn't pin many hopes on her. If she'd known anything, surely she'd have reported it already. Even anyone as retiring as that couldn't have missed hearing the news. As Spence remarked, you'd need to be as deaf as the famous adder for that.

It showed how desperate they were that they should pin any hopes on so frail a straw, but in fact if one of May's derelict cats had strolled in with even a whisker of evidence, it would probably have been provided with enough salmon to last it for the rest of its life.

Tom Myers, accompanied by a police officer, had made a search of his daughter's room, but it hadn't yielded a shadow of a clue. No letters, no cards, no telephone numbers, no diary—at least, if she kept one, which was improbable, she'd taken it with her to her last fatal rendezvous.

"Shows you how much she trusted Brenda Myers," said one of the men on duty.

A woman detective-constable attached to the branch startled them all by saying, "If Brenda Myers was my mother-in-law I'd keep everything out of her way, too. Lock and key wouldn't be good enough. I know her sort. Open your letters, suppress your telephone calls, and all in the name of virtue. If you ask me, virtue covers more faults than charity's supposed to do."

"What's up with her?" the men asked one another when she'd flounced out of the station. (Crook could have told them never to discount a woman's evidence, because often she talks sense when she doesn't even know she's doing it.)

"Roll on, Sunday," the men said. Sunday was the Lord's Day. Maybe they'd have a little bit of luck then. And actually, quite a lot of things and people were going to be involved during the next twenty-four hours.

On Sunday mornings Mrs. Politi rose later than usual; her Mass wasn't till twelve o'clock, but she liked to take her coffee and rolls and sit in the window to watch the world go by. Her bedroom looked as though it had been lifted clean out of a museum, good solid Victorian furniture that was rapidly coming into its own, and large china ornaments and vases. Not very much normally went on at this hour, but if there should be anything exceptional you couldn't hope to see it by lying in bed. The usual faithful few, little black net squares in hand, went down the hill to St. Aloysius. Others, primmer, wearing what Lilli called derisively a holy look, and carrying small prayer books as opposed to the enormous missals of the Catholics, plodded in the opposite direction. The nonconformists didn't surface until later, and last of all came the Christian Scientists—in Mrs. Politi's opinion, the best turned-out of the lot. She had no sooner settled herself than she realized that something unusual was afoot in the flat opposite. Usually May had a nice lie-in on Sundays, a breakfast tray in bed, and then off to the chapel where she helped to lay out the music. Mrs. Politi had hardly got over the surprise of seeing the light burning so early, when it was extinguished, and a minute later May emerged, not carrying a service book, but equipped with mackintosh and umbrella, and she turned, not in the direction of the chapel, but up a side street, walking purposefully and wearing the hat that she considered rather showy for chapel.

Where she go? wondered Mrs. Politi. There was only one place where she could be going and that was the station. The few food shops that braved the nonconformist conscience and opened their doors on the Sabbath wouldn't be stirring yet —but why a train on Sunday morning? It wasn't even as though she was carrying luggage—not that you could imagine May doing a flit, and what reason had she? But Mrs. Politi's feelings were outraged. Surely if you were going to do anything so out of character as catch a train at an hour when most of your neighbors were still asleep, you would confide in your best friend, the one who lives just over the way.

"That May, she getting sly," announced an indignant Mrs. Politi to an immense china horse that served as a doorstop. Considering, she decided that the metamorphosis had started on the night that May came back from feeding her beloved cats in the company of a strange man in an unforgettable yellow car. "Perhaps she go to meet him now," Lilli confided to the horse, a noble inscrutable creature, and would probably have dropped dead from shock if she had known she'd hit the bull's-eye.

After that everything started to go haywire. Mrs. Politi had just dressed, not because there was any reason to dress so early but because she felt restless, when a police car drew up at the house opposite and an officer got out. He rang May's bell, but of course there was no reply, and in the meantime the man who owned the lower flat had disappeared with his wife or the woman who passed as his wife, so there was nobody to answer the bell. Lilli pushed up the window sash.

"You want Mr. Eccles?" she shouted cunningly. "He gone out. With the car. And that woman go with him."

The officer came across the road and Lilli hurtled down the stairs to open the door.

"We're trying to contact Miss Forbes," he explained.

Lilli smirked. "She go too, but not with Mr. Eccles. I think she go to the station."

"Did you happen to notice if she took any luggage?"

Mrs. Politi looked surprised. "Why she take luggage? She have a conscience, she don't shirk her duty. Miss Robinson expect her tomorrow, so tomorrow she go to the shop."

"You don't know where she might have gone?"

"She not tell me," acknowledged Lilli, "but I think she go to meet the man, the one who bring her home the night Linda Myers is murdered."

The police officer was about to put another question, but she grabbed him by the arm and pulled him into the passage.

"Walls have ears," she reminded him, "and sometimes they don't hear right. I think she in plenty trouble. Never before she miss the choir—a nice voice she has, sometimes she sing the anthem, and I tell you this, never before does she miss chapel. Oh, she in trouble all right."

"Who is this man who brought her home, Mrs. Politi?"

Lilli spread her hands. "Do I know all her friends? She miss the bus, he give her a lift, put her down at the corner. That I see. Maybe she tell you tonight when she come back."

"Of course," said the officer rather nervously, "you didn't notice the number of the car."

To his surprise Mrs. Politi's face suddenly split into an enormous grin. "You know Elijah?"

"Elijah who?" He wondered if Elijah was the name of the mysterious driver.

"Elijah-taken-up-into-heaven-in-a-chariot-of-fire," gabbled Lilli. "This car like that, big and yellow. And very fast."

"And she didn't mention his name? Or where he came from? Or even where she met him?"

"She wait at the bus stop, the bus has gone, he come, he give her a lift." She chuckled again. "The Gingerbread Man, that who he look like." Then her manner sobered. "I tell you, mister, someone frighten May. Friday she don't go to the Common. A man speak to her, she say, she afraid, see? Well, I tell you she damn afraid not to go for her precious cats."

"I understand she leaves food for them in saucers."

"Saucers I give her." It wasn't quite the truth, but at a penny a time you could really call it giving them away. "Monday, Tuesday, Thursday, Friday she go to the Common; Wednesday we go to the pictures; Saturday she go to choir practice."

"But this Friday she stayed at home. You would recognize your own saucers, Mrs. Politi?"

"Plenty saucers I don't sell," said Mrs. Politi blandly.

But she finally agreed that the saucer he described was a facsimile of those she had sold to Solly, so that was one point out of the way. The police, who felt they were competing in a snail race, sighed with relief.

"You think May Forbes bury the girl?" Mrs. Politi asked.

"Of course not. But if she was down there that night she could have heard something. This man who spoke to her . . ."

"You think he the murderer? That May! So quiet and so sly."

"I don't know that it's such an advantage to have met a man who may have killed a girl," said one of the police officers severely.

"And then she meet Mr. Elijah and he bring her back." Lilli shook her head. "No need to marry to have excitement."

"Does she have a telephone, Mrs. Politi?"

"She say she summoned by bells—a funny thing that? —all day in the shop, so at home, she want peace."

"If she comes back before night . . ."

"She come back," prophesied Lilli serenely. "She not stay away with Miss Alice having her strokes. Oh yes, May back in time for work tomorrow."

She half rose to indicate that the interview was at an end. One of the officers remembered a film he'd once seen about Queen Victoria, just the same cocksure old aristocrat, though everyone knew Mrs. Politi didn't come of aristocratic stock.

"She say it was her duty to come back," Lilli wound up. "I tell her her duty to herself, but no, that May, she die for her duty and no one the better off, but"—she shook her huge head of brilliantly black hair—"no sense. I have a phone," she added delicately. "Maybe I give her a message. Maybe when you ask she tell you why she go off so early, desert her chapel —maybe."

"We must hope so," the officer agreed, thinking it would be nice to be told something for a change.

5

That same morning, while Mrs. Politi was bedeviling the police, Mr. Crook sat in his office tearing his way through the Sunday press and looking hopefully at the telephone. The notion that man should rest on the Sabbath had never found a sympathizer in him. "One seventh of life idled away," he'd have said. And, "The better the day the better the deed." And it seemed that quite a number of his clients agreed with him. He had finished reading about an invisible wolf, a sort of Loch Ness monster of the woods, that was ravaging a village in one of the northern counties, when his front doorbell buzzed, and he was on his feet with an alacrity that would have done credit to a prize army cadet. He pressed the release mechanism that opened the front door and came on to the upper staircase. His flat was at the top of the building, and leaning over the well he saw a small figure trudging purposefully upward.

"Will you walk into my parlor?" inquired Mr. Crook joyfully.

The small figure turned up a face as round as a plate. "It's May Forbes," called a voice no louder than a ghost.

"If you're afraid of waking the other tenants, don't give it a thought," bellowed Mr. Crook. "Judgment Day'll hardly wake some of them."

"Perhaps I shouldn't have come on a Sunday," apolo-

gized May, "but I couldn't very well leave Miss Phyllis all by
herself tomorrow, and though Jack Hardy means well, he's
something of a bull in a china shop."

Panting slightly, she reached the top floor. "Come in,
Sugar," Mr. Crook invited her heartily, "don't know when I've
been more pleased to see anyone."

She blinked at what seemed to her the confusion of the
room into which she was ushered, but Mr. Crook, with a wave
at the uncurtained windows, said, "Best view in London. All
those houses, all the houses full of rooms, all the rooms full of
people, and any one of them might need my help any minute.
Keeps you on the buzz, you know."

He looked as new-minted as if he'd been turned out
from some Machiavellian machine only that morning.

"It's about Linda Myers," said May, coming to the
point with a directness that delighted him. "You've seen the
news, I'm sure."

"I've read the pieces in the paper," Mr. Crook agreed,
"but when you're as old as me you'll know the important bits
are the ones they don't print."

May nodded. She felt suddenly dizzy. "Have any
breakfast?" asked the astute Mr. Crook. "Nice cup of tea, I
suppose? That's what I thought. I'll give you something better
than tea. Just for medicinal purposes, if that's the way you like
it," he added.

He poured some brandy into a glass. "They won't give
you better than that on the Health Service." He produced a
box of biscuits. "My first-aid pack," he told her, beaming.
"Now, Sugar, put yourself outside that, and then come clean.
You were holding out on me last time, and don't think I didn't
know it."

This direct attack made May blink. "I couldn't know
it was a girl he had in the boot," she protested. "I mean, you
don't expect—and it isn't as if I could recognize him again, because of the mask."

"So just what did you think he was doing?" inquired
Mr. Crook, taking this remarkable confidence in his stride.

"Chap in a mask at dead of night with something mysterious in the boot of his car. Didn't happen to see a spade, I suppose?"

"Actually, I did," confessed May. "That's really what alarmed me."

"Must be the understatement of the year. Just tell me, Sugar, and remember you'll have to tell the police, too, so it better be good, just what did you think the chap was doing?"

"I thought it might be a dog," babbled May. "A big dog."

"You don't generally put on a mask to bury a dog," suggested Mr. Crook reasonably.

"It would depend on the dog. I mean, if it was one you'd run down and you thought it might be valuable. You're supposed to report it to the police, but it might be someone who didn't want to—I mean, he mightn't find it convenient—and you can't exactly leave a dog lying in the road, though that does happen sometimes to cats . . ."

"So the fellow put on a mask and retreated to the woods, goin' to a place where no one was supposed to hang around, and there you are—why?"

"I told you, I feed the cats."

"So you did, Sugar. You must have given him a shock."

"He gave me a shock. I explained about the kitten—well, I told you that—and I couldn't get away fast enough. I suppose if I'd heard next day that someone was missing I might have linked it up, but no one was, not till the police went digging by the canal last night and found that poor girl. I knew then, of course, I'd have to tell them what I'd seen and heard, but I thought I should get some advice, and you had said—I mean, you gave me your card, and of course as a rule I don't need a lawyer."

"What do you expect me to tell you?" asked Crook.

"On the films," explained May shyly, "they always say I wish to speak to my lawyer . . ."

"That's when they're bein' accused of some crime. You don't think the police are goin' to suspect you . . ."

"Well, of course not. But it's nice to feel you have

someone *behind* you. Not that I don't trust the police, of course; I do."

"Mentioned this to anyone else?" asked Crook.

"Only Mrs. Politi. I told her I'd seen a man by the canal and he spoke to me. I had to tell her something because she saw me getting out of your car. She's my neighbor, a very kind woman, she sometimes gives me leftovers for the cats, but she does talk."

"It's when they make you talk you have to start watching your p's and q's," Mr. Crook commented.

"She's very curious . . ."

"No harm in that. Curiosity may have killed the cat but it's saved a lot of lives, whatever the moralists may tell you. Tell her much?"

"Just that I'd seen a man who made me nervous and then you saw me waiting at the bus stop and gave me a lift home. She wanted me to go to the police, but I said no one had done me any harm, the man didn't threaten me in any way, and they'd simply say I was asking for trouble, going down there by myself at night. And I suppose in a way they're right," added May honestly, "only nothing's ever gone wrong before, I mean, I've never met anyone. And it's not as though I can really help much. I wouldn't know the car again and I wouldn't know the driver. I don't know that I'd even recognize the voice. He spoke as though he had a sore throat or something, kind of muffled."

"If I was found burying a girl at dead of night I'd have a muffled voice, too," said Mr. Crook. "You still don't think there was something rummy about the mask? Or do they all wear masks for night driving in your part of the world?"

"I did think that a bit strange," May confessed, "but, of course, if it was a valuable dog he wouldn't want to be recognized, and that and the balaclava—did I say?—and the darkness, well, it would be difficult to know him again."

"You didn't answer my question," Mr. Crook pointed out. "Do your drivers mostly wear masks?"

"Well, of course, in the ordinary way—but this wasn't ordinary. You see, the Saturday before, I don't mean yesterday of course, the Saturday before that, there was this students' rag at Ainstown, that's the next town on the map to Churchford, about eight miles away, and there was quite a pageant, or would have been if the weather hadn't turned so bad. The students were going round in all sorts of disguises to get money for the Cottage Hospital. One of them was dressed like an ape" —she disregarded Crook's hearty suggestion that most likely he didn't find the change very different—"and frightened an old lady out of her wits. And there was someone on one of the floats dressed as Death—the archenemy, you see, and he wore a mask. And Linda was taking part, I remember, because she came to see Miss Alice—she came in occasionally to wash her hair after Miss Alice found it difficult to get about; of course, she made it worth her while, Miss Alice, I mean, she really did love seeing Linda, and you couldn't be surprised, she was so pretty and bright, and Linda must have had a good heart, because sometimes she'd stay on and read some of Miss Alice's letters to her, she kept all her old letters, she said her life, her real life, was all in the past . . ."

"So'll mine be, at this rate," commented Mr. Crook heartily. "Are you saying that the chap representing Death thought he might as well go a step further and put the theory into action?"

"Well, of course not." May looked shocked. "I don't even know which one he was and I daresay there was more than one. I only saw the floats as they went past the window. We don't close on Saturdays."

"Once when I was a kid I went into a maze," said Mr. Crook frankly. "Believe me, I thought I was going to die there before I found the way out. I'm beginning to feel the same way now. Let's recap. You stood in the doorway and watched the floats go by and there was this chap wearing a mask, and there could have been another . . ."

"I only saw a part of the procession, because a customer came in, and I never saw the return because of the rain —it really pelted down, and broke everything up. And, of course, I'm not naming any special person, I don't even know who was wearing the mask, I'm just pointing out that it wouldn't be so difficult for someone to have one. I mean, if he'd tried to buy it, or you can make them yourself with a square of felt and a bit of ribbon; we sell squares of felt at Robinson's, people buy them to make egg-cozies or children's toys, particularly at Christmas . . ."

"And you don't remember anyone buying one?"

"Well, no, but someone else might. Or I expect you can hire them at these theatrical costumers, people going to fancy dress parties or doing charades. I used to do quite a lot of amateur theatricals myself when I was younger, I loved dressing-up, and you don't have to believe the psychologists who say it's because you're dissatisfied with your own life and are looking for compensation. I went to a lecture at Ainstown Town Hall once, and that's what the professor said . . ."

"It's all very interesting," said Mr. Crook solemnly, "and I could listen to you all day, but it's going to be different when you're talking to a chap in uniform. Uniform does something to people—you remember the tribe in the Good Book whose yea was yea and nay nay? Well, that's what the police 'ull expect, so before we go down to set a light in their darkness, it might be as well to separate what you think it could have been from what you really did see."

"You mean"—May's eyes were brilliant; she must have been a fetching little thing as a girl, Crook thought—"you're *coming with me?*"

"I thought that was the proposition. I mean, you didn't make this journey on a cold Sunday morning just for me to warm your hands. And one more thing, Sugar. Just remember, the uniform ain't the man. There's something about a uniform that works havoc even with the innocent. But underneath it is someone who has to blow his nose and cut his toenails, same like you and me. The other thing to remember is that X may not have set out to murder the girl—a lot of murders I know have been no more than unfortunate accidents, but once you're loaded with the corpse, what are you to do? I don't say it's ideal to dig a pit in a dark wood, but it's generally more convenient than keepin' the body on the premises."

"I suppose she could be tiresome," May allowed, and

he marveled at her discretion. "I know she used to annoy Miss Phyllis by serving her own friends first, she said old people had plenty of time on their hands, and she did quote special prices to them. I think she really didn't understand that it wasn't honest, and Miss Phyllis couldn't make her."

"Wonder they kept her as long as they did."

"That was Miss Alice. I think she saw her as the daughter she'd liked to have had. If she'd been married, I mean."

"No secret romance?" asked Mr. Crook.

"I did hear a reference once to someone she'd lost and never really got over . . ."

She looked so woebegone that Crook clapped her on the shoulder. "Window dressing, Sugar!" he declared. "Of course, the world's changed a lot since I was a boy, but human nature don't change much, and when I was a lad every maiden lady had a gentleman friend who died on his way out to India. Funny how lethal journeys to India were in those days."

He wondered what the police were going to make of his client. They might start by seeing her as a woolly-minded old dear, who'd probably dreamed up half her story at least, but it wouldn't be long before they changed their minds. Even without his support he could see she wouldn't let herself be browbeaten, and she'd hold her own, all with an air so gentle and placatory than even a bluebottle would start feeling a brute if he pushed her too hard.

The police were still at sixes and sevens when Mr. Crook arrived with his client. As soon as the plainclothes branch heard that May had arrived, they even showed enthusiasm. When they heard about her escort, enthusiasm paled a bit.

"Trust Crook to winkle his way in, even outside his own manor," said Crowthorne. "Still, she's got something to tell us to make it worth his while coming down to Churchford. We'd better have 'em both in."

When he saw May he said they'd been hoping for this meeting.

"Hope don't always pay such rapid dividends," agreed Mr. Crook.

"I suppose you'll think I should have come to you right away," May acknowledged, forgetting everything Crook had told her. "But I didn't really know anything. I just saw a man in a car down by the canal, and he had a spade, but as I said to Mr. Crook, he might have been burying a dog."

"The police are like me," said Crook. "Imagination ain't their strong suit. I mean, they do like their facts in order. Start at the beginning, and if there's anything they don't understand they can stop you and ask."

So May told her story steadily, aware that to them it must sound absurdly melodramatic. "Mr. Crook says I might have known it wasn't a dog, I mean, he wouldn't have to display so much secrecy, but some dogs are very valuable, I met a woman once who told me she'd given £175 for a poodle, it wasn't even very pretty, one of those very sharp noses, and I don't know if insurance would cover running down a dog. And then, of course, there's the breathalizer. If it was someone whose living depended on his car, he wouldn't dare take risks."

"Did he sound intoxicated to you?"

"I told Mr. Crook his voice sounded odd, but that might be because he was afraid I might recognize it."

"Somebody you knew, you mean?"

May looked horrified. "I didn't say that. But—well, it was an English voice, I mean, you can always tell, however they try to disguise it, foreigners still retain a trace of accent. It might have been clever if he'd pretended to speak broken English, but I think I took him by surprise as much as he took me. I told him about my kitten in case he thought I was spying on him or something. Actually, I felt rather nervous."

"But you still thought he was burying a dog?"

"I thought it could be a dog. Well, you don't go for a walk and expect to meet somebody burying a girl you know. And it's no use asking me what he looked like, because what with the mask—what they call a domino, I think—and the balaclava which hid his hair, and the general darkness, well, it could have been practically anyone."

"You didn't mention this, not even to Mrs. Politi?"

"Well, especially not to Mrs. Politi, because—I daresay it's her foreign blood—she's like the poet who saw heaven in a wild flower, if you get my meaning, only in her case it wouldn't be heaven or a flower. And if I had told anyone else, before Linda's disappearance became public property, I mean, they'd just have thought I was crazy. You might even have thought so yourself."

"She's got you there," said Crook, grinning.

"But you didn't mind telling Mr. Crook?"

"He'd said—he drove me back that night and of course I didn't tell him then, because in a way you could say it was no affair of mine—but he said if I ever should need any help, here was his card. So when I heard about Linda, I remembered that—he had been so kind," she wound up.

"Oh, Mr. Crook's a very kind man," Inspector Crowthorne agreed. "But you didn't really need him to tell you where your duty lay."

"No. No, of course I didn't," May acknowledged. "But when you're on your own and you're a woman and not young any more, and you've never had much to do with the police, well, nothing really, except once when I slipped on a banana skin and an officer came up after a minute to ask if I was all right, and of course I was, and anyway, someone else had helped me to my feet by then—it's rather nice to have someone *behind* you. I've always thought that was the great advantage of being married. Someone else buys the tickets and asks the policeman the way. And naturally, Mr. Crook said I should come to you at once, even if I couldn't help you much, because you might be able to read something into the situation that hadn't occurred to me."

"Or to Mr. Crook? That's difficult to believe."

"He said I should just tell you what I'd seen and heard and you'd understand."

"Mr. Crook's got a very high opinion of the police all of a sudden."

"You should try living a blameless life yourself," suggested Mr. Crook heartily. "Virtue may get you extra points in the hereafter, but in this sinful world it has a very constraining effect."

"Has it helped at all?" pleaded May. "What I've told you, I mean."

"It's narrowed the field considerably," the inspector said. "We know that Miss Myers left her employment just after five P.M. on Thursday, and you saw this stranger digging a grave—what precise time would you say?"

"I couldn't be precise," said May, knitting her brows. "I left home about seven-thirty and I walked to the Common, and I didn't go very fast, because of frightening the cats . . ."

"Lady came into the Rampant Horse just after nine," said Crook.

"Mr. Crook means the Mettlesome Horse," May explained.

"Do I?" said Crook. "He'd been out to grass so long . . . how long would it have taken you to walk, Sugar?"

"About twenty minutes, I think."

"So Miss Myers was probably killed between five-thirty and eight—those are the outside figures." Six to seven or seven-thirty was his own idea.

"I'm sorry I can't help you more. Of course, the person you want is the person she was going to meet on Thursday when she left Mr. Polly. It doesn't prove he's the one responsible . . ."

"He?"

May looked honestly astonished. "I can't imagine Linda getting off early to meet a girl friend," she said. "But perhaps someone will remember seeing her with an escort that night and come in and tell you."

"I can see you believe in miracles, Miss Forbes," the inspector said.

"Oh, I do," agreed May. "The difficulty is one doesn't recognize them at the time. It's like angels, who come in the strangest guises."

"If you're looking at me," said Mr. Crook, "thank you for the kind thought. Now, you're going to be asked to sign a statement, and read it through carefully . . ."

"I'm sure it'll be all right if it's only what I've said," said May.

"That's why you have to read it."

At last he did take her away. "How does Crook do it?" the inspector murmured. "Has 'em all eating out of his hand, young and old. I could do with a miracle or two myself."

And at that moment, though he wasn't aware of it, his miracle was drawing nearer and nearer to Churchford.

Chris Wayland, tall, fair, twenty-seven years old, a bit of a rolling stone, explaining himself to himself as a seeker for the right niche in life, came out of his lodging at Hornby that Sunday morning at about eleven o'clock and walked down the main street looking for a news agent. He was in a strange town, shaping out one more of a series of articles—Primitive Life in the Twentieth Century, they were called—and his thoughts were running on his work. He by-passed the queue of the devout outside the Roman Catholic church and another queue waiting for the Sunday morning bus, and found a stationer and tobacconist that was open. And went in. And, in a sense, you could say he sealed his fate.

The girl behind the counter was small and dark, some might have called her dumpy, but Chris remembered a song about a nut-brown maiden which seemed much more appropriate. When she looked up to take his order he saw that she seemed to twinkle—no, he amended, to sparkle—not just her eyes, which were a kind of golden-brown, but her whole personality. He looked at her small capable hands slipping out a paper from a pile, reaching to a shelf for the cigarettes he preferred, and he asked, surprising himself as much as her, "What's your name?"

"Well, you didn't leave your tongue with the cat today," said the girl coolly. But the sparkle was like diamond-dew. He thought for an instant she wasn't going to tell him, then she relented and said, "It's Jennifer, since you're interested."

"And I suppose everyone calls you Jenny. Jenny Wren."

"How did you guess?"

He didn't smile, as she'd anticipated. "The inference of the obvious," he said. "How long does this shop stay open on Sundays?"

"As long as there's any call for goods. Say five o'clock."

His thick fair brows lifted. "No trade union?"

"My Mum says I don't need any union so long as I've got her."

He nodded. He took the change she offered him and folded the paper under his arm, slipped the cigarettes into his pocket.

"Are you promised?" he asked her, and she stared.

"Well, there's a way to talk!"

"I can see you're not wearing an engagement ring," he elaborated, "but—are you compromised by an understanding with anyone?"

"It means something to you if I say yes?" She was still laughing, but there was curiosity in her voice.

He said, "I don't like poachers, I'd always sooner persuade a man to go peaceably."

She leaned her elbows on the counter and met his gaze clearly. "Do you talk to all the girls this way?"

"I'd be wearing manacles long before now if I did," he pointed out. "I'm twenty-seven. How old are you?"

"Nineteen." She spoke before she could stop herself. "Though what affair it is of yours . . ."

"Half a man's age plus seven, that's what the philosophers used to say."

"I suppose you realize I don't know what you're on about."

A couple of other men came in for papers, and then a girl for cigarettes, and Jennifer served them, and out they walked, showing about as much feeling as if they'd got their purchases from a machine.

"It used to be the old recommendation—well, one of them, anyhow—for a successful marriage. Half a man's age plus seven. You see how well it fits."

"If you don't talk like this to every girl, why me, why today?"

"It's like Sir Isaac Newton and the apple." He paused, and she said, quite without sarcasm, "I went to school, too, you know."

"The point being he must have seen bushels of apples, growing on trees, too, before the day that was the turning point of his existence. Probably he'd watched them fall, but one had to crash right on his head to give him the notion of the law of gravity. Maybe it jolted something in his brain that was—well, a bit sluggish before then. In the same way," he continued composedly, and how should she guess that his heart was leaping like a hooked fish under his conservative jacket, "I've been seeing girls all my life. Nice girls. In the same way as Sir Isaac had probably eaten a lot of apples."

"We're open on a Sunday to sell papers and smokes," Jennifer pointed out.

"I'm not stopping you, am I? And you didn't answer my question."

"You ask so many."

"The first one of all. Are you promised?"

Her brows, very delicate and dark, drew together. "Promises are things to be careful about."

"I couldn't agree with you more. But you still haven't answered."

"Let's say I'm choosy."

"Then—will you have dinner with me tonight?"

"I don't know what my mother would say if she could hear you."

"Let's ask her then."

He had no sooner spoken than the door at the back of the shop swung back and a big commanding woman came in.

"Haven't we got what the gentleman wants, Jenny?" she said.

It was Chris who answered. "I want your daughter to come out to dinner with me tonight."

Mrs. Hart stood quite still. He thought Boadicea might

have looked like that, watching the slaves binding scythes to the wheels of her chariot.

"What we sell here are papers and cigarettes," she observed.

"That's why I came in. Now I'm wondering if your daughter would come out to dinner with me tonight."

"I don't know what you think my daughter is . . ."

"The girl I want to take out to dinner. I've told her, and she thought I should tell you."

Mrs. Hart turned to the girl. "Do you know him, Jenny?"

"Not till a few minutes ago."

"Well, young man, you've got your answer."

"I'd like to hear what Jennifer has to say."

"My girl's a good girl and does what I tell her. I've no mind for any daughter of mine to make a fool of herself, and maybe end up like that poor girl in the paper today."

He moved instinctively, as if already he felt the scythes grazing the calves of his legs.

"Which girl's that?" He unfolded the paper he had tucked under his arm. A pretty face looked out of the front page. Chris could actually feel himself turning pale. "Oh no," he ejaculated. "Oh no."

"What's the matter?" Mrs. Hart demanded keenly. "Is it someone you know?"

His face seemed to have stiffened and aged by ten years in as many seconds. His eye was running rapidly down the column of print; he might never have heard the question. He didn't even move out of the way of other customers, wasn't aware he was blocking the counter. At last he looked up, refolded the paper and pushed it back under his arm.

"I'm sorry, Jennifer, it can't be tonight, after all. I have to go to Churchford."

"You mean you did know her?" Mrs. Hart's voice rang with indignation.

"It was my ring she was wearing." It might have been a machine rather than a man speaking the words. No feeling there at all. And then Chris turned and walked out of the shop,

84

practically walking through a stout lady who had just entered with a yapping Peke on a lead. Perhaps the young man trod on its foot, because suddenly the yapping rose to a wild crescendo.

The owner's voice was almost as piercing. "Well, really, did you see that? No manners some people, and a poor dumb beast. If that's all education does for you—The Sunday *Record* and the *Gossip*, please, dear."

"Couldn't you see," demanded Jennifer, and her voice was almost as devoid of feeling as his had been, "he's taken the knock? He didn't even see you. He's taken the knock."

"What made you say that?" her mother demanded when the vociferous pair had left the shop.

"If he'd known—about her, I mean—he wouldn't have said. He'd have been like those soldiers in the hymn who had their armor girded on. He wasn't wearing any armor at all. I wonder why he gave her the ring."

"The sooner you forget about him the better, my girl," scolded Mrs. Hart. "Walking into the shop like Lord Highmuckamuck, asking you out to dinner, and you letting him . . ."

"How do you stop people asking you out to dinner?"

"A smart girl like you knows how to put a man in his place. I've told you before, my girl, I don't want to see you make the mistake I did. Anyone would have thought butter wouldn't melt in your father's mouth. He's not the man for you, my mother said, but I didn't listen. I knew it all."

"I don't know anything much," the girl agreed, "but someone has to teach you."

"The only good thing I got out of that marriage was you," Mrs. Hart continued, "and I don't mean to see that ruined, too. Now, stop daydreaming. We're here to sell papers, and goodness knows there's competition enough."

The girl moved a few steps down the counter to serve some newcomers. "He called me Jennifer," she said dreamily, as they went out. "No one's ever called me that before."

Inspector Crowthorne had only just got over the

shock of his interview with Crook and his intrepid companion when someone knocked on the door of his office and a constable came in to say, "It never rains but it pours, sir. There's a chap outside who says his name's Christopher Wayland and he's the one who gave the Myers girl the ring."

"What's he like?" Crowthorne asked.

"Tall, fair, late twenties, I'd say . . ."

"In short, Chris, the man of mystery."

"He says he only saw the news about two hours ago; he was staying in Hornby and he went out to get a paper . . ."

"And came right down to see us?"

"He said he wanted to hear at first-hand what we'd found out. Came in a car, sir," he added, "dark blue Martineau."

"Very considerate of him. We'd better have him in, and then send someone along to collect Miss Forbes. It's not much of a chance and I don't suppose any jury would wear it, but she just might recognize the voice or something—women are good at details—and what's more to the point, he might recognize her."

"Shock tactics? Yes, sir. He looks a pretty cool customer."

"Oh, they're all that," the inspector agreed. "And that wretched girl's the coolest of the lot."

"I'd have come before if I'd known," began Chris bluntly within a minute of taking a chair, "but I didn't see the news till about eleven o'clock."

"And you recognized the girl from her photograph?"

Chris looked surprised. "Well, yes. But I didn't actually need the photograph, it was all in the press. And then there was the description of the ring. I haven't seen it yet, but that was described too, and it sounds like one I bought from Mr. Gold to give to her."

Shown the ring, he identified it immediately. "We had heard from Mr. Gold about the man who purchased it," Crowthorne said. "Did it have any special significance? I mean, a ring's a rather personal thing to give a girl."

"It wasn't an engagement ring, if that's what you're driving at. There was never anything but a ships-that-pass-in-the-night relationship between us. I hadn't set eyes on her till I came to Churchford . . ."

"How did you meet her, sir?"

"As a matter of fact, she thumbed a lift. It was a wet night and there was no bus . . ."

"And after that you saw more of her?"

"Well, obviously. I don't make presents to every girl who asks for a lift. And even present is hardly the right word, it was more like payment for value received."

"What exactly does that mean, Mr. Wayland?"

"I've been commissioned to do a series of articles on ancient customs still obtaining in English village life, a sort of link-up with the past, and Miss Myers was remarkably knowledgeable. The difficulty isn't usually to find someone who'll talk about the past, but someone who can give you authentic information. The girl told me the legend of Hunter Scanes, for instance, that I was subsequently able to verify, and she knew about a number of other local superstitions. She said her mother used to tell her stories when she was a child. It was a snip for me really, it saved me any amount of research; that is, I wasn't plunging about in the dark, I knew what I was looking for. Then a TV company bought the rights to one of the articles, and I told Linda—Miss Myers—and she laughed and said didn't she rate something, or words to that effect."

"And you gave her the ring?"

"Yes."

"Did she ask for it?"

"I think she might have preferred the money, but I didn't want that. She hinted that a ring would be acceptable—I could be wrong about this, but I wasn't certain the idea wasn't to gear up some other fellow . . ."

"Make him jealous, you mean?"

"It was just an idea. If you're going to ask me for chapter and verse, then I can't supply it. I know she went around with quite a lot of men. I never thought it went very deep with any of them, she was just a girl wanting a bit of fun. I was always expecting to hear she was going to be married, she was very attractive."

"You didn't think of marrying her yourself?"

"I couldn't possibly support a wife on the standards she'd expect."

"And you don't think she could have misunderstood your attitude."

"She wouldn't have thought of me twice in that connection, and only once if I'd put the idea into her mind. 'You're tied down like a donkey pegged out in a field once you're married,' she said to me once. 'All kids and supermarkets. I don't mean to settle for that.' "

"And when did you last see her?"

Chris considered. "It must have been Thursday. It was the day I left Churchford. It wasn't by appointment. I'd just come from Mr. Warren, the man who has the garage at Churchford Point, but you know that, of course."

"We know Mr. Warren," conceded the police.

"I'd taken her—my car, I mean—for a general overhaul a bit previously, since I have the Ministry of Transport test coming up. Mr. Warren said I'd never get through with the tires that were on her, he had a couple in stock and he thought he could get me two second-hand ones in the next few days."

"He thought all four should be replaced?"

"He said I might scrape through with two of the old ones, but he didn't recommend it. I said I had to go on to Hornby to get material for this article, but I said I'd look in after that, probably about the end of the week."

"But no definite date was fixed."

"I wasn't absolutely sure which day I'd be back and he couldn't guarantee the tires, but he said to try the end of the week."

"And they were fitted?"

"On Friday morning. I got back from Hornby pretty late Thursday night."

"And you last saw Miss Myers . . ."

"Some time on Thursday. I knew I was pulling out and I told her I was going to look for the Thurleigh Castle ghost—a young woman who's said to have drowned her illegitimate child in the lake, and who wanders around after dusk calling for it."

"You seriously tell me you believe that sort of legend?"

"It's what I'm paid to write. And what I believe is beside the point. A lot of the locals believe it."

"And did you see the lady?"

"Actually I didn't, though I hung around a long time. I'd hoped to see the interior of the church too, it's got some very nice old brasses, but my luck was dead out. The old woman who has the key was away and there was nobody else."

"So you couldn't write your article?"

"Luckily I met two or three of the ancients who swear they've seen the lady—all I personally got out of it was the nightingales. Hornby nightingales are famous, but of course you know that. I stopped off at a drive-in café on the way back, one of these help-yourself places. It must have been about eleven P.M. when I returned to the Bald-Faced Stag, where I was staying."

"And all that time you didn't run into anyone who'd remember seeing you at Hornby on Thursday night?"

Chris looked skeptical. "Well, hardly. I'd never been there before; and I doubt whether you can call the nightingales as witnesses."

The inspector stiffened. "This is a murder case, Mr. Wayland, not an opportunity for wisecracks."

"I recognize that, naturally. Why do you think I came pelting back to Churchford as soon as I saw the news?"

"Even though you hadn't seen Linda Myers since you left Churchford on Thursday—afternoon?"

"If, as you suggest, she was murdered that night, the afternoon's about the latest time I could have seen her."

"Did you have much conversation with her?"

"She was going somewhere; anyway, she didn't seem disposed to loiter. I told her I was pulling out, she said good hunting or words to that effect. It doesn't seem as though I've been of much assistance," he added grimly. "Except that you know who gave her the ring . . ."

The inspector was doodling with a rather thick black pencil. "One more point," he said. "Mr. Wayland, were you aware that Linda Myers was pregnant?"

"What!" Chris stiffened as though he'd swallowed a poker. "The paper didn't say anything about that."

"The news will be released in the morning. She was about two months gone. How long had you known her?"

"Since I first came to the district."

"About three months ago?"

"Roughly that." He frowned. "I moved around, of course."

"I have to put this question to you. Mr. Wayland, is there any possibility that the child could have been yours?"

"Absolutely none. I told you, ours wasn't that sort of relationship."

"And you never met any of her family?"

"I knew she had a stepmother she didn't get on with, and a father who thought the world of her."

"You had no intention of meeting any of them?"

"It was never suggested."

"So if Mr. Myers says his daughter told him you were expected to midday dinner at his house today, he's got hold of the wrong end of the stick."

"Does he say that?"

"It's what his daughter told him."

"He must have misunderstood her. I didn't even expect to be in Churchford today. Could it be . . ." He hesitated. "If he knew about the child she might have said the father was coming to see him?"

"He didn't know about the child and he is sure you are the man the girl referred to."

"It doesn't sound like Linda, you'd expect her to have too much sense. Though I suppose . . ." He hesitated again.

"Yes, Mr. Wayland?"

"If her mother—stepmother—was on at her for going

about with strange men, she might have said someone was coming on Sunday."

"Why you?"

Chris shrugged. "Search me. Unless, of course, they were fussed over the ring. But it wasn't all that valuable. Did anybody know about the child?"

"No one has admitted to knowing. Of course, she may have hoped to persuade the father to marry her."

"And he didn't see it like that? And they had an argument and it got a bit out of hand? That's pretty Grand Guignol, isn't it? I mean, this isn't the Victorian era. Girls do actually have children without a wedding ring, and it doesn't wreck their lives."

"I hardly think Mr. Myers would see it that way. Where is your car now, Mr. Wayland?"

Chris looked surprised. "Well, outside. It's a blue Martineau." He gave the number.

"You said you'd had fresh tires fitted?"

"That's right. On Friday morning. You can check that with Mr. Warren," he added dryly.

"We have to do things by the book," the inspector assured him. "Did you have the car washed at the same time?"

"I generally polish her up myself, but as he was putting on the tires . . ." He stopped. "You are trying to tie me up with this, aren't you? Well, ask him. He'll tell you he didn't find any bloodstains . . ."

"I wouldn't expect it, not when the victim's been strangled." He doodled some more. "Do you carry a rug in your car, Mr. Wayland?"

"Well, I call it that. It's more of a blanket, really. Just in case I have to spend the night in her. It has happened."

"Yes. All right, Mr. Wayland. That's all."

"You mean I'm free to go? After this build-up?"

"Leave your address and telephone number with the sergeant as you go out," said Crowthorne. "I may take it, I suppose, you won't be leaving Hornby for a few days?"

"Not of my own free will," said Chris, elaborately polite.

He thought that Crowthorne might be a quite formidable enemy, though his appearance was ordinary enough. You could see him half a dozen times and not remember him on the seventh occasion. Coming into the general office or whatever they called it, he noticed a little woman sitting on a chair against the wall, like a rather dejected Patience on a monument. She peered at him from under the brim of a brown felt hat that half obscured her face. He wondered what sort of trouble she was in. But as he approached the desk she suddenly came to life, jumping up and hurrying across the floor.

"Sergeant," she said, pushing back her hat with a fluttery hand, "I'm sure this gentleman's business is very important, but I have been here some time, and naturally I'm anxious. Are you sure there isn't any news about Tom Jones?"

Chris turned to her. She looked as though she might have walked out of a nursery rhyme, swaddled in a rather too heavy coat for the time of year, with a collar that came up around her ears.

He felt an urge to say something shocking, like "Another poor soul gone missing?" and was appalled at himself.

"Go ahead," he advised her. And then to the sergeant, "Have you heard anything of Tom Jones?"

"He's my kitten, you see," said the urgent voice, and he thought he might have guessed, she was the motherly sort, presumably unmarried and so turning to an animal for company. "A Burmese. I lost him last Thursday night on Broomstick Common. I don't know if you know this part of the world, but it's a great place for wild cats and, well, he's so young and I don't know that he can look after himself—they say cats always know their way home, but it's quite a distance. I keep feeling he may have fallen into the canal."

"Oh, I shouldn't think so," said Chris. "Cats hate water as a rule."

"He could have slipped. And I'm sure he can't swim. If cats were licensed like dogs," she added uncontrollably, "there'd be a lot more notice taken if they vanished."

"If you'd sit down again for a minute, Miss . . ."

"Jones," she supplied hurriedly. "I told you."

"Is that why the kitten's called Tom Jones?" asked Chris.

"Of course. I suppose you think I'm making a lot of fuss about a cat, with all the trouble there is about poor Linda Myers—you did hear about her?"

"Yes," he agreed. "I've heard about her. Well, it's in all the papers."

"Yes. Of course. Such a pretty girl."

The sergeant intervened. Women never knew where to stop. She was quite the actress, all that yap about a kitten.

"If you'd wait a little longer . . ."

"I don't want to take up too much of your time. But family men and women don't always understand. The difference between a house and a home, I mean."

"I know just what you mean," said Chris. "The inspector asked me to leave my address and phone number in case he thinks of anything else," he added to the man at the desk. He concluded his business and went out. At the door he turned. "I hope you find your cat," he said to May.

His footsteps hadn't died away before she was back at the counter. "That's not the one," she said. "I couldn't be certain about the car when your officer pointed it out to me because I don't know anything more about cars than I know about horses. One has four legs and a tail and the other has four wheels and a bonnet. But that's not the man I saw in the wood on Thursday night."

"How can you be so certain, Miss Forbes? It was dark, beginning to rain, he was wearing a mask; obviously he'd do his best to stay out of sight . . ."

"He didn't know who I was or why I was here," May insisted. "Why, it stuck out a mile. I was just some poor old body who'd lost her cat, like—like in *La Mère Michel*," she added. "That was a French book we did at school. After all, even if I didn't see *him* very well that night, he got a clear look at me, and suddenly jumping up like a djinn out of a bottle, I mean, of course, a spirit, not spirits, he would have given himself away, especially when I talked about Tom Jones, but he was absolutely *fogged*. He never turned a hair when I mentioned Broomstick Common, and do you know why?"

"You tell me, Miss Forbes?"

"Because none of it meant a thing to him. He wasn't on Broomstick Common that night."

"I expect you're going to tell me just where he was," the policeman suggested.

"Oh, I daresay he hasn't got an alibi. My father used to say always mistrust a man with an alibi. Honest people don't carry them around like carnations in their buttonholes."

Heredity, thought the sergeant gloomily. Whole family seemed to have been round the twist. "Thank you for your cooperation," he said formally. "One of our cars will take you back."

"That's absurd!" cried May. "It's only ten minutes. And I shall enjoy the air. It's rather stuffy in here. I suppose you get used to it. It's like that in the shop sometimes," she added more kindly. "I'm really quite grateful to the thoughtless customer who leaves the door open, though Miss Alice used to feel the draughts so. Anyway, people will talk enough without me being driven back in a car. Mrs. Politi started plenty of gossip when she noticed Mr. Crook drive me home that evening."

"Oh, there's always plenty of gossip where Mr. Crook is," said the sergeant.

"To tell you the truth," May confided, "I've been shaking in my shoes ever since I got here, in case anyone I knew came in. I know I'm only here to assist the police, but it's like justice, isn't it? It must not only be done, it must be seen to be done." As though she had made her position crystal-clear she gave him an understanding sort of nod and walked out.

"She seemed pretty sure," the sergeant told Inspector Crowthorne, "and she could be right. If she isn't, he's wasted on his present job, he should be on the stage."

"He played it cool enough," Crowthorne agreed. "Talk about the three fates. That woman and Crook and Wayland all in the same day. I want someone to go out and bring

Warren in, he might remember something about the car—no hope of tracing anything from the tires, Wayland got them changed first thing next morning, but according to him that had all been fixed up beforehand. And get someone to keep an eye on Wayland. I don't want him leaving Hornby till we say so."

Lloyd, the officer sent to collect Warren, came back to report that the man was out, the garage wasn't open on a Sunday, and Warren, a widower, had taken his eight-year-old son for a drive.

"Sister keeps house for him, she said she'd give him the message as soon as he came in. She said right off she knew nothing about his business affairs, so it was no use asking her questions."

"Wonder why she said that," the inspector brooded.

"She's the kind that thinks the police bring bad luck just by crossing the threshold. Not that I got that far. And it's probably true, that he doesn't confide in her, but I'll tell you this, sir, she wouldn't tell us if he did. Quite steamed up about Albert being disturbed on his day of rest. Different for you, she said. That's what you think, I told her."

Warren, a short square man, with an open fresh-colored face, came in shortly after six o'clock.

"You've put my sister in a rare old tizzy," he told the inspector. "Next time you want me and I'm not there, send one of your nice lady policewomen. Martha thinks every man is an ape in human guise. I left her planning to get the priest in to exorcise the house."

"Let's skip the humor," said Crowthorne. "We all have our crosses to bear. Do you remember a young chap called Wayland coming in for a new set of tires on Friday morning?"

"That's right," Warren agreed. "And none too soon at that, only I hadn't got the complete set. You're never going to tell me he's crashed or something?"

"Not in the sense you mean. Know him well?"

"He's been coming to me for his petrol for about three

months, I suppose. A newspaper chap, goes around writing pieces for his paper." But his voice implied it wasn't likely to be the sort of paper he, the speaker, would subscribe to. "And there was the time some Mick ran into his car on the M.1. and he wanted a dent banged out. Not worth claiming the insurance, he said, it would cost more than the bill, and anyway, he hadn't got the other chap's number. Didn't stop, see?"

"You'd recognize his car again?"

"Why, what's up?" demanded Warren. "It's not been stolen?"

"When did you last see him?"

"Must have been when I fitted the tires. That 'ud have been Friday."

"Just fitted the tires—that's all?"

"I gave her a bit of spit and polish."

"Needed it, eh?"

"Nothing special. Here, what's up, Inspector? You're asking a funny lot of questions."

"You didn't notice anything unusual? She could have been involved in an accident."

"Here, wait a minute," said Warren, and he began to laugh. "I don't suppose this is what you want to hear, but when he fished out his checkbook to settle for the tires, he yanked out a sort of highwayman's mask, you know the kind of thing—two eyepieces and a band to go round the head. 'Hullo,' I said, 'what are you planning? Don't waste your time on my garage, I bank every night.'"

"Not trying to be funny, I hope," Crowthorne barked.

Warren looked startled. "Well, but it was funny."

"Didn't strike you as a bit ominous that he should be carrying a mask around with him?"

"Well, but there was this hospital rag they had the other week, he was in that. He said, 'Good Lord, I'd forgotten I still had it,' and when he went out he stuffed it into the litter bin I keep on the premises—don't want the station mucked up with cigarette cartons and ice-cream papers. My kid found it a minute or two later and brought it in. Martha, that's my sister, was all for chucking it away, not hygienic, she said, but the bin was practical empty and quite clean, and it's the sort of thing that amuses kids. Get more education from the telly these days they do than from their schooling; anyway, they pay it more attention."

"Wasn't it a bit outsized for a boy of—how old?"

"Eight. Well, but it was rigged up on a piece of elastic, adjustable, see, all very professional. Yes, I thought he must have had it for the student rag."

"But he's not a student."

"They're not that fussy. I suppose someone pulled him in. Not that it came to much, thanks to the rain, came down in sheets, sent everything flying."

Asked about the discarded tires, he said he sold them with a lot of other similar stuff to a rag-and-bone man who came around regularly. "It's that or taking them along to the dump," he pointed out. "What does he do with them? How should I know? Sells the stuff by weight, I should think."

"Anything to distinguish them from any other tires?" Crowthorne asked. "Well, no need to keep you any longer, Mr. Warren. We know where you are if we should need you again, and I expect your family's getting anxious."

"Not Brian," said Mr. Warren confidently. "That kid's a regular tearaway. 'Will you be in handcuffs, Dad?' he said. And if I was to go back in a police car . . ."

But the inspector didn't take the hint.

Chris Wayland had got nicely settled at the bar of the Ship Inn and was talking casually to the barman—no mention of Linda Myers on either side—when he was called to the telephone and told that Inspector Crowthorne would be glad if he could come in and clear up one or two other points that had arisen. The inspector offered to send a car, but Chris said he thought the landlord probably wouldn't care for that.

He suspected that the Hornby police had been alerted, and if he tried to oil out he'd be stopped before he'd gone a couple of miles. It was a quiet night, not much traffic on the roads, a moon tilting on her back, lights in windows showing like golden squares on a dark chessboard. A night for witches, he thought, and wondered what else the inspector had conjured up.

At the station he was confronted with the domino. "Where did that erupt from?" he asked, and the inspector said, "Mr. Warren brought it in. Found it in his litter bin. Could it be the one you wore to the pageant?"

"You don't miss a trick, do you?" murmured Chris. "I'd go a step further and say you can bet your hopes of a pension it's the identical one. I stuffed it into the bin on my way out. Funny, I hadn't thought . . ." He stopped. "Are you tying this up with Linda Myers' death?"

"We know that the man seen on Broomstick Common that night was wearing a black mask."

"Funny there's been no mention of it till now."

"We have a most reliable witness. Could you explain how it came to be in your possession?"

"I had it for the hospital rag," said Chris. "I was Death, the faceless enemy, confronted with Life, battling for an anonymous patient."

"I didn't know you were a medical student, Mr. Wayland."

"No more did I, but they're not that fussy. Actually, it was Linda Myers who suggested I should lend a hand. It was a tableau on a float, and if I say it myself, it was pretty effective, or would have been if the rain had held off. As it was it came down cats and dogs, and we had to belt for shelter. I stuffed the mask into my pocket . . ."

"Didn't it belong to the organizers of the show?"

"If they had to supply all the props they wouldn't have made much for the hospital. I bought it at a theatrical costumer's near Great Newport Street in London. As a matter of fact, I'd forgotten all about it. Quite a surprise when I found it in my pocket when I was at Warren's."

"His boy found it where you'd put it and took it for a lark, and when we were questioning him—Mr. Warren, I mean —he remembered and told us."

Chris grinned faintly. "Yes, I suppose he would. I don't suppose he sees one of these every day of the week."

"Highly unlikely," the inspector agreed.

"Who said your suspect was wearing it that night?"

"An unimpeachable witness. She happened to be on the Common . . ."

"Of course," exclaimed Chris. "That woman who stormed the desk when I came out to leave my name and address. Well, I can promise you one thing, whoever was wearing a mask that night, it wasn't me. Good thing for her it is a woman, isn't it?"

"What does that mean, Mr. Wayland?"

"If it had been a man I might have suggested it was a switcheroo. You know—criminal makes the discovery and informs the police. There was a case when I was a kid, a doctor had a woman die in his surgery from an illegal abortion, somewhere in the East End of London, so far as I recall. He dumped the body under a bridge on a black wet night and 'found' it in the small hours on his way back from visiting an emergency case. Reported it to the police, imagining they'd never suspect the chap who gave the information, I suppose."

"But they got him?"

"Oh yes, they got him. Still, you can't win them all."

"You can't supply the name of any other participant in the pageant who wore a mask?"

"How policemen love long words! Now, actually, I can't. But the organizers might remember. Or of course it doesn't have to be anyone connected with the pageant."

"Sheer coincidence?"

"Where would we be without it? Oh, come now, if what I think you think were true, wouldn't I have got rid of the thing the same night?"

He still wasn't taking the situation too seriously. Playing it cool, the inspector decided.

"You admitted you'd forgotten you had it."

"I wouldn't have forgotten it if I'd used it to conceal a body. Besides . . ."

"Yes, Mr. Wayland?"

"That was your witness, wasn't it, that woman who

yapped about a lost kitten on the Common and being afraid it might have fallen into the canal?"

"We're asking the questions, Mr. Wayland."

"And I've answered them. Now it's my turn. You ask your sergeant, he'll tell you she didn't know me from Adam. I suppose you'd briefed her? No, don't answer that. I remember, you're asking the questions. But I'll tell you this for free. She didn't recognize me because she'd never set eyes on me before, nor, so far as I know, I on her."

"It's not so easy to recognize a man wearing a mask, particularly in the dark."

"You want to get on the organizer of the rag and ask him who else was wearing a mask."

"We've done that, Mr. Wayland. He doesn't remember anyone else."

"Then the odds are it wasn't anyone connected with the pageant. Good heavens," exploded Chris, "you can get these things anywhere. They sell them at kids' joke shops. Anything else I can do for you, Inspector?"

"I'm wondering if you'd care to make a statement. I'm sure you know your rights, but all the same I'll remind you of them. You don't have to say anything, nothing you've said to date can be used against you, because you haven't been cautioned, but I'm cautioning you now. Did you see Linda Myers on Thursday night?"

"I've already told you I didn't. I saw her earlier in the day and told her I was moving on and she said good hunting or words to that effect. I went to hunt for this ghost—well, to try to track down the legend. I went alone, I didn't see anyone I knew, I got back about eleven P.M. The mask is mine, and I can tell you where I bought it. I don't know why Linda Myers was murdered, I had no motive at all to wish her any harm. I didn't expect to see her again, and I was absolutely staggered to find her picture in the paper this morning. That's the only statement I can give you, and I'm afraid it's not going to get you very far in finding the chap who's responsible. And if there's nothing more to ask me I'll be glad to be on my way."

But he didn't get back to Hornby that night.

6

The news that a man had been at the Churchford Police Station for a good part of the day, assisting the police in their inquiries, was part of the late news. (The further information that a man was being held for the murder of Linda Myers appeared in the first editions on Monday.)

"So they've got the chap who did it!" That was the general reaction, and a few people, notably those in the Churchford area who had young daughters with romantic ideas, sighed with relief. But in one household the police had never heard of officially, and which, therefore, they did not connect in any way with the crime, the relief was unmistakable.

Willy Stephenson—the Honorable Willy—was the only son of his mother, and she a widow. He had been to some extent a thorn in her flesh but recently had atoned for all the anxiety he'd caused her by announcing his engagement to Victoria Ebury, only child of that alarming tycoon, Sir Alfred Ebury. Willy was good-looking, red-headed and enthusiastic where his pleasures were concerned. He was also the son of a man who had gambled away an inheritance and then moved out with a fascinating actress, and had subsequently died abroad.

"Thank goodness you've shown a little sense at last,"

Blanche congratulated her son. "Now be sure you don't spoil everything by falling at the last fence."

On the Sunday after Linda's murder Blanche Stephenson rose at eleven-thirty and dressed with as much care as if she had been going to meet a lover, though her appointment was her usual Sunday one of having lunch with her sister, Louie. Louie was sixty-one, unmarried and blunt as a paper-cutter.

"I don't know why you always wear your finest clothes to come here," Louie said candidly. "You're not going to find your millionaire under my roof." She looked at her sister's elegant figure. "And you can't believe that you'll impress me at this time of day."

"I don't know why I bother to come," murmured Blanche restfully accepting a thimbleful of sherry in a cut-glass goblet. Louie would not have a bottle of Scotch in the house, but there were delicious smells coming from the kitchen. "If you were a cannibal and were going to feast me on a missionary you couldn't take more trouble with your pot roasts," Blanche went on. Her voice made the words sound like the compliment they were intended to be. "As for why I come, you know perfectly well that at our age there's nothing better than conversation with someone who remembers the world you knew when you were a child—and the people in it. It's as good as taking your hair down." She didn't mention the Honorable Theo but he was in the minds of both.

"How's the great romance?" Louie demanded.

Blanche looked grave. "To tell you the truth, Louie, I shall be glad when they've both said I will. They tell you it's difficult getting a daughter married. Believe me, it's nothing to getting your son settled."

"Particularly if his father was the Honorable Theo," Louie agreed robustly. "I hope this Ebury filly realizes what she's taking on. He's the dead spit of his father—as if you didn't know."

"Oh, I know all right," Blanche agreed with a sigh. "But if he wasn't he wouldn't have girls falling in love with him all over the place."

"Falling in love with the Honorable Theo didn't do you much good."

"You only say that because you haven't been married. If I could have foreseen the future, I'd still have married Theo. Oh, I know he was reckless . . ."

"To the point of criminality," Louie reminded her sternly, and really, Theo had only just escaped prosecution by the skin of his teeth. "And then going off with this bitch . . ."

"She wasn't a bitch, she was the most beautiful thing I ever saw. And it didn't do her all that amount of good. She didn't last more than about four years, four years that wrecked her as an actress. It's no use, Louie. You can't try and judge people like Theo and Willy by ordinary standards. You remember that song Mother used to sing: 'I lift up my finger and I cry Tweet! Tweet!'? Theo and Willy hardly need to lift their fingers, the girls come running. And if I ask Willy what he wants with so many of them, all he says is that you can't have too much of a good thing."

"Well, it's to be hoped Victoria will be able to keep him on the straight and narrow—for Willy's sake."

"The depressing thing is, Louie, that if she does convert him, though I admit it's unlikely, she probably will find he's no longer the man she married. I was like that with Theo. I knew he was no good before any of you told me, but I loved him the way he was. It doesn't make sense, does it?"

"You never did make sense," Louie assured her heartily, taking up the glasses and going into the kitchen to fetch in the first course of what was to prove a delicious meal. "Still, I suppose the girl knows her own mind. If her feeling for Willy can survive two months' absence—I suppose Sir Alfred only took her on that cruise in the hope she'd come to her senses . . ."

"And marry some tycoon of his choosing?" suggested Blanche dryly. "You have such a charming way of putting things, Louie."

And the conversation passed to other subjects.

Sometime during the afternoon Louie made a casual

reference to the finding by the police of the body of a girl in a piece of wasteland not more than fifteen miles away.

Blanche hadn't heard. "You'd better take my Sunday *Record* and read the whole story," offered her sister. "Strangled she was."

"The usual reason?" wondered Blanche.

"The paper didn't say. She was only found Saturday with the aid of a dog."

Blanche shivered.

"Mind you," Louie conceded, getting up to put on the kettle for tea, "she may have asked for it. Nine times out of ten these girls do. But that doesn't detract from the fact that she was somebody's daughter."

Nothing was said about the killer being somebody's son.

Blanche stayed till nearly six. When she got home Willy was out. He hadn't left a note, but she hadn't expected it. Men of twenty-eight don't have to account to their mothers for every hour of the day, and until he was safely married Blanche rode him on the lightest of reins. Like his father, he was capable of getting into trouble anywhere, but less likely under her roof than anyone else's. That's what she thought. Presently she put on the TV for the news. This was very much the mixture as before, one long record of violence. And the last item in a sense was the most violent of all, concerning as it did the girl whose body had been unearthed by the dog. The police, it said, were anxious to contact anyone who could give any assistance in the search for the killer of Linda Myers, and a picture of the girl was flashed on the screen. Blanche Stephenson, who had risen to switch off the set, remained standing, as still as Lot's wife turned into her pillar of salt. She had never heard the girl's name before, but she had seen the face, and with her heart giving sickening jolts, she remembered where.

Willy Stephenson came in shortly before eight. He said he'd been to the cinema at Axton.

"With Victoria?" Blanche asked, like an automaton, knowing the answer in advance.

"You're joking, of course," said Willy. "Sir Alf" (his irreverent way of referring to his prospective father-in-law) "wouldn't enter a place of entertainment on the Sabbath—you can hardly call chapel a place of entertainment— and he's brought Vicky up the same way. That's one of the things I shall have to cure her of," he added.

"Are you asking me to believe you went to a cinema alone?"

"Well, of course not. What's up, Mater? Was Aunt Louie more scathing than usual? I know what she thinks of me."

"I know what I think," retorted his mother fiercely. "I think you're a fool. Oh, Willy, couldn't you even take your engagement seriously? Did you have to go running around with a girl who's got herself murdered?"

Willy stared. "I suppose you know I haven't an idea what you're talking about?"

"This is what I'm talking about." She opened her stout black leather bag, and took a bit of paper out of the zippered pocket. "Now tell me you've never set eyes on this girl and I shan't believe you."

Like a man in a daze Willy took the photograph. It showed a girl, laughing and gay, her hair blown by the wind, her eyes full of mischief but shrewd for all that.

"Tell me that isn't Linda Myers."

"Well, of course it's Linda. Where did you get it?"

Blanche, feeling sickness beginning to overpower her, gripped the table edge with one strong hand. "You must have been a jackdaw in a previous existence. I found it with a lot of rubbish in the pocket of your sports coat that you asked me to send to the cleaners."

"I'd forgotten about it," Willy muttered. "Still, because I'd met the girl months ago . . ."

"You've only had that sports coat two months, so you must have been seeing the girl while Victoria was on her cruise with her father."

"Well, what did you expect?" Willy demanded. "Because I'm engaged to Vicky it doesn't mean I have to break with every other girl I know."

"A tactful fiancé would see to it that he doesn't know a girl who gets herself strangled."

"What's that you said?" Willy's voice was as sharp as the ping of a rifle.

"I told you—she's been murdered."

"So you did. I didn't take it in. Well, Ma, you must admit you are inclined to lay on your colors with a heavy hand. But murdered? Linda? Not that she didn't ask for it. Look, you're not playing some macabre joke."

"Read it for yourself," cried Blanche, half hysterical by now and quite unable to read her son's mind. Theo had been the same, the world's most convincing liar, though even he had had too much sense to get involved with murder. She picked up the *Record* that Louie had told her she could bring home and threw it in her son's direction. Willy took the paper and opened it so that his face was concealed while he read the hideous story. "And if you'd been back a bit earlier," Blanche continued, "you could have seen her on the television. That's how I knew . . ."

"Knew?"

"That she was the same girl, of course. I suppose she's the one who has been ringing you up this last two or three weeks."

"Girls are always ringing me up. You know that." Will sounded sulky.

"Not like this one. Willy, did she expect you to marry her?"

"Linda?" It was impossible to mistake the genuine amazement in his voice. "She wouldn't have put me at the foot of her list. She was just waiting for her millionaire to come along, and meanwhile anyone would do to go around with."

"How long had you known her?"

"I don't remember exactly. Oh, before there was any question of my marrying Vicky."

"But you went on seeing her?"

"What was I supposed to do while my betrothed was sunning herself in the Caribbean or wherever it was Sir Alf took her in the hopes of curing her of her infatuation? That's what he called it, an infatuation. Now, if he'd got himself murdered . . ."

"Willy, can't you be serious about anything? Here's a girl you've known pretty well—anyway, you were carrying her picture around with you . . ."

"I'd forgotten I had it. She showed it to me one day and said—and she was laughing—Take it as a souvenir. I tell you, she was no more serious than I was."

"I suppose that's why she rang you—three times."

"You didn't tell me."

"She didn't give a name. She just said, 'Say it's Lynn. I must try again, mustn't I?' As you say, girls are always ringing you up."

And she remembered those months before Theo eloped with his Fay, who also had been ringing him up at brief intervals.

Willy was recovering his aplomb. "I warned her that one of these days she'd overplay her hand," he observed. "She seemed to think her luck could never turn. Oh, Mater, that girl had as many boy friends as she'd had hot dinners. And she liked to be the one that did the ditching."

"So she didn't much care for it when you ditched her?"

"I didn't ditch her. But she must have realized that when I was married, things would change."

"She did know about Victoria?"

"Of course she knew."

"Did she mind?"

"I told you, she wouldn't even have thought of me as a husband. Any more than I ever thought of her as a wife."

"It says in the paper that she was a hairdresser's assistant."

"Not quite the way she put it. According to her, she was a partner."

"At eighteen? Not even you, Willy, foolish though you are, can have believed that."

"Well, perhaps not." Willy shrugged. "But it was no skin off my nose. She was just a pretty girl I played around with. Just one of a number."

"Only none of the others got themselves murdered."

"I can't help that. It's an odd thing, seeing how unalike they are but she and Vicky had quite a bit in common. They both expected to be able to play things their way. If I'd known at the start she was going to make such a nuisance of herself . . ."

"Willy, you're talking about a girl who's been murdered. I should have thought even you would have had the sense to leave her alone once you got engaged."

"I hadn't seen her for some time. The last time I told her my fancy-free days were over. I'm putting my head in the noose, I said. It happens to the best of us. Now, Mater, I can see this has been a shock to you, but even you can't have expected me never to see a girl for two months. It's Sir Alfred's fault, if anyone's, trying to break things up between me and Vicky. And though I mean to make her a damn good husband —well, that's part of the contract, isn't it?—even you can't pretend she's a sex kitten."

"And Linda Myers was?"

"And how. You know, I can't quite take this in yet. When did it happen, or doesn't the paper say?"

"They found the body on Saturday, following up information given by some schoolboys who found a ring that had belonged to her. She'd hardly have been buried in daylight, so they think she was strangled on Thursday. Where were you on Thursday night, Willy?"

"What on earth are you driving at, Mother?" It was only in moments of the gravest import that he ever used that word.

"It's what the police will ask."

"The police? What on earth are you talking about? They haven't been *here*?"

"Not yet. But when they know you knew her . . ."

"If they're going to follow up every chap she ever went out with they've got their work cut out till Christmas. You

haven't said anything about the photograph to anyone, have
you?"

"No."

"Not to Aunt Louie?"

"Least of all to her. And if you're shocked, give me a
thought, too. I didn't know that the girl in the picture and the
girl who'd been murdered were one and the same, not till I put
on the TV."

"So," said Willy, "where do the police come in? If
they'd been going to connect me with Linda they'd have been
round before this."

"Perhaps they did, and no one was here."

"Why on earth should they?"

"They want to contact anyone who knew her."

"That's routine stuff. My dear mother, I couldn't help
the police even if I wanted to. It was as big a shock to me to
hear she was dead as it can possibly have been to you. After
all, you'd never met the girl. She didn't seem to be made for
death."

"Oh, we're all made for death," said his mother in a
curiously calm voice, "only not all in such a violent shape.
You didn't answer my question, Willy. Where were you on
Thursday night?"

"How on earth am I supposed to remember? Hold everything. Yes, that was the night I was at home. Remember?"

"Thursday's my bridge night and has been for the past
six years. I go over to Marianne's about six, and we have a
snack and go on to the club. You weren't here when I left."

"That's right. I wasn't."

"You didn't mention you were going to be at home."

"I didn't mean to be, I meant to go round the pubs,
you can always meet someone there—well, it's hardly likely
I'd be taking a girl out, with Vicky just back from her cruise.
But I had this blinding headache . . ."

"At the prospect of marrying Victoria? Headaches
aren't up your street, Willy."

"I'd been lunching with my prospective father-in-
law, remember? That would give anyone a headache."

"I don't think the police are going to be very satisfied with that as an explanation. Unless, of course, you rang someone up to postpone an engagement."

"I told you, I didn't have an engagement. So naturally I didn't ring anyone up."

"And no one rang you? Not Linda Myers?"

"How could Linda Myers ring me if she was being murdered? Anyway, she knew we were through. And she had plenty of other fish on her line."

"So you just stayed quietly at home?"

"That's right. Well, till about nine-thirty. Then I thought a spot of fresh air might clear my head, and I went for a little spin."

"That's something else the police aren't going to like."

"I've told you before, the police don't come into this, so far as I'm concerned."

"How about the people, who knew you were friendly with the girl?"

"No one knew. Well, obviously I wouldn't take her around and introduce her to my friends. She was a pretty girl and good fun, but hang it all, she was a hairdresser's assistant—O.K., O.K., I never really believed she was a partner— her father was a commercial traveler, and for some reason that's always good for a laugh—and I was engaged to Vicky Ebury. She was just a fill-gap and we both knew it."

"And I suppose whoever killed her was also a fill-gap, only perhaps he didn't know it?"

"I don't know. She never talked about her other boy friends, except to let you know she had plenty of them on a string. The fact is, that girl was obsessed by the idea of power. She liked to think she could make chaps jump to her bidding, and I daresay it was a bit of a shock to her when she found I wasn't one of them."

"I hope when you're talking to the police you'll show a little more sense," his mother said.

"I've told you, the police don't come into this. Not that I've anything to fear from them, of course, so far as Linda is concerned, but there's bound to be publicity, and though Sir

Alf's nuts on it as a rule, this is the sort he wouldn't appreciate. And I don't propose to let a little golddigger like Linda muck up my whole future."

He made a swift gesture, and before his mother could realize what he had in mind, he had snatched up the photograph and was applying the flame of his cigarette lighter to one corner. Like a rabbit hypnotized by a snake she watched the paper blacken and curl; the ashes fell into a small china dish on the table. When the picture was utterly destroyed he took the dish to the window and blew the blackened ash out into the darkening air.

"Good-bye, Linda Myers," he said.

Blanche was appalled. "Your father did a lot of things to shock me," she said slowly, "some of them I couldn't find excuses for. But he'd never have done that. I daresay you were only having a bit of fun with the girl, but she was eighteen and she was living and now she's dead and in this hideous way. Can't you even show a little rational pity?"

"Well, of course I'm sorry," said Willy. "I'd be sorry if I'd never known her, just as sorry as if she'd been run down by a bus, but there's nothing I can do about it. If you brought the head of Scotland Yard in here I couldn't tell him any more than I've told you."

"He might think it odd you were so anxious to destroy her picture," said Blanche slowly.

"Not he. No one wants to carry the picture of a murdered girl around with him, particularly if he's engaged to someone else. I bet you there are quite a lot of chaps tearing up photographs of Linda Myers this weekend, and it's possible that one of them might be able to give the police some pointers. Only that chap isn't me. Now, Mother, do stop working yourself into a fever. By the time we get the late news they may have identified the chap she was with on Thursday night. Until then I propose we shelve the subject. We can go on arguing all round the clock and still meet ourselves going to bed."

The late night news carried the information that a man had spent a considerable part of the day at Churchford Police

Station assisting the police with their inquiries. (The news that Chris Wayland had been detained for the murder of Linda Myers didn't make the press till the next morning.) Willy was full of triumph.

"There you are, Mater. You know what that means. The police always play it cagey, but it means they've got the chap they think's responsible, so you can stop worrying yourself about an alibi for me for Thursday night."

It occurred to Blanche that he hadn't uttered one cry of pity or horror at Linda's fate, only displayed an immense relief at the thought that inquiries were virtually at an end, or, if not, wouldn't turn in his direction. And she remembered Louie saying, "She may have asked for it, but you can't overlook the fact that she was somebody's daughter."

Now, to her amazement, she found herself thinking of the unknown man who had been assisting the police with their inquiries, and remembering that he was somebody's son. And this one, this Anon, might really have cared for the girl, while she could have been running the two of them, Anon and Willy, on a string.

God help him! she thought.

There didn't seem to be anyone else likely to do so.

7

On Monday morning Miss Alice didn't appear in the shop. Miss Phyllis, her eyes sunk in her head, and looking like someone who hasn't slept for two nights, told May frankly, "I don't know what I should have done without Jack these last weeks. He's been a tower of strength, but I begin to think he was right, after all."

"Is Miss Alice worse, then?" May was scurrying around tidying and dusting, and rearranging stocks on hangers and stands.

"She's had another little stroke. And, of course, the news—about Linda—has upset her terribly. Is it true, my dear, that she was expecting a baby—Linda, I mean?"

"That's what the doctor says. Poor Mr. Myers! He must feel so responsible."

"I don't see that he can be blamed," Miss Phyllis objected. "He was in Wolverhampton at the time. That's two counties away."

"He'll probably feel he should have prevented it somehow. That's human nature. I wasn't with my father the day he tripped on the curb and broke his ankle—and he was such an energetic man he was a terrible invalid and he wouldn't hear of going into hospital—but I felt responsible just the same. If I hadn't had such a headache that morning I'd have run out myself and bought his tobacco, but he said he couldn't wait, and then—I've always felt guilty."

"My poor sister!" said Miss Phyllis with great feeling, not even pretending to be interested in a crotchety old man who'd been dead and gone for years, and no loss to anyone, least of all May. "She feels it quite dreadfully. Not responsibly, of course. I wished I didn't have to tell her, but if I hadn't, someone else would, and they might just have broken it quite badly, but of course nothing really softens the blow."

"What did you tell her, Miss Phyllis?"

"I said a terrible thing had happened to Linda, she broke her neck in the dark on Broomstick Common, which is more or less the truth; but of course my sister has too much sense to believe you can break your neck on a piece of comparatively flat ground. A leg or an arm—yes. But a neck's different. And then we've had the police here, asking questions. 'We can't tell you anything fresh,' I assured them, 'and no, you cannot see my sister, she's in a state of shock.' I got Dr. Mellish to say she wasn't fit to be questioned. It's not as though she could tell them anything. I'm afraid he told them no evidence of hers would be of value, because she's so confused. Which is true. I mean, she seems to have lost her sense of time. It's what's called living in the past. She actually addressed me as Amy the other day, though Amy's been dead for years, and we were never in the least alike. I suppose it was because of Jack, it sent her thoughts backward. I suppose I have a very selfish nature, because though I know it's terrible what happened to the poor girl, what chiefly concerns me is the effect it may have on Alice. It's not as though being distressed could help Linda now."

"I think it's perfectly natural for you to put your sister first," said May firmly.

"I wish everyone had your sense. It's odd how sympathetic people are for widows—and widowers too, of course— when they suffer a bereavement, but seem to think it's quite different if it's a sister. But if it's your sister who has made your house a home for more than thirty years, the sense of loss, of

—of having your second self chopped off, as it were, is just as acute."

"Poor Miss Alice!" said May respectfully, but she really thought, Poor Miss Phyllis. Alice was protecting herself, even if unconsciously, by retreating into a past where Linda couldn't penetrate, but Miss Phyllis could seek no such consolation. Hers were the present and the future and she could expect nothing but anxiety.

"In a way it eases things for her," May murmured, but Miss Phyllis said, "Oh no. If it had been anyone but Linda. Poor Alice, she did so long to have children, and Linda—I sometimes think she saw her as the daughter she didn't have. That's why she took to her so, because there's no use pretending she was much good in the shop. I've wondered so often what might have happened if our father hadn't put his foot down about young Percy Trivett."

"Is he the one whose letters she keeps and won't let anyone read?" asked May, frankly enthralled.

"She never minded Linda reading them, and I must say the girl was very patient, because young people don't want to hang about a sick person's room. And I think she used to confide in her. Percy was an assistant here in the twenties. Of course, we were a much livelier concern during our father's lifetime. We had a Mrs. Gordon, who was our buyer and manageress—for years neither Alice nor I ever served in the shop, our father wouldn't permit it, though we were allowed to assist in the clerical work behind the scenes. Percy came to us after the war. He'd gone to fight very young, and when he came back there was nothing waiting for him in the way of a position, no one seemed to care after that war; it was different, of course, the next time, I suppose you might say we'd developed a national conscience. He was quite glad to take a quite subordinate situation here; I think he really did hope to work up, not that he was brilliant in any way, but he was very honest and hard-working and customers liked him. But even if he'd been a second Gordon Selfridge, I don't think Father would ever have considered him as a husband for his daughter—well, not for Alice, anyway. He was quite devoted to her; you can't think, my dear, how lovely she was as a girl. Amy and I both disappointed him, he set all his hopes on her."

"Did she want to marry Percy?"

"She never wanted to marry anyone else. Father said he must have behaved in a very dishonorable fashion to have got acquainted with Alice at all, but I don't think that's true. And, since, I've sometimes wondered if Father didn't regret his decision, because there might have been children, and a man to step into Father's shoes in due course. But then"— Phyllis drew a long, sighing breath—"he didn't expect to die at sixty. After that Alice and I took things into our own hands. It was a bad time industrially, and no one was particularly interested in the shop. After 1918 Churchford developed so much, a whole new miniature town sprang up with bigger and flashier shops and restaurants, and then cars became so common, and people dashed up to town or went over to Axton and Maresford for goods. Mrs. Gordon had gone before then, and afterward we found any amount of goods she'd bought as bargains, she said, but they weren't bargains really, because nobody wanted long-sleeved combinations and wool vests and camisoles any longer. There are boxes of them down in the cellar, together with a lot of Father's effects, as I think they're called. We really never knew what to do with them. It seemed irreverent to give them to charities—there were six pairs of trousers—think of it, my dear, six pairs, and two never even put on. We packed them all in mothballs and they're there to this day."

"So that's what's in the boxes down there," May said. "I always wondered, when I take the wrappings and the wastepaper baskets down for the dustman. You have to go through the storeroom to get to the back door."

"We used to carry a lot of stock, millinery, too. And at one time we had a delivery service." (Miss Phyllis seemed happily, dreamily immersed in the past, and May hadn't the heart to remind her that this was 1969 and custom might be tapping on the doorstep.) "A boy on a bicycle with a little van in front. We used to feel so proud to see our name on the side of the van as he pedaled through the streets. But then people started having motor deliveries and our boy learned to drive and left us and we couldn't get another, so people started taking their own goods home. We got a different class of customer, too. The big houses got shut up or turned into flats. I often think it's a good thing Father can't see it now. The bicycle lived in a little shed affair, opening off the stockroom. I believe it's still there, though it must be thick with rust now."

"What happened to Percy Trivett?" asked May, who didn't care a button about the late Mr. Robinson's fads and foibles.

"We never heard. Father dismissed him at once. He did write a few times and the letters got smuggled in, then Father found out and there was a terrible scene. Poor Alice cried for days, but she wouldn't give the letters up, and, as you know, she's got them still. Father said he looked higher for his favorite daughter than an assistant in a provincial drapery, but, my dear, between ourselves, I've always thought his attitude would have been different if Percy had been after me. He thought the world of Alice. Nothing was too good for her."

"They could have eloped to Gretna Green," suggested practical May.

But Miss Phyllis shook her head. "You didn't know our father. When they arrived they'd have found him waiting for them. That was the sort of man he was."

May thought he sounded odious, never realizing he was cut from the same cloth as the late Mr. Forbes, only he'd seen to it that his daughter never had a chance of cutting loose.

Miss Phyllis was meandering on. "It's an odd thing, nothing was ever quite the same after Percy went. Father might have kept Alice in the flesh, so to speak, but she changed, and she's never changed back. There were other men who wanted to marry her, but she wouldn't look at any of them."

"He didn't mind your other sister getting married," May pointed out.

"Oh, Amy. Well, that was rather different. You see, she had this—this slight deformity . . . oh, nothing very serious, a club foot, she managed very well all things considered, but Father was such a perfectionist. And you may have noticed that someone a little handicapped often attracts a husband where perfectly fit people don't. It may be some element of compassion, I don't know. But when Mr. Hardy—Tim—asked for Amy, Father agreed at once. They went to Canada and she used to write very happy letters. When Jack was born, in a way that was the worst of all, it seemed to bring all Alice's disappointment back. Amy sent photographs, but Father wasn't really interested, and Amy died after ten years, some epidemic, I think. Tim wrote such a nice letter, I really think he was very upset, but all Father said was, 'I could see he was a careless kind of chap'—losing a wife after ten years, he meant, which wasn't really very logical since when dear Mother was killed in an accident, he said it was an Act of God. Of course, Tim married again, he couldn't bring up a child of nine, and I think his second wife must be a very nice woman because she always saw to it that Jack sent cards and presents at birthdays and Christmas, and when he'd gone down with scarlet fever she wrote to Alice to say he was doing all right. Those letters seemed to make up to Alice a bit for her own disappointment. She's a great hoarder, my sister. The letters and papers she keeps in that box in her room, well, you've seen them. She used to read them over and over, every letter she ever got from Percy, and all Jack's letters. I think she used to get Linda to read them to her sometimes when her sight began to fail. And you too, my dear, I'll never forget how good you've been to dear Alice. Reading the same letters over and over can't be very entertaining. I expect Linda thought them rather absurd, but it was better than working in the shop."

"She has that photograph of Linda on her mantelpiece," May recalled.

"Oh yes. Even after Linda decided she'd sooner be a hairdresser and went to that school in Axton and then started with Mr. Polly, she came in from time to time to wash my sister's hair. Of course, Alice made it worth her while. It's not that I couldn't have washed it, but it was such a change for her to see anyone young and pretty. I must say," she added wistfully, "it was like having a sunbeam round the place."

But practical May reflected that sunbeams are very un-reliable. They vanish as unexpectedly as they come and never seem to stay five minutes in the same place. Poor Miss Alice! She hadn't had much success with her sums, never able to count on anything remaining stable for any length of time.

Miss Phyllis seemed suddenly to realize the time. "Oh dear, what can I be thinking of, gossiping away like this, but you can't imagine what a relief it is to be able to recall the past—and really there was a lot of happiness, though it's difficult to put one's finger on the precise occasions—enough to make dear Father turn in his grave. You know, I think I'll run up and sit with Alice for a little, if you can hold the fort. We're never busy on a Monday, but if you need any help, just press that button and I'll come straight down. Don't call out, we don't want to give the impression that everything isn't all right. I don't know where Jack is. I did so hope he'd remember it's Alice's birthday, he's always been so good, and though she hasn't said a word, I know she's waiting."

"Perhaps he's gone out to buy something," suggested resourceful May.

After that brief quiet half-hour at the start of the day, there was quite a bustle of customers, though May shrewdly suspected they could thank poor dead Linda for a lot of the trade. Customers came in to make unessential purchases and stopped to comment on the tragedy. "What a shock for Mr. Myers! One can't help wondering . . ." and they looked slyly at May under thin or artificially thickened brows, but they got no change there.

"We don't know any more than anyone else," May told them firmly. "That'll be one-and-eightpence, please, Miss Shrubb. Yes, of course Linda worked here once but it's quite a long time ago." And she added with a rare touch of malice, "I wonder how many people are trying to get snap appoint-ments at Polly's this morning. Yes," she said to another nosy old biddy, "we did hear something about Linda expecting a baby, but you can't expect us to be able to shed any light on that."

But during the afternoon the blow fell. Old Miss Marsh,

who had a nose like that of the fabled princess, which ran down a long road and around a corner, came bustling in to look at dressing jackets, and said fruitily that she understood the police had nailed the man responsible for Linda's murder. He was at the police station at that minute. Helping the police with their inquiries—"And we all know what that means. I expect he'll appear before the magistrate tomorrow. It's Mr. Pantin, he's very severe on sex cases."

"I didn't know it was a sex case," said May repressively. "This is a Shetland wool, lined with nylon, four and a half guineas . . ."

"You're forgetting I'm a pensioner," riposted Miss Marsh roguishly. "I must say it's a consolation to think they've got this man under lock and key. I've hardly dared put my nose out of doors since I heard about that girl. You know what they say, *l'appetit vient en mangeant*, and the first murder's always the hardest. After that . . ."

"Do we know this is a first murder?" asked May, neatly refolding the shetland bed jacket. And if he was after more blood, she thought nastily, you wouldn't be in any danger. You wouldn't yield more than about half a pint in your whole stringy carcass. She was horrified at the violence of her own thoughts, but I'm right to be violent, she reassured herself, she's just a ghoul.

Miss Phyllis had been flitting in and out of the shop all day. Jack hadn't put in an appearance. At five-thirty May locked the door and started to neaten the place against the morning—collecting the empty boxes and wrappings and slipping down the stairs through the cellar to put them out for the dust collector—and it was just after six when she got home to find Mrs. Politi waiting in her own doorway.

She hailed May in a voice like a fog horn. "I hear the news—at six o'clock," she declared.

"What news?" murmured May, who suddenly felt as though someone had removed her spine, so that she simply couldn't remain upright any longer. All she wanted was to kick off her shoes and make a cuppa.

"About this man they take for Linda Myers' murder. I light a candle for you," she added magnanimously.

"Very kind," murmured May. "I don't know why, but all the same . . ."

"You see the murderer face to face—yes?"

"If I'd done that I could give the police an accurate description of him, I might even know his name," May pointed out.

"You fortunate you not see his face or you be in another grave with that Linda. But"—she leaned her enormous bulk toward her friend, who automatically stepped backward, anticipating annihilation—"maybe he see you, too."

"Since I don't know who he was . . ." May began.

"But I tell you. Why you not listen? The police have him . . ."

"Oh, that one!" said May. "He's not the one who killed her. I'm sure of that, even if he was wearing a mask. And what's more, Mr. Crook won't believe it either."

"You think this MISTER CROOK . . ." Her voice put his name in capital letters.

"He's like the man in the Bible—or Mr. Churchill," amended May, who wasn't sure that Mrs. Politi's authorities allowed her a free run of the Good Book. "The one who, having put his hand to the plow, never looked back."

"Better he look back to see who follow him," returned Mrs. Politi severely.

May thought she wouldn't like to be the archangel on the Gate when Lilli's turn came up for the particular judgment. But dropping with fatigue, she let her friend have the last word.

The next morning Miss Alice was worse and her sister said she meant to ring Dr. Mellish.

"I begin to think dear Jack is right, we shan't be able to carry on much longer, it's too much of a strain. And I could never agree to Alice's going into any sort of institution. She hasn't worked all her life to be driven out of her own home at the end."

The buyer from Bayman was due today or tomorrow and Miss Phyllis couldn't be sure how much to order, or if, indeed, there was any sense ordering anything. She was more downcast than May had ever seen her. May had decided to nip out at midday and telephone Mr. Crook. He would know, of course, about Chris Wayland and wouldn't need any advice from her, but she felt she must talk to someone, and she was certain he would understand. He might have a face like a professional pugilist, but that only went to show that you couldn't judge by appearances.

At about ten-thirty the shop door jangled open and Jack marched in, carrying some flowers. "I hear they've got the fellow for that girl's murder," he said. "If you ask me, he's lucky to be inside, getting police prótection at public expense."

"We don't know yet that he's guilty," said May calmly. "What beautiful flowers!"

He bowed and extended them toward her. "I had an idea you'd like this kind."

"You're getting confused," May told him. "It's not my birthday. At least, yesterday wasn't. Miss Phyllis was rather upset because you never do forget, but Miss Alice was so poorly . . ."

He looked at the flowers in his arm. May was right, they really were beautiful. "*Amende honorable!*" he murmured. "I better go up and make my peace."

"You might offer to sit with Miss Alice for a little, if you have the time," May suggested, quite without sarcasm. It didn't seem to her natural that a young man should spend all his time with an ailing old lady he'd never seen until a short time ago, even if she was his aunt. "Miss Phyllis probably didn't get more than catnaps all night."

She'd have liked to ask him to hold the fort for ten minutes while she ran across the Green and telephoned, but she decided against it. Jack Hardy might be very good at his own job in Canada, but he was like a bull in a china shop when it came to the haberdashery. Not that she blamed him, it wasn't a young man's job. Of course, there'd been Percy Trivett, but things had been different then. Life had been much drabber for the young and much more stereotyped.

"It doesn't seem very appropriate to say happy birthday, does it?" Jack murmured, diving for the stairs that led to the upper floor from the back of the shop. It was a dark morning, with fog outside that threatened to thicken, and May put on the light; no one was going to come into a shop that looked like a cave. Jack vanished, and the shop bell rang sharply. May turned; she'd always secretly resented that bell, people should be summoned by people, not a machine, she thought. An old termagant called Parrott came in to ask for handkerchiefs—the initialed kind, she explained, for her niece, Queenie.

It would be, May reflected grimly, explaining there really was no demand for personal lingerie with the letter Q embroidered on it.

"Well, really," bridled old Miss Parrott. "There's Queenie and Quentin and Quarles, and my best friend had a daughter she christened Quebec."

It was obvious to May that she'd come in for a gossip rather than a purchase, but "You shall buy some handkerchiefs if I have to stuff them down your throat," May adjured her silently. She ransacked a drawer and came up with a box of handkerchiefs with a colored design of ducks in the corner.

"Quack-quack!" she explained.

Miss Parrott laughed gaily. "What an amusing idea! Still, I don't know that my niece—everyone's sense of humor is different, isn't it?"

"If your niece has the right kind," asserted May, "she'll be tickled pink."

"You really think so! I must admit they're rather ducky . . ." She suddenly realized she'd made a joke, and began to giggle. While May packed them up she wandered to the opposite counter, where she began to finger gloves, disarranging the neat stand May had set up that morning. Suddenly she began to neigh like a horse. "Think of that," she said. "We were so busy talking we never even heard the postman come."

"The postman doesn't call at this hour," explained May.

"He's come this morning." The old horror contrived to look positively arch. "Or perhaps it's a *billet-doux*."

She stooped down, a great overgrown croquet-hoop of an old woman, and tugged the envelope out of the low letterbox that the postmen disliked—but where else can you put a letter box if you have a glass shop door?

"Why, it's for you," she discovered, more arch than ever. "And dear me—I was right—it's not stamped, so it must have come by hand."

May took the letter without even looking at it and put it in the pocket of her cardigan. She took a pound note from the clearly disappointed Miss Parrott, and returned her change.

"I mustn't keep you." Miss Parrott simpered. "I'm sure you're dying to open your letter."

And that, reflected May, putting away the box of handkerchiefs, is probably the first true thing you've said since you came in.

She stood well back in the shadow, where she was virtually invisible from the door but could herself keep a watchful eye on her domain. Miss Parrott was right, the letter hadn't come through the post. On such a foggy morning and with so much on her mind it wouldn't be difficult for anyone, under the guise of window shopping, to stoop and slip the envelope into the slot marked LETTERS. Either it wasn't there when Jack came or else he didn't notice it, she decided. But it would be so easy to overlook. It wasn't even a white envelope, but one of those cheap yellowish ones that in this light could easily go unnoticed. The address was printed in a backward sloping slapdash hand, and even May didn't suppose it was the author's normal writing. Anyway, it was kind of printed, had an uneducated appearance, but that could be cunning, too. She tore the envelope open, willing everyone to stay away until she'd digested the contents. The message was composed of letters and words cut from a newspaper and stuck unevenly onto a plain white sheet. The message read:

Ask Mr. polly where he was at 6 p.m. last Thursday. The sender had had some difficulty in finding a capital P. and Mr. Polly was fashionably named with a small letter.

May's first thought, as she pushed it deep into her cardigan pocket again, was Now I've got to get in touch with Mr. Crook. It never once occurred to her it could be someone playing a practical joke; it was someone who had evidence and couldn't or wouldn't come forward, someone who was afraid of the police pinning the crime on an innocent man, but fearing to put a name to his or her own suspicions.

There's no time to be lost, decided May, and as though fate grudgingly admitted that she deserved a small respite for her patience, Miss Phyllis could be heard to open a door upstairs and then down she came into the shop.

"Was that Miss Parrott?" she asked. "I thought I recognized the voice. I suppose she didn't buy anything."

"She bought six handkerchiefs with ducks on them," said May. "People talk about putting a purchase tax on goods. I think there should be a service tax, Miss Parrott would pay at about fifty percent."

"Poor May!" But Miss Phyllis's thoughts were clearly elsewhere. "It's about a quarter to one, I think we might close the shop now."

Since Alice had been unable to serve in the shop, they had closed for the midday break between one and two o'clock. "I doubt if anyone would be coming in," Miss Phyllis added, as though it didn't really matter much either way. "It's not so important. I could do with a cup of tea. I'll put on the kettle."

"I must run across to the chemist," May said. "My head . . ." It wasn't really a lie; her head had begun to ache abominably, the world seemed to be spinning around her, and her mind must be spinning, too, because she thought that if Crook stuck out his big hand and steadied it, everything would be calm again.

"I have some aspirin upstairs," said Miss Phyllis. "There's no need to go out."

But May said desperately she was allergic to aspirin, Allen's kept a tablet that was just the job, she'd only be five minutes anyway.

She didn't suppose Miss Phyllis would try and check up on her, but conscience made her dive into Allen's and buy twenty-five tablets she didn't need, before slipping across the Green into the Ancient Mariner by the restaurant entrance. They had a telephone halfway up the stairs, which insured privacy, not like those you saw in French films where the instrument was in the bar and you had to shout to make yourself heard. If she should be seen and recognized, it would only be supposed that she was nipping up for a bit of lunch. The bar was filling rapidly and there was plenty of noise, which gave her an odd feeling of concealment. She had her money in her hand and now it only remained for Mr. Crook to be in. And this time luck was with her and he answered the phone himself.

"I've only got a minute," she whispered. "I'm in a call box . . ."

"I could have told you that, Sugar," said Crook, who had heard the coins fall.

"There's something I've got to tell you, it's urgent."

"If it's about Young Lochinvar being taken for the girl's murder, I've heard that," said Crook, and she didn't stop to wonder how it was he could be so sure of her identity.

"Well, yes, I suppose so, but this is different. I've got something to show you, only I can't get away, not this afternoon, with Miss Alice so ill, and no one but me in the shop, so . . ." She paused, because her breath had suddenly run out.

"I get the message," said Crook soothingly. "Mahomet can't come to the mountain. Well, Sugar, you're speaking to the most traveled mountain in the business. What time's your tea break?"

"We don't actually have a break then . . ."

"You should have a word with your union," Crook advised. "Then say I come along for a pair of gloves, or . . ."

"We don't sell men's gloves."

"I didn't say I was buying them for myself. I daresay my auntie wouldn't mind a nice surprise. And if you don't serve in the glove shop she'll have to put up with a nice silk scarf or a pair of bedsocks."

She thought he was considering a comparatively long journey in bad weather with less ado than most people make about having to go down the road in the rain for a pint of milk.

"I wouldn't ask you if it wasn't urgent," she began, and he said well, it hadn't occurred to him she was ringing just because she had cold hands and wanted someone to warm them for her. Then he added, "Be seeing you," and he set down his receiver with a resolution that would have aroused the envy of King Canute who couldn't even stop an advancing wave, let alone a distracted female in full spate.

When May got back to the shop she found Miss Phyllis sitting with her hands folded in her lap and the electric kettle puffing away fit to burst. May switched it off, drew herself a glass of water and ostentatiously swallowed two tablets, then fetched some teacups from the cupboard.

Miss Phyllis opened her eyes. "I believe I was dropping off," she confessed. "But it's all right. Jack's upstairs with Alice. Did you remind him about its being her birthday yesterday? I mean, he came in with an armful of flowers."

"They were entirely his own idea," May reassured her. "I saw them. They were lovely."

"I must have given him a fright because he tried to give them to me and they *were* lovely, but oh dear, they made me think of funerals, all so white, you know. Somehow it seems wrong for a young man to bring white flowers to an old woman. Youth should go for the strong colors. And then Alice saw him and she must have been half asleep, because she started to call him Percy, though they aren't in the least alike, and she said she'd kept all his letters, and if he didn't believe her, they were all in a box under the bed. And then she saw me and said hadn't I better make sure Father didn't want anything. Poor Jack! I'm afraid he's not going to have very happy memories of his aunts, when he's back in Canada."

"Did Dr. Mellish come?" asked May, because the doctor naturally would go to the side door, which was the private one. The shop stood on a corner, with a long narrow lane running down to some recently built maisonettes grouped around a little square.

"I talked to his partner. Dr. Mellish was out, and he

said—Dr. Durant, I mean—that I should try and keep her quiet —not that she's in the least violent, you understand. He did ask if she had a temperature, but I said no, I didn't think so, she didn't seem feverish, so he said if there was an emergency to ring again and he'd tell Dr. Mellish as soon as he came in. Not that I think there's much he can do if she's suffering from loss of memory, and if she's happy believing that Jack is Percy Trivett, why should any of us try to prevent her having a little pleasure? She hasn't had much in her life, poor Alice."

"She's had you," said May simply, unwrapping a packet of sandwiches, and she spoke with so much sincerity that her companion was startled.

"It's not a great deal to show for a life," she said humbly. It didn't seem to occur to her to wonder how much she herself had had.

Mr. Crook turned up about three o'clock. Miss Phyllis was at the glove counter, so he diplomatically asked for a silk scarf instead.

"Pick the sort of thing you'd like yourself," he suggested.

May produced her favorite, pale pink with a design of small groups of kittens in shadowy gray at the corners and an erect mother cat in the center. She spread it on the counter, and Mr. Crook lifted it, bunching it in his hand in a professional manner. On the counter, underneath the scarf, lay the letter.

"Got the envelope?" murmured Mr. Crook, dropping the scarf and sleeving the scrap of paper apparently all in one movement. "I'm not so sure about the kitties, how about a nice poodle? Or a picture of Buckingham Palace? She's very patriotic, is Auntie. So maybe not a poodle, after all. French dogs, ain't they?"

"I believe they were originally seen in Russia," said May, playing up like mad, and hunting through the folder of scarfs.

"When did it come?" whispered Mr. Crook, demanding of fate a fresh customer who would distract Miss Phyllis's attention. She was looking at him rather oddly, as if she though at any minute he was going to produce a gun and yell put 'em up, though May could have told her that men of his caliber, even if they have criminal intent, don't waste their energy on a tatty little haberdashery run by old maids. And an instant later the doorbell tinkled and someone came in to buy some Fair Isle mittens for a granddaughter.

"This really is something," Mr. Crook acknowledged. "Make with the scarfs, Sugar. Something with flowers, maybe. My auntie loves a nice bunch of flowers. Too bad all the words have been cut out of a popular morning daily. There can't be more than a thousand locals or so who take that one. Or it could even have been bought for the occasion."

"You think whoever left it knows something?" whispered May, shaking out scarfs like someone plucking a fowl; they seemed to be flapping in all directions.

"Well, I don't think it's a practical joke," Mr. Crook retorted. "My guess would be that whoever sent that knows you've pulled me into the case, and you ain't done that in your own interests because you don't even know the young chap. So, if Wayland's out, someone else has to be in, and X wants to be tooting sure it ain't him."

"But why Mr. Polly? I mean, he's a married man . . ."

"That could be why. Who was it said a man with a wife and children had given hostages to fortune? He can't afford to laugh it off like some young chap might be able to. What's she like?"

"Mrs. Polly? Well, she comes to the chapel. Very— forceful, I think is the best word for her. And decorative in a sort of Roman matron way. About twice his size and very competent. I mean, if a fuse blows in the house she's the one who knows how to put it right, and if the car breaks down she could probably mend it much more quickly than he could. She was a schoolmistress before she married."

"Wonder she stooped to trade," murmured Mr. Crook, snatching up a scarf with a Beefeater design, and bunching it under his chin as if he were trying to learn if he liked Beefeaters the way children hold buttercups to decide whether they like butter. "Or maybe she didn't like the notion of having Miss writ on her tombstone."

"It can't have been that," objected May. "She was a widow—she's some years older than he is—with one daughter. She's married, the daughter, I mean, and the Pollys never had any children. Did you say your aunt likes flowers? How about this one with lilies of the valley on a pale green ground?"

Miss Phyllis's customer had chosen her gloves, but curiosity being strong in her, too, she was making conversation in the hope of catching the sense of what the brigandish creature was saying to Miss Forbes. Mr. Crook blessed her. He said he thought not the lilies of the valley, his auntie was superstitious, and May went on to explain about a customer finding the envelope, etc., etc.

"Likely to open her trap?" inquired Mr. Crook sympathetically, meaning the customer, of course.

"Well," said May innocently, "she is a Parrott."

And Mr. Crook put back his head and roared like any bull of Bashan. "Lucky she was here, though, and was the one to take it out of the box," he suggested.

"I don't understand."

"Then no one can say it didn't come straight dinkum through the slit, not a home-grown article," he elucidated kindly.

"But why on earth should I want to implicate Mr. Polly?"

"Maybe you put half a dozen names in a hat and that was the one you drew. Well, use your marbles, Sugar. You're backing Young Lochinvar, wearing his colors, so to speak."

"Only because I know he's innocent," urged May. "You see, the police set a trap and he didn't spring it."

"You have to hand it to the police, they wouldn't let a little thing like that stop them," acknowledged Mr. Crook generously.

"Even though I didn't really see *him* that night, whoever it was must have seen me, and if I'd sprung up at his elbow like—like a ghost, he'd need to be Sir Laurence Olivier not to show even the smallest sign of surprise."

"I'd like to see you standing up to the attorney-general," offered Mr. Crook, meaning just that. "You know, I think I'll have the kitties, after all."

"I thought you said your aunt didn't care about cats."

"Wherever Auntie is now, God rest her soul"—Mr. Crook made a reverent gesture toward his abominable brown bowler hat—"It won't matter to her what sort of scarf I buy, so maybe I'll take this one, and if I find I need a bit more info I can bring it back and you can find me a nice view of Lake Windermere or something. Is it a fact you ain't got a buzzer?" He sounded quite incredulous, he'd as soon have been without his clothes as without his telephone. "Well, then, how about your lady friend over the way? The one like the Eye of God that never sleeps?"

"She would always take a message," May agreed, reflecting, as she folded and packed the scarf, that this was the first time in years she'd sold anything without the thrify customer inquiring the price. "Are you going to see him now, Mr. Wayland, I mean?"

"Have to find out first if he wants to see me. May have a legal beagle of his own."

"He hasn't had much time, and he doesn't sound the sort of young man who would have a lawyer." Her voice made them sound as rare and valuable as diamonds.

"Might have a word with Mr. Polly," conceded Crook, offering a five-pound note. "Where does he hang out?"

May told him while she made change. "But he's not a gentleman's hairdresser," she pointed out. "Mr. White, at the corner of Mill Street, is said to be very good."

"I need a barber like I need a hole in the head," said Crook graphically. He pocketed his change and picked up the little parcel. "If Auntie don't like the kitties I'll bring it back," he promised. "By the way, got a chain on your door at home?"

"No," said May. "I've never needed one."

"Maybe not, but now times have changed. You're obstructin' someone's plans by being so tooting sure the police have got the wrong man, which makes you a person of importance, whether you know it or not—important to young Wayland and important to me, to say nothing of being important to yourself. And one more thing, don't let anyone in, not even if he says he's a rozzer, not without he shows you his warrant through the crack. Faith is one of the great trilogy, as we know, but blind faith is just blanketty stupidity. I sometimes think," he added more calmly, "that's one of the things that's got faith such a bad name; the faithful do have a tendency to shunt responsibility onto the Lord God, and though I ain't a theologian, I don't recall any place in Holy Writ that tells you to do that."

"Casting all your care upon Him," murmured May.

"Sounds like heaving bricks to me," said the outspoken Mr. Crook. "And me, I'd have a better use for bricks. Still, you bear that in mind and drop into Woollie's or whatever on your way back and don't forget to buy a chisel while you're about it. When you've finished putting in the screws, just remember there are a lot of worse weapons than a chisel, if some nasty chap does manage to insinuate himself over your threshold."

8

Leaving May to ponder on the wisdom of that suggestion, Mr. Crook got back into the Superb and breezed along to Polly's Parlour, where he found himself confronted by a female with a face like a human lemon, who had just fitted a setting helmet over a mop of pinned-up hair. When she saw the newcomer she quickly pulled the cubicle curtain, as though it would be sacrilege for him to see a client in what might be called a state of undress, and an instant later came into the shop with a nice trimming of frost around the lemon-face.

"I'm afraid you've made a mistake," she told him icily. "This is a ladies' salon."

"And you don't think I look like a lady? And you'd be dead right." He gave her his friendliest smile. "Boss around?"

Miss Buxton stiffened. "If you mean Mr. Polly, he is not available."

"How do you know he doesn't want to see me?"

Her expression said that this was something beyond the bounds of likelihood.

"I mean," pursued Mr. Crook, "I might have come to tell him he's won £25,000 in the draw."

Miss Buxton didn't unbend. "Draws are made on Saturdays and on the first of the month," she pointed out. "In either case your timing is wrong."

"I bet the boss sets his watch by you," observed Mr. Crook respectfully. "All the same, I'd like a word."

"He is giving a blue rinse to one of our most important clients."

"Blue hair to match her blue blood?" suggested Mr. Crook. "Well, but I can wait." He dropped down on a hard chair and picked up a women's magazine.

Miss Buxton looked dismayed. "I'm afraid it won't be any use," she said.

Crook pulled one of his fantastic professional cards out of his pocket. "Maybe if you were to get him to cast his eye over this . . ."

Unashamedly Miss Buxton read it. "Is it supposed to be a joke?" she inquired.

"Chaps who get one don't normally think so."

Miss Buxton's client, who, after the way of women, realized there was something funny going on, began to fidget under her drier and call out something about its being too hot.

"Turn it down, dear," said Miss Buxton crisply. "But it'll mean staying there all the longer . . ."

"I can't find the screw," whined the client.

Mr. Polly, attracted by the unusual clamor, darted out of the cubicle where he was performing the miracle of turning drab gray into a sparkling lilac-blue. Crook was on his feet like a bouncing ball. "Mr. Polly? My card." He removed it from Miss Buxton's nerveless hand. "Representing young Wayland, if you know who I mean, thought you might be able to assist inquiries . . ."

"Are you from the police?" demanded Mr. Polly, looking baffled and outraged at the same time. "May I remind you this is my place of business . . ." Then he noticed the card in his hand and paused to read it. The bafflement disappeared, the outrage swelled. "Really, Mr. Crook, I consider this an unwarranted intrusion. Miss Buxton, I think your client is endeavoring to attract your attention." Reluctantly Miss Buxton departed. "If you have come for information, I can only assure you that I have told the police all I know about Miss Myers."

"Ah, but maybe the police and me wouldn't ask the same questions. They were thinkin' of a guilty man, I'm out for an innocent one. So, how about you and me havin' a little get-together, at your convenience, of course. How about after you shut up shop?"

"I go home—naturally."

"Maybe I could call around there." He waited for that to sink in, then continued affably, "Or if Mrs. P wouldn't be agreeable, how about you meeting me for a nice glass of something at some convenient rendezvous? I daresay you'd know the local ports of call better than me."

"I've already told you, Mr. Crook, I have already told the police everything they wanted to know, insofar as lay in my power."

"Such as—where you were Thursday night?"

"Thursday is the night I stop late at the shop to do the week's accounts."

"Every Thursday?"

"Every Thursday."

"So if my informant says he saw you at six P.M., outside the shop, he's a liar?"

"A case of mistaken identity perhaps." Mr. Polly's hands stole out and caught at the back of the chair.

"He don't seem to think so."

"May I ask the name of your informant?"

"That I can't tell you at the moment," returned Mr. Crook truthfully. "But he seems dead sure. And the only way of proving him wrong is to prove he ain't right."

Mr. Polly hesitated. His worst enemy couldn't accuse Crook of a threatening attitude, but the hairdresser recognized the look in that wide-open right brown eye. He'd seen it too often (though hers were a refined shade of blue) in Mrs. Polly's. To cap everything, the titled client began to make chattering noises. "I cannot wait," Mr. Polly said hurriedly. "A tint—a case of the little more and how much it is. Very well, Mr. Crook, if you insist—yes, Lady Pitt-Marten, I am coming immediately—the Flying Fox at the top of Aldershot Hill, it's a short distance, but my wife doesn't care for me to be seen in the local public houses, she's the chairman of our Temperance Association—no doubt you have your car—shall we say six o'clock?"

Mr. Crook found himself wondering whether Mrs. Polly had ever been jealous of the dead girl. A bit older than him, Miss Forbes had said. And according to the evidence, the girl had been quite a beauty. All the same, there was something odd about the situation, an ancient and fishlike smell. Not for the first time Mr. Crook thanked the powers that be for his own single status. Everyone concerned seemed to him eager to cover up something, but when all the flat stones were lifted and the flat creatures they concealed released, it wouldn't surprise him if quite a lot of people had quite a lot of shocks. Come to that, he was prepared for a shock or two himself. He drove direct to the prison where Chris Wayland was kicking his heels, quite unresigned to his situation.

"Is Wayland expecting you?" an officer inquired when Crook had made his errand known.

"Mr. Wayland," amended Crook. "He ain't convicted yet, you know. And lots of chaps have been taken unaware, some of 'em by angels. Lawyer," he added patiently. "Even an accused man has his rights."

The officer stiffened. "We've no instructions about legal aid."

"You're getting 'em now. Want I should call the boss?"

He produced his official card, and the man gave it and him a quick, suspicious glance. It was clear he'd heard of Crook and didn't much like what he'd heard. But Crook continued to look about him with a guileless air until, after some apparent consultation, he was told he could see the prisoner. The jailer wasn't the only person to be surprised by Crook's appearance. Chris Wayland stared at him as though he were a denizen from the deep.

Once more Crook produced his card. "My friend, client really, Miss May Forbes, asked me to come and see were you fixed up. She's the one who knows you didn't do it," he added persuasively.

"I'm glad there's someone besides me," Chris agreed.

"That makes three of us, because, naturally, my clients are never guilty. Four, if we count the chap who really is. Guilty, I mean. Now Sugar—Miss Forbes to you—she's as good as gold, and you can't have better than that."

"Why should she concern herself?"

Crook saw the young fellow really wanted to know. "I'll tell you why—and hold on to your hat—because she believes in justice, and she knows the rozzers have pulled a boner. No hope of showing you couldn't have been there that night, I take it? No, I thought not. Mind you, there are probably a few chaps who did see you go by that evening, without actually *seein'* you, if you get me. Well then, let's try another tack. Stop off at a bar or anything? Petrol station? Ask anyone the way?"

"No to all those," said Chris. "I went into a help-yourself hot-dog café—I didn't even remember the name of that, though I suppose I could track it down again—but no one 'ud remember seeing me there, and then on to meet my ghost, who failed to keep her appointment. I tried to call the church caretaker, but she was having a day off, and no one answered the rectory phone. I'm afraid I'm a dead loss to you, sir."

"Oh, I don't know," murmured Crook. "If you don't give the police any facts, at least they can't twist 'em into the wrong pattern."

"So how do you start convincing them I'm not the chap they're after?"

"Only one way I know and that's to find a substitute. You don't want to be known as another of the chaps that got away with murder. Doesn't seem to have occurred to anyone that if you'd laid the girl in her pebbly bed, the odds are you'd have removed the ring first."

"I suppose they'd argue I was panic-stricken and didn't think till it was too late, or was taken unawares by the prowler and dropped the ring and couldn't find it in the dark. You know, if Miss Forbes hadn't been out feeding her cats that night, the odds are the police wouldn't have found Linda Myers yet."

"It wasn't the police found her, it was Solly Gold's dog, but no one's going to give him a medal. I take it, by the way, you're not legally represented?"

"Well, not till you drifted in." The young man actually grinned. "It's hard to make these old chaps understand that while you're still working on your first million, the odds are you don't have any need of a lawyer—even if you could afford one."

Crook said instantly, "Payments by results, that's my motto, and Robin Hood was one of my ancestors."

Then he took his new client through his story in detail. "It figures," he said at last. "I mean, that's virtually what the police got, too. Now, about the young lady. I've had her stepmother's opinion, second-hand of course, and Sugar's. Linda worked at Robinson's for a while; I understand the old lady took the news very hard. And Mr. Polly's going to open up tonight, whether he believes it or not."

"Polly? That's the chap she worked for?"

"It ain't likely there'd be two. Ever mention him?"

"She said once it was nice to be the one that called the tune. I suppose she'd got him tied to her shoestrings, too."

"Ever wonder why?"

Chris looked surprised. "You never met her, of course, but she is—was—the kind that just puts out her hand, not grabbing exactly, but expectant that whoever she's with will put whatever she wants into it."

"If he didn't, would she try and get it by force?"

"Not force, but—I'd say she didn't give up easily."

"According to one of his assistants, she wound Polly round her little finger."

"I wouldn't be surprised."

"Never tried anything of the sort with you?"

"You're joking, of course. I mean—perhaps this isn't a thing one should say of the dead, but you're asking the questions—she wouldn't have thought I was worth it, and she'd have been right. I hadn't much to lose, living more or less from hand to mouth—the TV payment was a bonanza and it wasn't all that generous—not even much of a reputation. No, she'd reserve her energies for bigger game."

"No touch of little Dan Cupid, I take it?" murmured Crook.

"Not on my side, and certainly not on hers."

"Knowing how many beans make five?"

"Knowing that, and knowing, too, where to pick the beans. No, I don't know in whose yard; if I did I'd tell you, I can't do her any harm now. But I gather she could pick and choose her escorts, though I couldn't put a name to any of them for you."

"Know the most difficult job the police ever find themselves up against?" Crook asked. "The murder of prostitutes. Because there's never a clue pointing in any definite direction. Same with maniacs. What the police need is motive. And if the chap stops at just one—if Neil Cream had had that sense they'd never have named him, but he went on and on. It's a hard saying, but missing women are still two a penny. And that's when chaps begin to think they're safe. Smith (George Joseph) might have lived to get the King's reprieve if he'd stopped at one bride in the bath, because one bride's a misfortune, but six is plain ridiculous. By the way— you're bound to be asked this one way or another—got any other girl in your eye?"

The question was so direct, so unexpected that the young man looked as though he'd been kicked by a mule, and kicked practically insensible at that. After a moment during which Crook made no attempt to hurry him, he said, "You don't have to drag her in, I hadn't even met her at the time of Linda's death. And that's one thing I can prove, if I have to."

"I like a quick worker," Crook approved. "All the same, the rozzers 'ull be grasping at straws, seein' that's all they've got to grasp at. Well, that's all for the time being. I've got a date to see a man who might be able to throw a bit of light on the situation, only my guess is he's going to claim he's lost his matches."

Chris grinned appreciatively. "And you're going to do

a conjuring act and produce them from behind his ear or something?"

"You catch on quick," Mr. Crook congratulated him. "Take care of my client," he adjured the outraged officer who saw him off the premises. "And be sure you vet his visitors. Anything happens to him and British justice could go right down the drain." Leaving the man speechless, he hopped into the Superb and drove gaily off to keep his appointment at the Flying Fox.

There was no sign of Mr. Polly when Crook reached his rendezvous, so he perched himself up by the bar and asked for a pint.

"Not had a message for a chap called Polly, I suppose?" he offered with that first pint safely under his belt.

The barman, who had been watching him fascinated, said, "You mean the hairdresser? No, we don't see him here. You should ask at the Black Sheep, or so they tell me."

"Mrs. P runs the Temperance League, I hear," remarked Crook, ordering a second pint and adding, "Have one yourself."

"Strong drink is raging, wine is a mocker," intoned the barman, who clearly saw himself as a bit of a wit. "Still, here he comes."

Out of his business premises, Mr. Polly looked taller and better turned-out than Crook recalled him. But then shackles of servitude hardly ever do a fellow justice, he reminded himself.

Crook picked up his tankard and hopped down from the bar. "Give it a name," he encouraged.

Mr. Polly said a glass of dry sherry, adding that he couldn't stay long, his wife was expecting him. And he added that he'd told the police everything he knew. He'd said it so often by this time he sounded to himself like a gramophone record, and he wondered if that was the way he sounded to Crook, too.

"You may find it hard to believe this," Crook assured him, "but the police don't always confide in me."

The barman brought the drinks and Crook came straight to the point. "It's about Thursday."

"Last Thursday?"

"So far as I'm concerned, that's the only Thursday there is. So tell me."

"Tell you what?" Mr. Polly swallowed almost all his sherry in a gulp.

"Anything that occurs to you that could help us to track down Linda's killer. We both know the police have got their finger on this chap, Wayland, but for the sake of argument, let's assume he's innocent. So—who would you suggest we might put in his place?"

"Why ask me, Mr. Crook? Linda was nothing but a temporary employee. I never expected her to stay very long, she's the restless kind, always wanting change."

"What kind of change?"

"How do I know? She never discussed her future with me. I know at one time she was anxious to go to London, only Mr. Myers prevented it."

"I didn't know they could do it, these days. Fathers, I mean."

"Well!" Mr. Polly looked down at his folded hands. "I suppose there were some advantages in her situation. She was living rent-free, so anything she earned was hers to spend."

"Not the saving type?"

"I don't think she'd have known what the word meant."

"Was she a good employee, good at her job, I mean?"

Mr. Polly considered. "I wouldn't describe her as a devoted hairdresser, in the way Miss Reith is, for instance, or, if I may say so, as I am myself. But when she gave her mind to it she could turn out a very pretty job. I sometimes wondered if there wasn't some feeling among the other members of my staff when some client of quite long standing would ask for Linda, explaining that she knew the trendy ways of doing hair, and really she produced some remarkable results. Some of those middle-aged women can't have recognized themselves when they looked in the glass."

"Didn't they like themselves the way they were before?"

"You know how women are, Mr. Crook, always something for a change. And no one likes to be thought to be stuck in a rut. Miss Buxton and Miss Reith both turn out neat, accomplished jobs, but even elderly women get tired of the tidy parting and the careful waves. I've had clients say to me, 'I almost feel as if I was wearing a wig.'" Delighted they were. And they'd give Linda a bigger tip than usual. Of course, that's partly the age. The older ones are afraid to give the youngsters what they'd think sufficient for their own contemporaries."

"You seem to have made quite a study of it," said Crook. "Still—I know jealousy's a green-eyed monster, but you need rather more motive than that . . ."

Mr. Polly looked horrified, as well he might. "You're not suggesting that I should attempt to involve Miss Reith or Miss Buxton in this tragic affair? They're—I could call them dedicated women."

Dedicated to a hair dryer, reflected Crook ribaldly. "Well, let's come on to Thursday," he suggested. "She left at her usual time?"

"Actually, she asked if she might leave a little early. She had no further appointments and she had what she'd call a date."

"And you agreed?"

"I've said she had no other appointments, and it was only a matter of, say, twenty minutes—well, perhaps half an hour."

"And that's the last time you saw her?"

"I've told the police that."

"And now you're telling me?"

"That's right."

"You mean, that's right, that's what you told the police, or that's right, it's the last time you saw her?"

"Well, both. Naturally."

"You couldn't have made a mistake?"

"What's all this in aid of, Mr. Crook?"

"So if my informant says he saw you together at six

o'clock that night he's a liar? But I asked you that before, didn't I?"

"It must be a case of mistaken identity," insisted Mr. Polly. "She went around with a good many men."

"So I've heard. Do you know a pub called the Black Sheep?"

"The—I've told you, I'm not a drinking man. I owe it to my wife . . ."

"That wasn't what I asked."

"I've heard of it, of course."

"But the barman there wouldn't recognize you? Oh, come on, it's simple enough. He does or he don't."

Mr. Polly hesitated. Then he said desperately, "I have been there occasionally. But I've never gone there to meet Linda Myers."

"And you didn't see her there last Thursday?"

"If you're trying to link me up with what happened to her . . ."

"I'm trying to find out who killed her, if Chris Wayland didn't."

"That's a big if, Mr. Crook."

"The Black Sheep's quite a way out from Churchford," murmured Mr. Crook.

"It doesn't do for me to be seen drinking at the locals," blustered Mr. Polly.

"So when you tell your wife you're stopping late to do the books, what you really mean is you're on a bit of a pub-crawl. Ain't you afraid she might ring you at the shop?"

"Thursday night is the night of the Temperance meeting. That's why we decided it was a good time for me to work late. Otherwise I should have to clear the books on Saturday afternoon, and naturally she expects my company then."

"You know all the answers, don't you?" said Crook in an admiring tone. "Now let's stop going round in circles, and you tell me what she had on you."

"Are you talking about Linda Myers?"

"She didn't make any secret of it, you know. She knew she could get off early or have an elastic lunch hour. She told one of her boy friends it was nice to be the one with a bit of power. Well, I suppose her stepmother ruled the roost at home."

"I've told you already, Mr. Crook, I wouldn't dream of taking that girl out anywhere. She was nearly young enough to be my daughter and I'm a married man."

"I don't say you set out to meet her on Thursday. Maybe she just turned up uninvited, knowing you often went to the Black Sheep that evening."

"I'm sure she knew nothing of the kind, it was purely fortuitous . . ." Mr. Polly, gasping and floundering like an inadequate swimmer suddenly finding himself out of his depths, stopped and picked up his empty glass to cover his discomposure.

Crook looked across to the bar. "Same again," he called. "Yes, of course you will. You're going to need a bit of Dutch courage. Not that I blame you for wanting a pull now and again. Man wasn't made to live on water. And don't tell me that all she had on you was knowing that you sometimes dropped in for a glass or two. It's who you dropped in to meet. Now just consider. It wouldn't be too difficult to get you identified, a chap as well known as you, and maybe they could identify your companion as well."

"I won't have her dragged into it," cried Mr. Polly sharply. "The girl meant nothing to me, and Monica—my friend—knew it. Nor do I know what happened after I left the bar. I can only assure you that Linda Myers was in excellent health and about to join whoever she had come there to meet."

"What makes you so tooting sure about that? Now, let's not waste any more time. That's a nice suit you're wearing, fits you a treat, but the coat wasn't cut for you to sleeve aces. So let's have a few cards on the table. You went to the Black Sheep, as per usual . . ."

"I was a little early, also as usual. To my surprise Linda Myers suddenly appeared at my table and sat down uninvited. She said something like 'Someone standing you up, too?' She's not the sort of girl who likes being kept waiting."

"Didn't drop a hint who she was there for?"

"I daresay I shouldn't have been enlightened if she had. But she was put out and—it was more than that. I knew that girl well enough to realize that if someone really kept her waiting she'd march off with her nose in the air."

"But instead she decided to fill in time talking to you? And you couldn't shake her off because, like I said, she had something on you. Could be she knew your friend's name?"

"No. No, I'm sure it wasn't that. But—she did see me out one Thursday evening with someone who wasn't Mrs. Polly. As a matter of fact, she tried to thumb a lift."

"Seems quite a habit of hers. That's the way she got acquainted with Wayland. If her stepmamma knew so much, shouldn't she have warned her that's the way to make trouble for yourself?"

"It was unfortunate that the lights were against us, so I couldn't drive on, and of course . . ."

"She got a good dekko. And she didn't see why she shouldn't turn her knowledge to good account. She sounds a real charmer. What did she take you for?"

"You make it sound so melodramatic," stammered Mr. Polly. "Blackmail and all that. But there was never anything of that sort; she just liked to be able to pull a string, like asking to get off early, and, well, subbing on her salary."

"And forgettin' to pay when Friday came round?"

"Quite small sums," Mr. Polly insisted. "A pound or two here and another pound or two there. I think in a way she thought it was all rather a joke, the sort of thing she'd seen on TV."

"From what I hear of her she was never home often enough to watch TV. And it ain't my idea of a joke. Anyway, it must have been pretty important to you." He had a sudden vision of Mr. Polly's existence—the salon where he worked and bowed and booked appointments, and the home where he wasn't even allowed to take a bottle over the threshold. No kids, May had said, no stake in the future, and for entertainment endless chitchat with elderly dames all fancying themselves the Jersey Lily or Miss Floradora. It shouldn't happen to a dog, he thought.

"Not just to me. There was Monica to consider."

"Never thought of asking Mrs. P. for a divorce?"

"It wouldn't have been any good. Monica's husband wouldn't have let her go, and there's the boy, Teddy; he's fourteen. You can't drag a fourteen-year-old through the divorce court. I'd always been sorry that Mrs. Polly and I never had any family—her daughter by her first marriage is married and in the States—but I wouldn't do that to a child, even if Monica had been prepared to take the chance, which she wasn't."

The aces were falling out of his sleeve all over the table now.

"Know anything about Linda's baby?" Crook asked. It was brutal, but you can't afford kid gloves in his line. Knuckle-dusters, are more like it.

"I don't think anyone knew. It's a funny thing, even the police haven't been able to turn up a doctor who told her what her trouble was."

"Could be because she didn't see a doctor. Could be she came to the Black Sheep to meet the father and hear what he had to say. Sure you didn't see him come in?"

"The place got pretty full; it's a popular bar, which is one reason we used it. There are so many people, coming in and out—it's near a station and quite a lot of commuters drop in and have a quick one while waiting for a train—I wouldn't notice any particular person. But I'm sure he had arrived, because suddenly Linda became much more animated. She threw her voice out and waved her hands, and laughed in a confiding sort of way, wanting to let him know he wasn't the only pebble on the beach."

"She sounds just a kid," Mr. Crook exclaimed, surprising himself as much as his companion. "Showing off. How about your friend?"

"I saw her come in. Of course. She went to sit at a table by the wall, as she always did. Then I'd go to the bar and get the drinks. By that time the barman would have served an orangutan without noticing. Of course, she saw Linda with me, so she couldn't come up. She must have recognized her from that meeting in the car. I don't think Linda saw her, she was too much engaged in her act. 'Are you sure your friend hasn't come?' I asked her, and she said, without moving her head, 'I don't see him. And even if he is here it doesn't matter. Do him good to see he isn't the only daisy on the patch!' "

"Didn't occur to her you might be keeping your friend waiting?"

"That sort of consideration wouldn't weigh with her. I said I couldn't stop long, and she laughed. 'Let her wait for once,' she said. 'It's what we all come to.' Really, I could have —well, you know what I mean."

"If you have to give this evidence in court," suggested Crook, "leave that last bit out. It's the sort of thing juries are so inclined to misconstrue."

Mr. Polly, who had been plugging along like a man trying to climb a steep hill without sufficient breath for the ascent, came to a dead stop.

"What do you mean—juries? I can't afford to appear in this case. And I won't have Monica's name mentioned."

"Tell me something," said Crook so earnestly that the question was robbed of offensiveness, "how did you expect it all to end? Not allowing for Linda, I mean, but you and the two ladies?"

"One doesn't look ahead in a situation like that. One doesn't dare. But it means a great deal—everything, in short— to me. Well, I couldn't actually get up and leave Linda—I wasn't absolutely certain that she would recognize Monica, and I certainly didn't want the two to meet. We were always so careful, two short drinks, and then we'd leave—not even together. She always had to be home before ten-thirty—that's when her husband's train came in, he had these Rotary meetings . . ."

"Everything happens on Thursday. Well?"

"After a while I saw Monica get up and go toward the door. I suppose she thought she looked too conspicuous, sitting there alone. I couldn't let her go without a word. I said to Linda, 'In that case, how about another half?' and I snatched up our glasses and marched up to the bar. I just dumped them and slipped out, and there was Monica waiting beside my car. She doesn't have a car of her own, comes in by bus and I drive her back to the nearest bus stop and let her out at the corner, so if she does meet anyone they'll think she's just alighted."

"Do you mean to say her husband never tumbled?" asked Crook.

"She tells him she goes to an upholstery class, and now and again when I couldn't make it—things crop up in spite of yourself—she really went. And when the classes were over she'd say she was meeting her sister . . . Oh, it was balancing on a knife-edge, but what choice had we? If he had an inkling of the truth he wouldn't hesitate, he'd take the boy from her— I don't know who spread the story about the delights of illicit love, but it was someone who'd never been through that particular mill. Sometimes she'd even wonder if the game was worth the candle—what with her husband and my wife, and never being sure if we'd be recognized . . ."

"And you have been," capped Mr. Crook neatly. "And it can't have been Linda this time, because she's past all mischief-making, and it wasn't my client because he was in durance vile . . ."

"You mean you don't actually know—you've been leading me up the path all this time?" Mr. Polly was as white as the proverbial sheet.

"This arrived at Robinson's, by hand, this afternoon," Crook said, producing the anonymous letter.

Mr. Polly stared. The white gave place to red. "You mean that's all you had to go on?"

"You're a glutton for punishment. How much more did you want?"

"You tricked me," Mr. Polly accused him wildly. "You let me think . . ."

"Calm down," Mr. Crook advised him. "Suppose I hadn't called you up, just consider the alternative. The finder of the letter would have taken it to the police. They might have thought it was somebody's idea of a bad joke, but they'd have had to make inquiries, and it's my belief you'd do better to talk to me than to them."

"They wouldn't have taken any notice of it," Mr. Polly declared thickly.

"You don't do them justice, honest you don't. I don't say me and them always see eye to eye, but they're no slouches."

"Who do you suppose wrote it? The murderer?"

"I think it was someone who knows I'm on the trail and thinks it would be a good idea—realizing that my clients are always innocent—to point the police to a different direction."

"Why not go to the police station, instead of all this mayhem."

Crook stroked his big pugnacious chin. "It's a funny thing—how shy even the most boastful chap can be when it comes to taking the limelight, particularly where the law's concerned. You note there's no signature. You or me could have sent that if we'd been daft enough."

"Mr. Crook, promise me one thing, you will keep Monica's name out of this? That girl was alive and well when I walked out of the pub. Sam, the barman, may have seen me. He must have known me by sight at least, we'd been going there quite a long while."

"Point is, would he know Linda by sight? Well, Mr. Polly, thanks for your help. And try and have a bit of common. I mean, an accident with your razor wouldn't be any use to anyone."

Mr. Polly glanced at his watch. "I must get back. Mrs. Polly will wonder what's happened."

"Simple enough. Defense counsel—not that it quite amounts to that, but it sounds well—wanted to ask you a few questions. Come now, you've been juggling quite a long time, a little thing like that shouldn't unseat you. I won't be getting along myself right away," he added cheerfully. "I'll stay and have another pint. You never know, the stuff at the Other Place may be what they keep to drown the mice in." He smiled, a big affable alligator smile, and called for another pint.

The door had hardly swung to behind Mr. Polly when

a young man who had been standing at the far end of the bar moved as it were casually in Crook's direction.

"Come right up and take a pew," invited Mr. Crook. "Feel like declaring an interest or is it just that I've got a smut on my nose?"

"You don't miss much, do you?" said the young man. "Is your name really Crook?"

"So my mother always told me, and I've never had any reason to doubt it," returned Mr. Crook heartily.

"I'm Hardy, Jack Hardy."

"The nevvy from overseas. Yes, I've heard of you from Sugar. Fill the gentleman's glass, Sam. Do things always happen when you're around, or is it just chance?"

"Just chance. I say, though, you're not trying to pull Pretty Polly into this, are you?"

"Pretty . . ."

"That's what Linda used to call him."

"So you knew the young lady."

"Seeing Aunt Alice looked on her as a sort of dream-daughter—granddaughter really, I suppose—oh yes, I heard a lot about her. Mind you, I don't think the old lady really knew Linda at all, but there's no doubt about it she got a lot of pleasure out of the acquaintance. Poor Aunt A, she's gone downhill definitely since she heard what happened to Linda. They talk about cushioning the shock, but there's a limit to the amount of cushioning you can do."

"Any chance of me seeing her?" Crook inquired.

Young Mr. Hardy frowned. "The police 'ull have your guts for garters if you do. They weren't accorded the privilege." He thought. "I don't believe she'd seen Linda just recently, but Aunt Phyl might know more about that than I do. She could fill in a few gaps, unless, as I say, you've got your eye on Polly."

"It occurred to me that as the girl's employer and the last person who admits to seeing her, he might be able to give me a pointer or two."

"I thought he'd confided everything to the police."

"Everything he was willing to tell," Crook conceded,

"but the police and me could have the same facts, and the results 'ud be quite different."

"Must be a fascinating job, yours."

"So long as you're well insured. But he couldn't help me much."

"I don't suppose he could. Mrs. P's a terror by all accounts. Any husband of hers would have about as much freedom as a cat with a tin can tied to its tail."

"If I was a cat and anyone tied a tin can to my tail, I'd go around with my claws unsheathed day and night. Young lady didn't confide in you, I take it."

Hardy grinned. "She made it clear from the start I was no more than a fill-gap while she waited for Lord Highmuckamuck to come riding along and carry her off to his castle. For a hard-boiled girl she was really very romantic. Funny thing is she believed what she told you. 'I'll surprise you all yet,' she'd say. 'A mini's all right for them that like small cars' . . ."

"But her taste was more for a Rolls?"

"Got it in one. And talking of Rolls, there's a remarkable specimen outside, a big yellow job . . ."

"Don't say it," begged Crook. "If I had a sovereign for every time I've been asked which museum I've been robbing, I could retire tomorrow."

"Not you," scoffed Jack Hardy. "All the same, I wouldn't mind getting my hands on her wheel."

"I'll put you on the waiting list," promised Crook generously.

"And I suppose I could hope for a Council house before you reached my name."

"Don't look round," said Crook with no change of tone. "But you're a native, temporarily anyway, so—what's Coppernob's name when he's at home?"

"Coppernob?"

Crook indicated the broad sheet of glass behind the bar. He'd heard that publicans put it there so that even when the barman had to turn his back on his customers he still had 'em in view, and a very wise precaution, too, in his opinion.

Jack's glance followed his. "Oh, you mean the Dishonorable Willy. It's only a joke," he added quickly. "I don't suppose he does any more fiddling than the next man, but his mother's the Honorable Mrs. Stephenson, so you see?"

"I'm not so sure I would in his shoes," murmured Crook. "Come here often?"

"I couldn't say," Jack acknowledged. "I'm not often here myself. Hullo, you seem to have flushed him."

For the red-headed man had pushed back his chair and was moving toward the door.

"He's got better hearing than a bat if he could hear what I was saying," Crook protested. "Unless, of course, he lip-reads. Anyway, why should he care?"

"Don't overdo it," begged Jack. "The modesty, I mean. Everyone knows you aren't even temporarily a native, and I reckon most of them know why you're here."

"Don't see why that should bother him, unless he was a friend of the dear departed."

"That's another thing I wouldn't know," Jack conceded, "but it 'ud surprise me if there was a chap under forty Linda didn't know. Not that he'd be much good to her. For one thing, he's engaged, and for another—if you were going to suggest that engagements have been broken off, he'd be even lower on the list than yours faithfully. Any worldly goods he has will come to him through marriage."

"Like that?" murmured Crook. "I didn't know."

"I suppose if the Archbishop of Canterbury were to walk in and take any notice of you, you'd put him on your list of suspects, too," hazarded Jack. "Hullo, look who's here?"

As he thrust powerfully against the swing-door, Willy found himself practically barging into another chap who was coming in.

"What's up, Mr. Polly?" inquired Crook cheerfully. "Thought of something you forgot to mention just now?"

"I—I seem to have mislaid a glove," muttered Mr. Polly. "Just wondered . . ." He dropped down and made a feint of looking for it under the bar.

Crook obligingly dropped down beside him. "I should

take another look in the car," he murmured. "What's the real reason?"

"It's just—if you should meet Mrs. Polly, I'd be obliged if you wouldn't mention where we met, I mean. I'm not suggesting she's an unreasonable woman, but . . ."

"Mum as an oyster," promised Crook generously. "Well, wherever you dropped it, Mr. Polly, it wasn't here."

"I must take another look outside, only it's part of a pair Mrs. Polly gave me and . . ."

"If you had to lose it she'd prefer it to be Ann's Parlour or Prue's Pantry. Well, good hunting."

Mr. Polly went out. Willy was staring at the big yellow Rolls. "That's Mr. Crook's car," said Polly, going past.

"I knew it wasn't local," Willy agreed. "That was Crook inside?"

"That's right. A Londoner, I understand."

"They say in London you could go about naked and no one would notice you," Willy said.

He watched Mr. Polly get into his neat blue car and drive off. When Jack Hardy came out a minute or two later, Willy had disappeared, too.

Mr. Crook was still sitting up at the bar. "Give you a toast, Sam," he offered. "You choose your own vintage."

When both glasses were charged he lifted his a little and, looking Sam in the eye, announced, "We'll drink a toast to X, the mystery man in the Linda Myers case. Because it's my firm belief you've had him drinking in your bar this very night."

9

By the time Mr. Crook had finished drinking his toast, Mr. Polly's smart dark blue Rover, Willy Stephenson's racing model and Jack Hardy's jalopy, as he liked to call it, had all disappeared from the car park. It was an inhospitable sort of night, a damp mist turning to fog, and Mr. Crook found himself hoping that at the Black Sheep, where he proposed to follow up Sam's tip, they'd have a nifty steak-and-kidney pie with all the trimmings. Or, failing that, a nice steak would do. And seeing he was going to grill Joe or whatever the barman's name might be, it could be appropriate if they were to grill something for him in turn. (This was the crude sort of pun he enjoyed.)

Of course, he told himself, turning the Superb out of the yard and facing her down the hill, there's steak *and* steak. The name was like charity, it covered a multitude of sins. There was goat steak, whale steak, and he remembered a place where he was convinced they kept a stableful of mules for the dubious benefit of clients.

And there was that chap who always swore he had a kangaroo steak at a lush-up in Brighton, he reminded himself, looking down at the distant lights in the valley, which seemed to be approaching him rather more rapidly than he expected. "Whoa, Emma," he adjured the Superb, but for once she seemed as deaf as the famous adder that laid one ear to the sand and put the tip of its tail into the other. "This ain't the Monte Carlo rally," he protested.

Mr. Crook wrestled with brakes that mysteriously failed to respond. "I'm not fussy," he protested to no one in particular, "but I do aim to reach the bottom in one piece."

Only by this time he was pretty sure someone else didn't intend that he should.

The Superb was winging her way downhill like a drunken bird. The hill was long and pretty steep. The Superb had been made in a day when everybody expected value for money, good solid metal and insides made to last, not like the tin and wire contraptions you saw all round you nowadays. Two-Ton Tessy ain't in it with her, reflected Mr. Crook grimly. Mind you, he hadn't the smallest doubt what had happened. Cars like the Superb don't put themselves out of action for a pettish whim, they don't go on strike; they're a lot more dependable than many of the human agencies responsible for their make-up. One of these days, he supposed, some genius would invent a car that went bleep-bleep if she'd been interfered with, but long before then he (Crook) would be bones and dust in some anonymous churchyard. With so many chaps coming and going, no one, particularly on such a night, was going to notice just one standing beside a car in the car park, with the hood raised, doing a bit of repair work. That's how it would look to the man in the street. And he himself, like the braying ass of the Scriptures, had sung out to all and sundry that he'd be staying on and having another pint or two, which would give an enemy all the time he needed. And when the crash came it wouldn't be easy to say just when the damage to the brakes occurred, and there'd be the fellow at the Flying Fox to remember how many pints he'd had, and another victory would be chalked up for Demon Drink, which he wouldn't deserve.

Biter bit, thought Mr. Crook, his mind working almost as fast as the car. Going to see a man, I said. Person I'm most likely to see tonight is the Recording Angel.

He remembered there was a sharp bend at the foot of

the hill, and at the rate she was going, even the Superb wouldn't be able to negotiate that. "Eternity, here I come," announced Mr. Crook, remembering with the clarity of desperation one of his late Mum's favorite aphorisms about dealing with a fool according to his folly. Even at this extremity he couldn't really blame anyone but himself. A chap with the most rudimentary notions of preservation doesn't drive with his eyes shut, which was precisely what he had been doing.

He heard a furious yell behind him, and in the driving mirror he saw a lorry thundering down the hill. The driver's lips were moving, though Crook couldn't distinguish what he said. Still, you could forgive him anything in the circumstances; the Superb was bouncing all over the road. Then the door of the cab opened and a few words became audible.

"You blurry fool!" said a voice. "Pull in, can't you?"

It was too much to suppose there were two of them out of control at the same time and in the same place, but no sense both of them getting clobbered, so he pulled in recklessly toward the wide ditch to his left. The Superb would crash into that and then through the narrow hedge, and it would be curtains for Arthur Crook and quite likely a lifer for young Wayland. He was aware of a great dark bulk on his right-hand side; for an instant he thought the lorry was going to crush him, just to make sure of the job, only it wasn't reasonable to suppose everyone was in league to put out his light, then he tipped sideways into the ditch. But the Superb didn't make the break-through he'd anticipated, because the great bulk of the lorry was there to slow him down. It was a chance in a thousand, and like many reckless chances it brought home the bacon. And he needed bacon now as he'd seldom needed it before. Automatically he'd shielded his head—hands were given men for more than lifting tankards—he'd shut off the engine without realizing what he'd done. He felt like a porpoise in a gulf stream, any moment he'd go over and over, always assuming porpoises haunted gulf streams. He heard glass shatter, and the world darkened, someone screamed, he couldn't think who. The lorry driver hadn't seemed the hysterical type, and anyway, hysterical night drivers don't last long on the roads of Britain. Crook wasn't, he assured himself, a murderous type, just a cozy hard-working chap who liked his job, but at this instant if he'd had a carving knife in his hand, it would have been bad luck for the chap who'd put this insult on the Superb.

A voice broke through the mist that had assumed a reddish tinge. "He's coming round," it said.

"About time, too. Wake up, mate."

Crook opened a cautious eye. He wondered if these were the holy angels he'd heard about in his childhood; they sounded uncommonly like members of the base-born human race. He opened a second eye; now he could see a girl with a long shining tail of fair hair bending over him.

"Crummy!" he ejaculated reverently. "They do exist, then?"

"And you can thank your perishing stars they do," said a voice that clearly never emanated from a celestial being. "Lucky for you there isn't a copper waiting around with his breathalizer apparatus. Who did you think you were? Waltzing Matilda?"

To his surprise Mr. Crook found he could function comparatively normally. He looked at his hands; they were both there, like outsized chestnut-colored starfish. He moved one foot, then the other. They were cramped, but at least they hadn't fallen off. True, one of his arms felt as though a giant had twisted it, and at the same time had mistaken his conk for a tenpenny nail and tackled it with a hammer with angelic zeal. He shook it experimentally.

"Take care it don't come off," said the same grim voice.

Mr. Crook swerved slightly. The angel was still in evidence, wearing a sort of abbreviated shirt that came nowhere near her knees and what his Mum used to call a smicket. Behind her the lorry bulked very solid and dark in the half-light.

"It wasn't you driving that?" he suggested vaguely.

"For Pete's sake!" It was the avenging angel again this time. "Women have enough daft ideas in their heads without you giving 'em any more, free, gratis and for nothing. Here, Beryl, you nip back into the lorry before some Nosey Parker comes along and starts calling the police."

Mr. Crook drew a deep breath. "Praise the pigs!" he said. "At least you're no angel, even if you are wearing your invisible cloak."

A tall, cool young man came into his line of vision. "What's she made of?" he asked, touching the Superb with a reverent hand. "Cast-iron? I wouldn't have backed my lorry to come through that, and she's brand-new."

Mr. Crook said, "Here, give me a hand out of this thing and we might try and assess the damage. Maybe if you could give her a tow, she might run down the hill on her own."

The lorry driver looked at him in admiration. "You don't half expect miracles, do you, mate? Anyway, she's about as safe on the road as a charging rhino."

"If you found yourself deprived of the law of gravity you might be hanging upside down in a tree," pointed out Mr. Crook, defending his darling with spirit. "And that's what's happened to her. No use blaming a fellow whose foot's been chopped off for not coming in first at the relay."

With some difficulty and with assistance from Rod, whose second name he never learned, he got himself into a perpendicular position, and they examined the extent of the damage. This was less than might have been anticipated. She'd lost a good deal of paint and her hood and front mudguard were a bit cockled, but given a bit of expert doctoring she'd soon be on the road again.

" 'Tain't so easy to put the Superb out of action," exulted Crook.

"What's that you called her?" said Rod.

"The Superb. Comes out of a poem, so they tell me." Crook was patting himself all over to find out if there was an odd bone sticking up somewhere that he hadn't noticed. Now he said, "How about a few introductions?" and produced one of his fantastic cards.

It was a pity, really, that visibility was so poor; he

couldn't see Rod's face properly in the light of the pocket torch the fellow produced, but his voice filled in all the gaps.

"This straight up?" he asked. "Here, Beryl, come out a jiff and meet someone who might be useful to you one of these days."

"Not in with the police, are you?" asked Beryl.

Crook didn't think it worth answering that one.

"What happened?" Rod inquired.

"Some chap's been reading the statistics about over-population and thought he'd rid the world of one specimen. Lucky for me you were taking the same road. I don't know what your work of mercy has done to her innards, but there's something screwy about the brakes, that was done before-hand." He looked thoughtfully at the Superb, who even in her hour of defeat maintained her air of dignity. "Any hope of pulling her out?" he inquired.

"No harm trying. There's a tow rope in the van. Here, Beryl, be a doll and fetch it out. Don't mind traveling heavy, do you?" he added to Crook.

"Hark who's talking!" murmured the lawyer.

"What's it feel like, driving a Rolls?" Rod continued.

"If she wasn't in the towing-class this 'ud be your chance to find out," said Crook generously.

Beryl reappeared with the rope, and between the three of them—and never tell him no more that ladies don't know how to pull their weight, reflected Crook—they got the Superb back on the road and hitched up to the lorry.

"Here, doll, you keep a weather eye open," Rod told his companion. "I reckon to know something about the inside of a car. Fact is," he confided to Crook, "we're not supposed to take passengers, even the non-paying kind. The bosses think we talk to ourselves to keep us awake, I suppose. There's the radio, of course, but they don't even like that much. Bad for the concentration. And if they knew I had a girl up with me . . ."

"Would they know the difference?" asked Mr. Crook. "Honest, I saw a chap down Fulham way last Sunday, ever such pretty brown hair, parted and plaited over the shoulders, two-thirds to his middle, and tied with blue bows. And he *was* a chap, what's more!"

"There's nothing of that sort of chap about my girl, only I don't want to marry her on the social security, and if you're outs with one lorry boss, you're outs with the lot. The word goes round. Mind you, it's not your morals they're troubled about or the doll's for that matter, no, they're afraid something may happen to their precious van. Well now, let's take a dekko."

He had the hood up and was peering inside with all the ardor of a Jacques Cousteau investigating some newly found ocean creature. "You're right, Mr. Crook," he acknowledged. "She never did this to herself. Someone don't love you, Mr. Crook."

"Point is—which one?"

"Going to report this to the police, Mr. Crook?" Rod asked.

"And see 'em split their sides laughing, those who ain't weeping into their mooshwars—handkerchiefs to you—because the plot didn't come off? Not something likely. Besides, me and the police so often don't see eye to eye they might take steps I wouldn't approve. No, heaven helps them that help themselves, and heaven's on my side, wouldn't you say?"

"Don't mix me up," pleaded Rod. " 'Rithmetic was never my strong suit."

"If you hadn't been coming down the hill, some undertaker might be having himself a ball," Crook pointed out. "Had you thought of that?"

"Tell me something," asked Rod, in the voice of the man who really wants to know, "do you have much difficulty getting life insurance?"

"What for? When I hand in my dinner pail there'll be no one to benefit but the State, and why should I pay premiums to cosset them? And over and above that, it's tempting providence."

"What are you going to tell the garage that puts that right for you, then?"

"I had a breakdown—brakes wouldn't work—or will they now?"

Rod lifted his head from under the car's hood. "If all the rest of her was as good as her brakes, you could drive her off yourself," he promised. "Funny how simple it is to put a car out of action if you've got the know-how."

"Lucky for me you carry the spare parts," said Crook.

"My old man runs a garage, wanted me to come in with him. I've got better things to do with my time than fetch and carry for all the barmies who drive a car these days, I told him. Anyway, it 'ud be a case of always the bridesmaid, never the bride, if you read me."

"Loud and clear," agreed Mr. Crook. "All these nits driving cars on the petrol you supply 'em with . . ."

"And me with no more than a motorbike. You tell a girl you work for your Dad and you've only got a motorbike, and she doesn't want to know. Now we'll tow you down to the bridge, there's an A.A. phone there, you tell anyone who you are and they won't be able to come fast enough." He would hardly have been surprised at this juncture if the Superb had unfolded invisible wings and taken off on her own account.

"You from the Smoke?" asked Mr. Crook, getting behind the wheel, an operation that gave him a bit more difficulty than usual.

"However did you guess?"

"They know me and the Superb in my own local, and maybe in a few further out, but this is beyond my normal perimeter, and you recognized her right away. Sure you ain't making trouble for yourself, bringing her along?"

"Well, she can't stay there, brother, not without you want to be run in for obstruction," Rod explained. "There's a caff on the corner beyond the bridge. Mostly only serves drivers, but they'll let you in, I'll pass them the word."

"Well, you've been in the wars," commented the A.A. man candidly. "What did you do? Try to jump a wall?"

"Don't confuse me," begged Mr. Crook. "I was tool-ing down the hill as nice as you please, when suddenly she went out of control, never ask me why. Next thing there was this chap stopping and giving me a hand. No, I don't know who he was, he didn't say, but we got her out of the ditch and he helped me roll her down—risked his own future, I wouldn't wonder. Something wrong with the brakes, he thought," he amplified vaguely.

"And you didn't get his name?"

"There's no record that the Good Samaritan left his name, either. Now, if I can get her back to Churchford, Mr. Warren 'ull doctor her for me, if he has to stop up all night."

"Don't mind expecting miracles, do you?" suggested the A.A. man. And that made two of them in one night.

"You want to look out for yourself, Mr. Crook," offered Warren. "That's a nasty bang you've got on the head. You should see a doctor."

"Join the army and see the world. Visit the doctor and see the next," improvised Mr. Crook. He dropped into a late-night chemist's and got a bit of plaster and some more advice (that he left behind on the counter), tracked back to the Bald-Faced Stag and decided to call it a day. May Forbes and the chap at the Black Sheep could both wait till the morning.

Someone's precious anxious young Wayland shan't get off the hook, he reflected. Still, we're coming along nicely. Funny how often chaps think they're blocking your road, when all the time they're giving you a hefty shove in the backside that gets you over some of your worst bumps.

Having been assured the next morning that he couldn't expect the Superb, even at double time, before mid-day, Crook mounted the bus for Axton and paid his promised visit to the Black Sheep. The fellow behind the bar was loath to help him till Crook suggested that his boss would probably prefer to answer his (Crook's) questions to those of the roz-zers. Then he acknowledged, a bit churlishly, that he knew Polly by sight and that he came in from time to time.

"Always the same time the same day of the week," Crook suggested. "Think, man, this is a murder case, some chap's going to get life and I'm out to see it ain't my client. Try and put yourself in his shoes . . ."

"I get bunions enough with the ones I'm wearing," said Joe, still only half mollified. "We don't like answering questions about clients, Mr. Crook, not if they're well-behaved and don't cause any trouble."

"Someone caused me a hell of a lot of trouble last night," Crook observed, more grimly than usual. "And I don't want to make trouble for innocent chaps any more than you do, but you know what they say, we're all one big family, members one of another . . ."

Joe gave up. "You'd talk the hind leg off a goat, Mr. Crook. All right then, he used to come in Thursday nights, not every Thursday, but if he did come, it would be a Thursday. When chaps are that regular you get to notice, and of course he's lived in Churchford a long time."

"And the lady? O.K., he's admitted she exists."

"I can't tell you anything about her. They just used to have a couple of drinks and off they'd go. I didn't think much about it, you get all sorts in a bar, and, like I said, they never made trouble."

"This girl who got herself murdered . . ."

Joe looked horrified. "You're not on about her?"

"Ever see her here?"

"Not that I recall, which isn't to say she never came. But she's not the one *he* used to meet."

"No, I didn't think she was. Well, it's a wicked world, you have to check up, don't you? You a believin' man?"

"Come again," said Joe.

"Our Father which art in heaven," amplified Mr. Crook.

"With the world in its present state? You're joking."

From which Crook deduced it mightn't lie too heavily on the fellow's conscience to bend the facts a bit, if it suited the management. But the way things were going at the moment, there didn't seem much sense trying to involve him.

He had reached the Black Sheep soon after opening time and hadn't stayed long, so he reckoned he could squeeze in his red-headed neighbor of the previous night before returning to Churchford and giving May Forbes the wigwag. Since the mysterious "accident" to the Superb it occurred to him that May herself might do with a bit of protection. If both of them were out of the way, X could count on going as free as air, and Chris Wayland would likely languish in a jail, having no one to speak for him.

She, he reminded himself, referring to May, is as trusting as a puppy. Look at the way she came with me that first night. All this mock-up about seeing, hearing and believing no evil might have been all right in the days of Victorian innocence, but it was out-of-date in the twentieth century, when the fellow to survive was the one who never let his ears or eyes off duty.

He didn't phone to announce his coming. It's not only trick cyclists who believe in the value of shock treatment.

The Honorable Blanche Stephenson might have had what Crook in his plebeian way called a handle to her name, but her house looked like anybody else's, and when he rang the bell she herself came to the door. She had two "obliging" women four mornings a week, but this didn't happen to be one of them.

When she saw Crook she started to close the door at once, but something seemed to have got in the way—in fact, the toe of Crook's glossy chestnut Oxford shoe.

"We don't buy on the doorstep," she said crisply.

"Suits me," Mr. Crook agreed, "seeing I've come to get rather than give. You'd be Mrs. Stephenson?"

"That is so, but I don't think . . ."

"It was really your son I came to see," Crook explained.

"My son is out."

"Expecting him back soon? I could wait."

"I really couldn't tell you. I don't keep tabs on the comings and goings of a grown man."

"Saw him in the Flying Fox last night," offered Mr. Crook.

Blanche's face froze, though the fascinated Mr. Crook hadn't thought it possible it could assume a wintrier aspect.

"If you have come to collect a debt or anything of that kind . . ."

"No money involved," Crook promised. "Well, I'm not mug enough to play cards with a chap I don't know."

"I don't understand what you intend to insinuate, Mr.—"

"Crook—Arthur Crook." He didn't offer her one of his cards. He knew she'd simply drop it in the nearest trash bucket. "Had an idea he might be able to give me a bit of info."

"Really, Mr. Crook, I cannot imagine . . ."

"What me and your son could have in common? Well, for one thing, we're both human, and for another, I fancy he might be able to help me about some inquiries I'm makin' on behalf of a chap called Wayland."

Blanche Stephenson looked at him as though she couldn't believe the evidence of her own eyes. "It's not possible—I mean, you are not here in connection with the man who murdered that girl, Linda Myers?"

"Got it in one," beamed Crook.

"It is quite impossible for my son to be able to help you."

"Go on," invited Crook. "Tell me he never knew the young lady and I shan't believe you. Why, he had his ears on sticks last night when two or three of us went into a huddle. Anyway, it ain't likely an enterprising girl like Linda Myers would overlook a distinguished-looking man like the Honorable Willy."

"Have you any proof that this—this Wayland is innocent?"

"If I had proof I wouldn't be bothering to ask questions, would I? But the courts won't take my word, they want facts, and facts is something your son might be able to give me."

"In what connection?"

"Well, for instance, he might have seen the chap who tried to disable my car last night. You don't do a thing like that for fun, and whoever was responsible was pretty keen I shouldn't continue to cumber the earth and wreck his future."

"If, as I suppose is the case, you are a lawyer, you must be aware of something called slander."

"I should, seeing how much I've experienced it. But you tell me how I slandered your son. I just said he might be able to give me some—well, might have seen someone showing a bit more than normal interest in the Superb. If he gave me a few particulars I daresay I'd be able to fit a name to them."

Somewhere in the house a telephone rang. Blanche hesitated. It rang again. She looked pointedly at her visitor.

"You go right ahead and answer it," Crook assured her blandly. "I'll wait here. Even if you don't like my mug or my moniker, you must admit I couldn't uproot one of the pillars." He looked about him with a glance that said there was nothing else worth pinching.

Blanche Stephenson acknowledged her first defeat. "You had better come in, though I warn you, you may have to wait a long time."

But if he was going to wait, it would be better to do it inside where he was invisible to passers-by. A man like Crook can't hope to escape comment, and she didn't fancy the kind of comment she would get if he were seen lurching about on her doorstep.

Crook looked interestedly about him. Gracious living, he supposed, observing the copper bowl of spring flowers, the scarred rug chest and the rug itself, so shabby it had to be valuable or a rag-and-bone-man wouldn't give you the time of day for it. He was examining a Victorian lithograph entitled "Twixt Love and Duty" when Blanche came back, closing a sitting-room door behind her. It was clear he wasn't going to graduate further than the hall.

"You spoke of a second attempted crime," she began.

"Well, not successful, or I wouldn't be here now,

would I?" beamed Crook. "But that's not to say the chap won't try again."

He could read her thoughts like goldfish swimming in a bowl. She was inwardly cursing the bungler who'd messed up his first attempt.

"You make it sound very melodramatic, Mr. Crook."

"Well, but murder is melodramatic. Maybe it ain't come your way much to date."

There was the rattle of a key behind him, and the Honorable Willy came in. When he saw Crook he blinked as though he were seeing visions and not the kind you'd hanker after. When he'd recovered he said, "Didn't know you knew Mr. Crook, Mater. If I'm interrupting anything I can push off."

"Mr. Crook came to see you, Willy. He appears to think you met at some bar last night."

"Flying Fox," explained Crook. "Chap I was with told me your name. You shouldn't have sat there drinking on your owney-oh, you should have joined us at the bar."

"My son is not in the habit of joining people he doesn't know." Blanche again, with the temperature below zero.

"How does he come to enlarge his acquaintance?" Crook wondered aloud. "Happen to notice anyone in particular in the bar last night?" he added to Willy.

"The Flying Fox isn't actually one of my pubs."

"So it was just chance you were there last night?"

"It's a free country, isn't it?"

"So they say, but you don't have to believe all you're told. Couldn't have anything to do with the fact that I was goin' to be there last night?"

"How on earth should my son know where you, a perfect stranger, would be drinking last night?"

Willy wished the old girl knew when to keep her mouth shut.

Crook was cheerfully answering her question. "Well, not because I told him," he agreed, "but you know the one about the chap who was following a tiger and all the time another tiger was following him?"

"My son being the second tiger?"

"I see you catch on," said Crook. "Most people around here know why I left the Smoke—London town to you," he added, seeing her perplexed expression. "On Linda Myers' account. So it's easy to guess I'd be of interest to anyone who knew the young lady, if only to keep tabs on my movements."

"That's the second time you have suggested that my son knew the girl. Are you not aware such a statement might be actionable?"

"You take the action, go right ahead," Crook advised her. "What interests me—I can find out about the girl for myself—is who went mucking about with my car last night. Your son was there—came by car, I suppose? he added to Willy.

"I didn't walk," Willy agreed.

"And you could hardly have flown. Funny—even a sparrow can do that, and yet we go around thinking ourselves superior to the bird world. And you left the Flying Fox before I did. Happen to notice a yellow Rolls standing in the forecourt?"

"You could hardly miss it," said Willy. "Anyone else taking any interest in it?"

"Some chap told me it was yours. Not many fellows about."

"It's like the Ancient Mariner," explained Crook, who could sport a culture-vulture hood himself on occasions. "He stoppeth one of three. Point is, which one should I be stopping?"

"If you car was really damaged, willfully damaged, which I take it is, what you mean to imply . . ."

"I said you caught on quick," interpolated Crook admiringly.

"How is it you were not injured?"

"The Lord looks after His Own," said Crook piously. "Likewise, angels come in strange disguises. Mine wore denims and talked a language that might fox even the Heavenly Host. Well, so you don't think you can help? But you don't blame me for trying, do you? I mean she was O.K. when we got there, and a car like the Superb don't put herself out of action. So I'll have to inquire in another quarter, won't I?"

Willy, who was expecting questions about the dead girl, was looking a bit dazed. "Oh," said Crook, turning back from the door, "don't happen to have a bus timetable handy, I suppose?"

"I'll run you back," offered Willy suddenly.

Crook looked more like an alligator than usual. "I may not look it," he said, "but I'm about the downiest bird in the business and I wouldn't dream of troubling you. There's bound to be a pub near a bus stop, where I can hang around, and having come so far on the road it 'ud be a pity to fall at the last fence. Oh, and two gems I leave with you. If you're thinking it's a thousand pities I didn't get fatally tangled up with the Superb last night, let me tell you, that wouldn't have been the end of it. There'd still be Sugar, Miss Forbes, and out and beyond her there's Bill Parsons, my partner. Remember the king in the Old Testament who said his father had chastised the mob with whips but he'd chastise them with scorpions. Well, Bill's the original King Scorpion, and it don't pay for anyone to forget it. No," he mused happily, opening the door, "I wouldn't say there was anything civilized about Bill."

He went out, leaving mother and son speechless. When they were past that phase, Blanche said, "What do you make of that?"

"Man's as mad as a hatter," said Willy.

"It's the mad ones who do the most mischief. Was he really in the bar of the Flying Fox last night?"

Willy nodded. "Carrying on like nobody's business about Linda Myers. That chap was born to put his feet into things; lucky for some people, I suppose, he only has two."

"Willy, you didn't say anything that he could get hold of?"

"I didn't speak to him, and I wouldn't have spoken to him today if I hadn't found him over your threshold. What d'you mean, Mater, by letting a chap like that in?"

"It's what he means that matters," retorted Blanche, "and a blind man could see that what he means is trouble."

. . .

It was ten minutes' walk to the pub and twenty-five minutes to wait when he got there, but he thought he'd just make Robinson's before it closed for the half-day. He remembered that May usually spent Wednesday afternoon with the redoubtable Mrs. Politi, and he'd prefer not to muscle in on any private arrangement of hers. But when he reached the shop he found it closed already, and a handwritten notice on the door to the effect that the business would be closed temporarily for family reasons. He rattled the handle but nobody came, and then he went round to the side, where the private or family door was, but the blinds were still open, which seemed to him to prove that though that Angel of Death might be flapping his wings on the threshold, he hadn't yet gained entry. May, presumably, had gone back to her own place, so he beetled round to Main Street, but when he pressed the bell nothing happened. No one looked out of a window or opened it and shouted; there was no sign of life there at all. Still, the woman had to be somewhere. Probably gone direct to Mrs. Politi and was at that very moment on the back premises knocking up some tasty nosh. Mrs. Politi's shop was still open, though there wasn't long to go before she, too, put the shutters up.

The junk store bore an imposing scroll over the door —*Antiques, China and Glass.* Mrs. Politi was clearly getting ready to close down; she regarded with some asperity one or two stragglers who had just stepped up to where the cheapest goods were laid out. She had a desk at the back of the shop, where she could see everyone without actually thrusting her presence upon them. People who're going to buy cheap damaged goods don't like to feel they're under too close an inspection. Crook picked up a plate decorated with an improbable tiger lily, with a bit of the rim missing, and marched up to the desk.

"Seen anything of Sugar?" he asked casually, handing the dish across. It was marked two-and-sixpence.

"Why you want this?" demanded Mrs. Politi, wearing her Rock-of-Gibraltar air.

MR. CROOK LIFTS THE MASK

"Wanted a word with you," explained Crook carefully. "Cheap at the price." He put his hand in his pocket and produced a half-crown.

"What word?"

"What I came for was Sugar or news of her. She ain't at the shop, they've shut down temporarily owing to illness of proprietor. I rang the side-door bell, but no soap."

"They put a piece of paper between the clapper and the wall," explained Mrs. Politi. "Then the bell not ring."

Crook nodded. "That figures," he said. "Still, don't tell me no one would be watching the street—well, they'd send for the doctor, wouldn't they? Anyhow, occurred to me you might know where she was."

Mrs. Politi didn't touch the half-crown. She laid the dish on the table. "You make a joke?"

"Never felt less like joking in my life."

"So—you ring me up, you say Miss Forbes not able to meet me this afternoon, she is lending you a hand, and then— But perhaps you forget," she added, elaborately sarcastic.

"Who's the philosopher who says you can't forget what you never knew? Look, is this straight up? I mean, you got a message said to come from me to the effect that Sugar and me— It's all baloney, you know."

Mrs. Politi looked over Crook's shoulder and bellowed, "You take that wolf off my premises. You think they a zoo?"

The startled customer, who was leading a Labrador not much larger than a Shetland pony, said stiffly, "Bruce wouldn't hurt any of the junk you've got here. Difficult to see how he could. A rag-and-bone-man wouldn't make you an offer for this stuff."

"You go before someone make an offer for you," threatened Mrs. Politi. To Crook she said, still speaking in a loud voice, "I show you a better dish, perfect condition, those I keep here." She backed him into a room behind the desk where there were some quite good pieces of china and glass. But she remained with her gaze on the street. "I take off my eye," she explained. "What happens? Someone help himself to a glass, a jug, a little dish, maybe. They talk of the magpie being a thief, like the one at Rheims . . ."

Crook opened his mouth to point out it had been a jackdaw, then prudently shut it again.

"I tell you," Mrs. Politi continued, "I not insult the magpie likening him to some I see go up and down this street. One of these days, believe me, some magpie write his story and let us know what he think of the human race. That will be worth reading." She nodded and her four chins quivered.

Regretfully Crook abandoned a desire to take her up on the subject of literary magpies, and got back to his first question. "What's this about me and Sugar?"

"You don't remember? Perhaps you take a little drink."

"I could drink the sea dry before I forgot a date with her," replied Crook simply. "When was this?"

Lilli considered. "I hear the church bell ring for Mass of the Dedication—that will be twelve o'clock. I have a customer about ten minutes later, the telephone ring. 'Excuse me,' I say. 'Please to wait.'" She indicated the telephone that was strategically placed so that she could get a reasonable amount of privacy and still be able to keep the shop under her eye. "Then the voice say, 'Mr. Crook? You remember? May's friend. She ask me to tell you she cannot come this afternoon, she will be helping me.'"

"You're sure that's what he said? May's friend."

"That is right."

"No, it ain't," contradicted Crook. "If it had been me I'd have said Miss Forbes or Sugar. I don't call a lady by her first name, not without I'm invited. What did he sound like?"

Mrs. Politi flung out her big arms. "He sound like a man." She said it in the same way as she might have said, "He roar like a tiger."

"Where did you suppose I was ringing from? Or didn't I say?"

"You ring from a call box. I hear the pips."

"Any reason why Miss Forbes shouldn't ring you herself? I mean, she didn't say she was bein' pressed into service with the invalid, only that I wanted her. Why bother to ring at all?"

"Because if May not come I ring the shop."

"And X don't want you to do that. How about doing that very thing now? They may not answer the front-door bell, but . . ." He looked at the huge watch he wore on his wrist, gift of a grateful client—and about as reliable, he sometimes reflected. "It's time you shut up shop," he added encouragingly.

Lilli looked at her watch, then surged forward, turbulent as a wave of the sea. She swept away the last of the lingerers and started to pull out huge faded green shutters. You wouldn't have believed a woman of her size could have handled them so deftly. Mr. Crook, on a point of honor, went to help her and was immediately made to feel like some beetle that got in the way of an Amazon forebear. Lucky if he only got his wings bruised, he reflected ruefully, wasn't completely trampled underfoot. Mrs. Politi locked the shutters, pulled another key from a chain she wore round her neck, and opened her side door.

"A private phone for my room," she assured him, as the stairs creaked under her monumental tread. It was a good thing it was an old house; a new one, run up as so many of them were, would have crackled like a twig in the smoke and precipitated them both into the cellar.

Either both Miss Robinsons were incapacitated or there'd been a wholesale holocaust at the house, for even Crook could hear the bell shrilling away, while no one answered. Lilli hung up, waited a couple of minutes and dialed again.

"Bet you an even pint you get the engaged signal," prophesied Crook, and that's just what they did get.

"I'll do the next call," Crook offered.

"You not put the police on to May," threatened Mrs. Politi.

"Who said anything about the police? I'm going to ring the doctor. If the Angel of Death has run amok in that household, it's time someone found out. If not, I want to know why no one's answering the phone."

Mellish was in, but in no very good mood. "Don't you know I don't take calls between one and two?" he demanded. "If it's an emergency, there's the hospital; if not, this happens to be Wednesday, when there's no surgery."

"So far as I'm concerned there don't have to be any surgery Monday to Saturday either," Crook assured him briskly. "The police have got their knife into me and I don't need any medicos doing likewise. Just want an answer to a question."

"Who's calling?" demanded the belligerent voice. "If it's you, Petersen . . ."

"If that's who I am my mother never told me," Crook assured him. "Who's Petersen, anyway?"

"Miserable little pipsqueak acting as garbage collector for the local *Argus*," shouted the doctor.

Give himself blood pressure if he carries on all his conversations at this pitch, Crook reflected. Nice, though, to find a chap out in the wilds who spoke your own language. "Name of Crook, representing Miss Forbes," he introduced himself. "Been round to the shop—Miss Robinson's, that is—no answer. Tried the phone—there's someone there because the receiver was taken off, but no dice conversation-wise. Been to Miss Forbes' place in Mill Street, no dice there either, and a neighbor says she had a message canceling a regular date."

"So?" suggested the doctor, but with rather more interest and rather less ferocity. "What are we supposed to make of that?"

"I don't know about you," returned Crook at his bluntest, "but my guess would be murder."

"You do like your dishes with parsley round them, don't you?" the doctor approved. "Or do you really have anything to go on?"

"Don't they say three's the magical number? Listen, then. We've had one murder, even the rozzers agree to that. Last night someone took a swipe at me—well, the Superb, if you like, but it comes to the same thing—and it ain't his fault it's no case of 'The angels in heaven are singing today, Here's Johnny, here's Johnny, here's Johnny.' And now Miss Forbes goes into a vanishing act."

"She could be doing some shopping or something," murmured the doctor vaguely.

"Or saying her prayers in the parish church, I suppose," amplified Crook tartly. "You tell me how she could be going round the markets on a Wednesday, with the boards up everywhere? And why ain't she with Mrs. Politi, because they have a standing date every Wednesday afternoon? And—no, I ain't finished yet—here comes the crunch. Who rang Mrs. P and said, in my name, *my name, mark you*, that her and me 'ud be walking out together today?"

Crook's breath ran out, to the doctor's relief, as he'd been trying to get a word in edgewise for the past thirty seconds. "Are you suggesting she's joined Linda Myers?" he demanded brutally.

"Not X's fault if she ain't."

"And this plot against you—sure you don't write whodunits in your spare time?"

"You give me some," challenged Crook, "and maybe I will. And for your information, cars like the Superb don't put themselves out of action. What's the situation at Robinson's, anyway? There's a notice on the door—closed till further notice— Old lady taken another step downhill?"

"Whizzing down on a toboggan," agreed the doctor grimly. If chaps talked Choctaw to you, you had to talk Choctaw back to them. "Miss Robinson had another and to my mind a final stroke this morning, no sense trying to keep the shop open. I told the sister I'd try and get her a nurse, but with all this flu about I'd need to make one myself with cardboard and a gold-paper halo. And by the time the glue was dry you'd find it was too late, her services wouldn't be wanted."

He stopped abruptly, startled to realize he'd been so confiding to a perfect stranger. Still, he reflected, the news 'ud be public property by tonight, unless he was much mistaken, so no harm done. And anyway, his correspondent didn't seem the sort of chap to take no for an answer.

10

At this juncture they were interrupted by the operator saying, "There is an urgent call for Dr. Mellish. Will you hang up your receiver, caller, please."

"Ringing from Mrs. Politi," added Crook rapidly.

"What he tell you?" Lilli demanded as Crook put the receiver down.

"He don't know much, just that Miss Alice had another stroke and he reckons it'll be her last. Shop closed by his advice. Next visitor likely to be the undertaker, and I only hope," he added savagely, "it'll be for Miss Alice and no one else."

"He tell you about May?" Mrs. Politi insisted.

"He don't know anything. Still, he'll come through again, told him where I was ringing from. Yes, of course he will. He's human, ain't he, and so being, he's also curious."

Sure enough, within five minutes the doctor was on the line. "On my way to Miss Robinson," he said. "I'll ask her about Miss Forbes. Not that she'll probably know much, gone shopping perhaps, Miss Forbes, I mean. Anyway, Miss Phyllis is on her own. You didn't happen to mention who you were," he added.

Crook told him. "And at the moment I'm standin' in for Miss Forbes' guardian angel." To Mrs. Politi he said, "We know Sugar didn't come right away off, "because you'd have seen her. And she didn't stay behind to hold Miss Phyllis' hand. I'm away to the House of Usher," he added, coming briskly to his feet. "I don't say that doctor ain't twenty-two carat, but I do like to come in on the ground floor. I don't suppose Miss Phyllis will be able to tell me much, but if young Clyde should surface . . ."

"No one called Clyde living there," insisted Mrs. Politi stubbornly.

"Bonnie and Clyde—Yankee gangsters," supplied Mr. Crook. "Well, if he should put in an appearance he might be able to fill me in a bit. Y'see, it ain't no joke. After last night's little adventure I rather fancy Sugar 'ull be the next on the list. Come to that, X may not know I'm still breathin'. Be a bit of a shock, I wouldn't wonder."

"You not breathing?" commented Lilli scornfully. "You breathe so hard you blow open the lid of your coffin."

"I don't know when I've had a compliment that's pleased me more," said Crook. "Well, I'll keep in touch."

"You keep in touch," repeated Lilli scornfully. She seized a sort of black mantle from a hook and swung it around her huge shoulders; she jammed a black woolen scarf on her head, and, her fingers digging into Crook's arm like an outsized crab, she demanded, "Why do we wait?"

Crook recalled that somewhere in the dear, dead past there was a chap who had his liver chewed up by a vulture; he felt a strong affinity with him. Vultures wouldn't be in it with Lilli Politi.

Feeling as conspicuous as if he were walking with his own guardian angel, Crook processed up the street and around to the side door of Robinson's Drapery.

The private door opened suddenly and Jack Hardy appeared.

"How you do get about!" he said. And then had the grace to look ashamed. "It's not exactly the best day for visiting, you know."

Mrs. Politi fixed him with an avenging eye. "What you done with May?"

"I was just going to try and fetch her back," the young man told them. "Aunt Phyl said to shut the shop at midday, she was expecting the doctor; well, it was obvious it was just a matter of hours, and she felt it wouldn't be respectful to carry on business in the circumstances, so she asked me to put a notice on the door."

"We saw that," Crook agreed.

"I'll tell you something," Jack added with a sudden sparkle, "your friend Coppernob is on the warpath."

Crook for once was taken off balance. "You mean he's been here?"

"Well, not here, but in Churchford. Miss Forbes was just putting up the notice when his car went by—well, either of them is noticeable, but the two together—and Miss Forbes said a rum thing. 'I've wondered sometimes if he knows more about Linda than he'll say'—meaning about the baby, I suppose. There isn't much she misses, for all she looks so innocent."

Hearing voices from below, Miss Phyllis came down the stairs. She seemed surprised but not outraged to find she had visitors.

"Do you know where Miss Forbes is?" she asked her nephew. "Not that I think Alice will recognize her again, she seems to have gone past a sort of curtain without looking back, but I think Miss Forbes would like to be here."

"As a matter of fact, I thought the same thing," Jack agreed. "I was going down to collect her."

"You know where May is?" Mrs. Politi spoke like a great brooding bird of prey.

"She said, as she had a bit of unexpected spare time, she thought she'd nip down to Mr. Polly and see if he could fit her in. She's quite an old client of his and says he's very obliging."

Miss Phyllis looked distressed. "When I said I didn't want the telephone used, I didn't mean May to carry it to that extreme. She could have rung up Mr. Polly, and perhaps saved herself a fruitless journey."

"Well, I did suggest it," said Jack, "but she thought she

might only get one of the juniors, who'd say right off it was
no good coming without an appointment, whereas if she came
down in person she might see Mr. Polly and he might squeeze
her in. They don't shut Wednesdays," he added for Crook's
benefit. "Saturday's their half-day."

"And perhaps Mr. Polly phone me that May not come
this afternoon because she out with Mr. Crook."

Jack shook his head. "Why on earth should he?"

"I ask you."

Jack looked hopefully at Crook. "I don't quite get the
drift."

"Someone rang Mrs. Politi, a voice she didn't recognize . . ."

"Some man," bayed Mrs. Politi disdainfully.

"And said the afternoon's entertainment was off—on
my account."

"But—was that meant to be a joke?"

Mrs. Politi gave an impression of the Three Weird Sisters rolled into one, rising to her feet. "So you think it a joke!
Miss Alice gone, Miss Phyllis left with no protector, May vanished, and you think it a joke."

"Let's you and me go along to Polly's and fetch
Sugar," suggested Crook diplomatically. "We might look in at
Warren's on the way and see how the Superb's coming along."

"I was in there this morning getting juice," reported
Jack, "and she was being given VIP treatment. You must have
had a nasty smash—on the hill, was it?"

"Not as nasty as X intended." He clapped on his horrid brown bowler hat. "You keep your auntie company till we
get back," he suggested.

"I don't know what we should have done without
Jack," said Miss Phyllis simply. "Sitting with my sister this
morning . . ."

"She thought I was Percy Trivett," confessed Jack,
looking a bit sheepish. "I hope it was all right, Aunt Phyl, she
made me tear up all those old letters, his, mine, the whole ca-
boodle. 'Now I have you I don't need them any more,' she
said."

"May say Miss Alice say she have them buried with her," intoned Mrs. Politi.

"I'm sure there's a precedent for it," agreed Miss Phyllis hurriedly. "There was a poet or someone . . ."

"That's right," agreed Mr. Crook, "I read about him in the papers. Only it wasn't letters, it was his original unpublished manuscript, and later, a lot later, when the wolf came baying at the door, he wanted to dig up the coffin and get the poems back. For the lolly," he explained. "I don't think they let him, though, and serve him right. All this shilly-shallying."

"I do hope I haven't pulled a boner, Aunt Phyl," said the young man anxiously. "Miss Forbes was here when I brought the wastepaper basket down and she looked a bit blue. Was I sure I'd torn them up very small, it wouldn't be nice to think of strangers reading them."

"Well," observed Mr. Crook heartily, "I've never been a dust collector, but it's news to me they'd have either the time or the inclination to piece together a lot of old letters . . ."

"You did quite right, my dear," said Miss Phyllis to her nephew. "For all we know, my dear sister has already established some form of contact with Percy, though, to tell you the truth, for many years now he has been more of an—an amorous ghost to her than a real person. I don't think she ever accepted the fact that if he were alive now he would be a man of about seventy. She remembers—remembered—him as he was when they were both young. And one of the tragic things about bereavement is the clearing up of the lost one's possessions. Alice and I never had the heart to destroy our dear father's lares and penates, as he liked to call them."

"Is that all his stuff down in the basement, Aunt Phyl? I took the rubbish, the torn papers, I mean, down there, Miss Forbes told me that's where they should go . . ."

"A lot of it is old stock, quite worthless now, I suppose, but there are his personal clothes there, too. We knew we should give them to a charity, he always had the best of everything, but somehow we couldn't feel he would agree—it's strange how some people don't seem to disappear just because you see them no more . . ." She conjured up a vision of the horrid old man lurching over a cloud, prepared to transfix his daughters with thunderbolts if they dared give away so much as a shirt he couldn't use any longer. "And by now, of course, they'll all be so outdated even the Salvation Army wouldn't take them."

"It was while I was down there I heard the shop door close," Jack continued. "Miss Forbes had told me about trying to muscle in on Polly, and seeing she wasn't around when I came back, I assumed she'd gone off. You did say," he added to his remaining aunt, "there was nothing more that she could do."

"Our exit line, I think," murmured Crook, getting to his feet. "You're sure she didn't phone or anything before she left?"

"Not that I heard, and I don't think she had the time. I just heard the door clang . . ."

"No voices?"

Jack looked surprised. "Unless she was talking to herself . . ."

"O.K.," said Crook. "How long does it take a dame to get her hair fiddle-faddled?" he added to Mrs. Politi when they were on the pavement.

"You ask me?" demanded Lilli scathingly. "I don't have to pay no man to do my hair. I brush, I pin—not more than ten minutes, say, maybe less. But that Polly . . ."

"Say an hour," suggested Mr. Crook peaceably. "And she'd get down twelve-thirty at latest. Should be pollydoodled all right by now."

When Mr. Polly saw his visitors he looked like a man perceiving the opposite of the Heavenly Vision.

"Mr. Crook?" he whispered, as though he feared all the elite of Churchford would pop their semi-dressed heads out of their cubicles and see the type of person now invading their privacy. "This—this is a surprise. I mean—I had heard you were involved in an accident last night, no details, mind you, but I did see your car, a striking machine, if I may say so, being—er—doctored at Warren's this morning. I left mine there for a small adjustment—not much of a mechanic myself," he added in the voice of one who puts art at the head of his list and manual dexterity nowhere.

"She's been havin' a face-lift, too," Crook agreed cheerfully. "Sorry if we gave you a shock. Did you think I was a ghost?"

Mr. Polly offered him a sickly smile. "I think you do know we don't have a gentlemen's salon," he whispered.

"Wouldn't find me in it if you did," Crook assured him ungallantly. "No, we've come to see if Miss Forbes is through."

"Miss Forbes?" Either the man was genuine or he'd have put Henry Irving in the shade. "But why should you suppose you would find her here?"

"Mainly because she left a message that she was on her way. Mean to say she never surfaced?"

"But she had no appointment, Mr. Crook, and Wednesday is a particularly heavy day, because of all the other establishments that close at one o'clock. We get positively swamped."

"She thought you might manage to fit her in."

"Dear me, that sounds remarkably unlike Miss Forbes. In any case, I can assure you . . ."

"Couldn't be that one of your staff . . ." hinted Mr. Crook, leaving the sentence unfinished.

Mr. Polly looked outraged, but he crept from one cubicle to another, putting the question.

"No one has seen her and there is no message," he announced on his return. "In any case, in the circumstances, poor Miss Robinson, though possibly a merciful release—she would not be thinking of personal beauty treatment at such a time, I do assure you."

"My, my, you're on the grapevine all right," commented Mr. Crook. "Nothing escapes you, does it? Me last night, Miss Alice today . . ."

"Perhaps that young man get it wrong," interposed Mrs. Politi, speaking in the sort of voice that once summoned Moses to the Mount of Sinai.

"Somebody got something wrong, that's for sure." Of

course, May might have told the young chap a tarradiddle to account for wherever she did propose to go, and wherever that was, he was willing to bet it wasn't doing Sugar any good. Obviously she knew something or thought she knew something or X believed she knew something, you could play the cards half a dozen ways. Crook was well aware that a number of people die every year, by violence or by stealth, because they possess information they don't know they've got or whose value they don't appreciate, and murderers, by and large, are a cowardly lot, sneaking up behind the unsuspecting and doing a bit of garroting (only nowadays it was more likely to be ka-rate) or pulling a gun on an unarmed man, if they could find him in or coax him to a sufficiently remote place, or even asking a neighbor to wet his whistle and lacing the drink with something that never came out of any honest bottle.

"Maybe the young man not listen," suggested Mrs. Politi.

"And maybe the moon's made of green cheese, though the lunanauts seem determined to prove otherwise. And how about the message you got? Come on, Sugar, we'll collect the Superb and go back to square one."

"You back again?" exclaimed Jack when the wanderers returned. "Aunt Phyl thought you might be Mr. Erskine."

"He bury you," explained Lilli, "like a beetle or a king, according to what you pay."

"You must have misunderstood Sugar," Crook told the young man. "She never went near Mr. Polly. And don't tell me he had her bundled away under a washbasin, because that's plain daft."

"I only told you what she told me," expostulated Jack. "Anyway, why should anyone want to do her harm? She was the most inoffensive creature living."

"She was the one who saw X in the wild wood," Crook reminded him.

"I thought the trouble was she didn't really see him."

"Could be X is afraid that when the police have given her another going-over she may remember something that 'ud point in his direction. And if you've already killed a lamb you may as well get picked up for killin' the sheep, too."

"So we are talking about sheep now, is it?" said Mrs. Politi.

"Skip it," Crook begged. He had the feeling of a man in a darkened room with the shutters fastened and bolted from the outside. Down in the street below vigorous life goes on, and the very chap you want may be standing on the step, but it don't matter a row of buttons to you if you can't see him.

Mrs. Politi intervened in a fine deep mannish voice that could have been heard a couple of streets away. "You talk and you talk like the Houses of Parliament and all this while no one looking for May."

"Where do you suggest we look?" Jack inquired. "We know she left the shop . . ."

"Well, not exactly," murmured Crook. "You heard the door clang. That's all you heard? No voice, no nuffin'?"

Jack thought. "That's all," he agreed.

"She might have been shutting the door after putting up the notice."

"But in that case . . ." Jack sounded as puzzled as he looked.

"She'd still be on the premises," concluded Crook.

"The toilet!" exclaimed Mrs. Politi suddenly. "Maybe she go to the toilet and the door stick."

"She's got a voice," objected Crook.

"Then maybe she faint." She darted away to investigate.

Hearing voices, Miss Phyllis reappeared. If anyone was going to faint she looked the chief candidate. Her one-time rosy face had a crumpled look, as though someone had taken a piece of pale brown paper and scrumpled it up and half-heartedly smoothed it out again.

Jack hastily pushed a chair in her direction. "You look absolutely tuckered up, Aunt Phyl. How about me putting the kettle on?"

Mrs. Politi came back, her big hands spread.

"No soap?" murmured Crook.

"Where is she, if she didn't go?" Jack demanded. "When I came back from putting out the debris the shop was empty, and she wasn't up with Aunt Phyl because I went straight up to see if there was anything I could do."

"You don't really think anything—terrible—can have happened to her?" whispered Miss Phyllis. "Losing dear Alice is bad enough, though not unexpected, but May is a tower of strength."

Mrs. Politi had her second brain wave. "Maybe she go down to the cellar, she slip on a stair . . ."

But Jack demurred. "She can't have done that, I'd have seen her. Besides, why should she want to go down to the cellar. It's like going into a world of ghosts," he added candidly. "All those overcoats hanging on hooks—were they my grandfather's? The sort they called redingotes?"

"It was fashionable at one time for gentlemen to wear their coats very long," Miss Phyllis explained.

"So perhaps you think May play a trick, she hide in an overcoat."

Mr. Crook didn't seem to have heard. "Whatever it was she knew, it made her suddenly dangerous," he said. And he had a vision of himself saying to the Stephensons, mother and son, "Blotting me out wouldn't do the trick" (or words to that effect), "because there'd still be Miss Forbes." He wandered over to the door, where the notice was still displayed. "She put this up when she'd written it . . ."

"I wrote it," murmured Jack.

"And gave it to her. And you think you saw Willy Stephenson's car go by. Then you went down the stairs and while you were there you heard the door close, but not anyone come in or any voices. It don't make sense."

"Unless, when she saw Willy, it went through her mind that he could have been the one in the wood that night."

"So she went out, complete with bag and brolly, to accuse him?"

"She might have gone to the police," Miss Phyllis said.

"Jack dear, we shall have to put up another notice to say that my dear sister has passed away. And add something about no inquiries either at the door or by telephone."

"Well, so she might," agreed Crook, answering Miss Phyllis's unexpected supposition. "We shall look the greatest if that's where she is all this time and we've got our thoughts on Murder Mile."

"Here, hold on," exclaimed Jack. "You're alarming Aunt Phyl."

"No harm giving them a word," Crook went on, taking no notice of the interruption. "They might have caught a glimpse of Coppernob, too. Anyone know if he has any sort of record?"

But, like Pilate, he didn't wait for an answer.

"I wonder what he is saying to the coppers," speculated Jack, who was carefully printing out the fresh notice. The original one had been in ordinary longhand, but it had been written in a hurry; perhaps, he thought, death commanded the utmost respect. He looked hopefully at the door through which Crook had passed, leaving it slightly ajar. The telephone was in a narrow passage behind the shop, an old-fashioned instrument set on a table, with a plain wooden chair for the benefit of users.

To his surprise, Miss Phyllis rose and closed the door. "If Mr. Crook has something private to say to the police he would prefer us not to listen," she said. "In any case, eavesdropping . . ." She left the sentence unfinished.

Jack was unabashed. "I'd say that one was born with his ear to a keyhole."

"That man think he God," asserted Mrs. Politi. "Perhaps he tell the police to pick up Mr. Polly."

"But we know Miss Forbes didn't see Polly. She never turned up at the shop," protested Jack.

"That's what Mr. Polly say."

"I thought all the assistants agreed."

Mrs. Politi merely shrugged.

There was an uneasy silence until Crook came stamping back. "No, she didn't turn up at the station, and if she had I doubt they'd have rung Mrs. Politi to say she was spending the afternoon with me. So we're left with one solution." He looked at them expectantly.

"She take wings and fly into a tree?" offered Mrs. Politi scornfully.

"You don't think she legged it to the railway station and just ran off?" suggested Jack.

"Why should she?" inquired Miss Phyllis simply.

"A very good question," corroborated Crook.

"If she was being threatened," suggested Jack uncertainly.

Mrs. Politi intervened. "You think May run out on her friend in time of trouble?" she demanded.

"I know she never carried much money with her," Miss Phyllis added.

"Well, of course she ain't run out," said Crook. "Leopards don't change their spots this late in the day. Well, there seems only one answer, and that is that Sugar never left the premises."

"Well, but I heard the door," protested Jack.

"But you didn't see her go out. Which way did you leave the house yourself?"

"Well, through the private door, the side door."

"So if she'd still been in the shop . . ."

"If she was in the shop, why isn't she there still?"

"I was wondering," confessed Crook. "These letters you destroyed. She knew Miss Alice set a mort of value on them?"

"I only destroyed them at Aunt Alice's request."

"But maybe she thought the old lady might have second thoughts. Which day does your dust collector call?"

"Tomorrow," Miss Phyllis told him.

"So if she got the notion she might rescue a few of the letters and piece them together . . ."

"Isn't that a bit improbable?" murmured Jack.

"I think she may have done just that thing."

"Why didn't she stop me chucking them out, then?"

"She may not have thought of it right away. When did you say you gave her the notice to put on the door?"

"I brought down the basket of torn-up letters from Aunt Alice's room, and I wrote out the notice and gave it to her, and while she stuck it up I went downstairs."

"And meantime you'd seen Coppernob?"

"He flashed past. I recognized his sporting model—well, it would be hard to miss."

"So . . ." Crook took the newly printed notice and moved toward the door. "Sugar goes this way—you didn't actually see her put it up?"

"Well, no. I'd gone down to the basement. She told me where to dump the stuff, and while I was down there I heard the door shut."

Crook tore down the original notice and affixed the later one. He walked slowly back with the first slip in his hand. "She wouldn't be carrying the brolly and bag while she put up the notice, so she'd come back here, collect her things—you're dead sure you only heard a door close, no other sound at all."

"No," said Jack consideringly. "That was all."

"And you didn't look in the shop on the way back?"

"I went straight up to Aunt Phyl. Well, I thought Miss Forbes had gone."

"And when you left the house . . ."

"I went out by the private door," said Jack, anticipating Crook's question.

Mrs. Politi took a hand. "If May go down to the cellar, why she not leave by the back door?"

"The only reason I can think of is that she couldn't," Crook told her.

Miss Phyllis stood up rather shakily. "You mean, you think she may have gone down to the cellar, had an accident, and—but this is terrible, Mr. Crook. She may be lying there now, unconscious."

"Those steps are like a precipice," Jack agreed, looking anxious.

Mrs. Politi had already waddled over to the door that

cut off the cellar stairs from the ground floor of the shop. "This way?"

"But surely, wouldn't she have called out?" suggested Jack.

"Again, maybe she couldn't. I don't say she is there, but she ain't home, she ain't at Mr. Polly's, and nobody's seen her. When you've tried all the likely places you have to start looking in the unlikely ones. Now," to Jack. "Lead on, Macduff. Ladies stay upstairs," he added. "Yes," this to the protesting Lilli, "Miss Phyllis is waiting for a caller, and she don't want to wait alone. In times like these one member of your own sex for company is worth a dozen bumbling males."

11

They made a combined sortie for the head of the cellar stairs.

"Youth before beauty," said Crook, pushing the young man in front of him. "You're right about them being steep. Still, this way, if I fall, I'll have something soft to fall on." He motioned to the two women to remain at the head of the stairs.

Mrs. Politi started to call like some giant bird trying to attract her mate. "May! May! Why you play hide-and-seek."

"If Sugar had the use of her voice we should have heard it before now," was Crook's rather grim comment.

That cellar seemed an eerie place. Boxes of goods, years and years old, yellowing and probably all moldering within, Crook thought, were piled on shelves. There was a stone floor, but at this moment, at all events, no signs of even inferior life—rats, mice, beetles. From some nails in the wall hung the late Mr. Robinson's coats, three of them: a long dark speckled frieze with a velvet collar that suggested the era of Edward the Peacemaker; a green tweedy affair, though no one had ever suggested that its once-owner had been a sporting type; and a plain-faced black cloth—"Moth and rust do corrupt," said Crook oracularly. "What's wanted down here is a nice fire, with all the goods insured first." The floor was cold to the touch, yet the cellar seemed less icy than he'd have anticipated. Patches of damp showed on the walls. "What was that you said about a charnel atmosphere?" Crook inquired. The surroundings seemed singularly devoid of hiding places, unless, of course, some of the paving stones were loose.

"There was a story I read once," Crook told Jack, "about someone else missing, a little chap, this was, practically had the town crier out for him. Know where they found him eventually?"

"I'm sure you're going to tell me," said Jack.

"Hangin' on the hatstand under an outsized ulster, like it might be here." He twitched one from its hook. Not that one. He made the same experiment with the green tweed.

"Third time lucky," gibed Jack Hardy. "Honestly, Aunt Phyl, the chap's daft."

Miss Phyllis came down a couple of steps. "Are you saying—are you telling us—that May is *there?*"

"Well, no," acknowledged Crook, "she ain't. But she's been down here, that I do know, at least . . . Mrs. P, come down a minute, can you?" He was standing with his back to the area door. "Catch," said Crook, and he tossed something in her direction.

Lilli caught it neatly. "That May's handbag."

"That's what I thought. And I daresay this is May's umbrella. And where did I find them? Hanging under a gent's overcoat. And who put them there? Well, not Miss May Forbes. That's for sure." He turned to Jack.

"It all sounds very elaborate," Jack murmured. "How do you work it out? X comes by, sees the notice, Miss Forbes lets him in—she must have done. I come up the stairs and go right on to speak to Aunt Phyl, he—what does he do, Mr. Crook?"

"Well, he don't take her out for a nice spot of lunch," returned Crook grimly. "Where does that door lead to?" He pointed to the door in the whitewashed wall.

"Oh, that's where we kept the delivery cart, oh, thirty, forty years ago. And later on, our bicycles. No one's opened it for ages."

"I wouldn't be too sure," said Crook. "Who has the key?"

"There's a nail," offered Jack uncertainly. "Shouldn't it be there?"

"Oh no!" said Miss Phyllis. "I mean, it was at one time. Then some tramp came in by the back—we never quite knew how—and he—well, he camped down there—dossed, I think, is the right word. It was extraordinary that no one knew he was there, but it wasn't as though we came down to the cellar often. Then one day we heard the police were looking for an escaped convict, it was thought he'd been seen in the neighborhood, and Father said, 'If that man's in my cellar,' but of course it was meant to be a rather dreadful sort of joke. But the police came round and when we went down—it was clear that someone had been there, though we never knew if it was that man. It must have been very uncomfortable, there was no light once the door was shut. But we found a little old rusty brazier and a tin kettle and one ragged sock. I've always believed it was a tramp myself, it was terribly cold weather, and as soon as it warmed up—or perhaps it came to his ears somehow that the police were making a search. Anyway, he'd disappeared. Or—we had a woman to scrub and so forth in those days, and one of her sons got into trouble, it could even have been him, and she could have smuggled food in. But you were asking about the key. After that, Father locked the shed, that's what we called it, and kept the key in a drawer upstairs, and so far as I know it's there to this day. It's probably so rusty it wouldn't turn in the lock now."

"Let's try it, shall we?" said Crook, and his assistant, Bill Parsons, would have realized how strung up he was by the very quietness of his voice.

Miss Phyllis pushed past Lilli and hurried up the stairs. Crook stayed where he was. Lilli did likewise.

"It's a bit far-fetched, isn't it?" murmured Jack.

"He must have forgotten about the umbrella and bag or found them afterward and thought it would be pretty safe to leave them there. Any luck?" he called up the stairs to Miss Phyllis.

"It isn't here, and I've no recollection of moving it. But, of course, Alice—but we can't ask her. Or I may even have thrown it away, it was a big key, and I suppose I decided we'd never need it again . . ."

Something like the hissing of a mighty serpent filled the cellar. "You think May in there?" hissed Lilli Politi. "You get a locksmith—pronto."

"Oh, I don't think that'll be necessary," demurred Crook. "I think a certain chap may have got it in his pocket."

He stuck out an immense hand right under Jack's nose. "Give," he said. "Unless you want to go to quod in sections."

Jack stared. "Have you gone stark raving bonkers?"

"Maybe up till now, but not any more. Give me that key."

"I didn't even know there was a key," Jack protested.

"So you won't mind turning out your pockets. Come on, man, we haven't got all day."

"Aunt Phyl," exclaimed Jack, "this man's a raving maniac."

"You know what they say about madmen," said Miss Phyllis, and even Crook was shocked by the change in her voice. "They should be humored. Besides, it will save a lot of time . . ."

But she got no further. Mrs. Politi, moving with a speed of which even Crook wouldn't have believed her capable, hurtled from her position near the foot of the stairs and fell on the young man like a tidal wave. One hand caught him by the necktie, half choking him.

"You tell where May is," she hissed.

"He can hardly do that while you're throttling him," Mr. Crook pointed out.

He put two fingers in his mouth and emitted a whistle that might have been heard on the other side of the town. Heavy footsteps sounded outside, and someone pounded on the door. Jack made a gurgling sound.

"Hold him, Ma, but don't quite kill him, we're going

to need his evidence," implored Crook, tearing open the back door.

A uniformed bobby stood outside. "What's going on?" he demanded, just like any stage policeman.

"Don't they brief you before they push you out?" Crook demanded. "We've some reason to believe a missing lady—Miss Forbes to you—is incarcerated in the Black Hole of Churchford"—he indicated the locked door in the wall— "and equally we've reason to believe the key may be in this gentleman's pocket. All we're asking him to do is prove we're wrong by turning out said pockets."

"Do you know anything about the key, sir?" said the constable to the red-faced and disheveled Jack Hardy.

"Of course I don't," gasped Jack. "If only they'd listen —I told them I didn't even know the door had a key."

"Then, just to save time, you won't mind obliging this gentleman by showing us the contents of your pockets."

"Mind you," put in Crook, "it don't have to be in his pocket. He could have slid it down the back of his neck. A good-sized key, would you say?" he added, turning to Miss Phyllis.

But before she could answer, the volatile Mrs. Politi had taken matters into her own hands. She had little respect for men at any time, and even less when they wore a uniform, and now she created a diversion by banging the wretched young man's head against the wall.

"Here, you can't do that," cried the constable, jumping forward.

Quick as lightning Lilli thrust her hand first into one pocket, then into the other.

"By the living God," said Crook in a soft, reverent tone, "she's got it." He held up the key. "This right?" he asked Miss Phyllis.

But Miss Phyllis seemed to be beyond speech.

Silence gives consent, they say, so Crook shoved the key into the lock of the shed door.

"It'll be rusty after all these years," whispered Miss

Phyllis, finding her voice, or at least some semblance of it. It sounded as rusty as she claimed the key would be.

"And keep your hands off that chap, Ma," Crook added over his shoulder. "If he's going to be knocked about, let the law do it. It's what we pay 'em for."

"Will it open?" whispered Miss Phyllis again, in that thread of a voice.

"You'd be surprised," said Crook. He had fists like legs of mutton, but he could manipulate with a surprising delicacy even a key that looked as if it might have come out of one of the Grimms Brothers grimmer tales. After a moment's struggle the key turned, the door swung back, releasing a great wave of warm air. It was too warm, though. It had a suffocating effect.

"My God!" ejaculated Crook. "You don't believe in doing things by halves, do you?"

He dashed into the sealed-off apartment and came out, coughing a bit and carrying a lighted brazier in his hand.

"Years since I've known anyone use this method," he gasped. "Must be—oh, better part of thirty years ago—in Norfolk . . . Here"—he extended the brazier to the startled constable—"take care of this, and for the Lord's sake don't let Lady Macbeth get at it. She's quite capable of dousing the young man with the contents, and he don't give me the impression of being the martyr type."

The constable gingerly accepted the burning brazier, and Jack, seeing his opportunity, wrenched himself free and went flying up the back steps.

"You let him go," screamed Mrs. Politi.

"He won't get far," promised the constable. "We've got one of our men leaning on his car, and if he goes the other way, there's another officer at the Main Street junction."

Crook thought if Jack had any sense he'd be grateful for police protection. This harpy would like to see him torn limb from limb, and wouldn't object to initiating the exercise.

Lilli said something about bulls trying to catch eels, but no one was listening. Against the wall of the shed room leaned an ancient bone-shaker, stiff with rust, and behind the bone-shaker, flung down on the floor, partially concealed and looking like a bundle that should have been deposited outside for the garbage collector, was the missing woman. There was a strip of material over her mouth, her wrists were bound behind her back, her ankles were fettered.

"We want an ambulance," said Crook, not taking his eyes off the figure. "Not you, Miss Phyllis, they'll come quicker for the police. But first of all give me a hand with this. Where's that blasted brazier?"

The constable indicated he'd put it outside the area door, where it could do no harm.

"Except collect a pack of ghouls all hoping for a drop of blood," grumbled Crook. "Well, if any blood's being shed, let's hope it's theirs."

Together they bore the unconscious form into the cellar, where the door was left wide open. Crook had his arm under her shoulders. "Feel in my pocket," he said to Lilli. "Maybe a snifter would help her to come through."

"You want to make her drunk?" But Lilli was deft enough in withdrawing the flask and unscrewing the top.

"Are they building that ambulance?" Crook demanded of the policeman, who had reappeared. "Don't hover, man. Get some coffee."

"I think the lady . . ." the constable began, and when Crook looked up he was surprised to see Miss Phyllis coming rather shakily down the stairs, carrying a tray with a coffeepot and some cups on it. The constable moved forward to take it from her.

"I'm sure I've always heard that black coffee with plenty of sugar is what the doctor ordered," she said.

"Well, but Sugar ain't suffering from a hangover. Ambulance coming?" he demanded again.

The constable thanked his stars men like Crook don't come in pairs. "On its way. How is she?" he added hastily to prevent further comment.

"She's breathing," said Crook, "and lucky at that. A lighted charcoal brazier in a cupboard, which is more or less what that place is, asphyxiates in a matter of hours. Don't ladies carry smelling salts or anything these days?"

To everyone's surprise, Miss Phyllis dashed at one of the yellowing packages and tore open the end. An instant later she had yanked out a pillow, its cover rotten with age, and with a minute pair of scissors that she apparently carried around her neck, she started to make a jagged hole in the ticking. Feathers began to float. Mrs. Politi, who seemed to read Miss Phyllis's mind, started to gather them up.

"Burnt feathers," said Miss Phyllis, piling them onto the enameled tray containing the coffee pot. "I know it's an old-fashioned remedy . . . Has anyone got a match? If not, I can get a spill from the brazier."

Crook thought they must look good enough for Grand Guignol. While Miss Phyllis started to wave the scorching feathers under May's nose—and if ever he'd come across a kill-or-cure remedy, decided Crook, this was it—someone pushed a cup of coffee into his hand.

"If that's for Sugar it's a waste of good coffee," said Crook sensibly. "If she can't take the real article—he indicated the flask whose contents she had rejected—"she won't be likely to take a substitute." He took a mouthful or two of the coffee himself. It was hot, strong and sweet. Very acceptable, he pronounced.

Now came sounds from without as an ambulance drew up, stared at in owlish or ghoulish fashion, take your choice, by the few passers-by who always seem to spring up from the paving stones or drop out of a tree whenever anything melodramatic's in the offing. Two young men in blue uniforms ran down the steps carrying a folding chair. Getting a stretcher up even half a dozen steep stairs would probably result in the unfortunate patient standing on her head. They stopped for an instant, though they'd have told you they were immune from the quality of surprise.

Mrs. Politi had dropped on her knees beside her friend, and was breathing at her. "May, you not die, you not *dare*," she proclaimed fiercely.

"Lady isn't conscious," said one of the ambulance men, but, "By golly, you've done the trick," ejaculated Mr. Crook. For May had sleepily opened her eyes. She looked about as sane as a March hare. Her gaze moved from Lilli to Mr. Crook. It was obvious she was trying to focus. She opened her mouth. Crook made a sign to the ambulance attendants and they waited meekly.

"He told me," she said in a voice like a wandering wind. "Only I didn't get the message." Her lids drooped again over her eyes.

"She's all yours," said Crook.

Lilli followed the men up the steps, puffing like a great black porpoise. She made it clear that she intended to accompany her friend to the hospital. "When May wake up," she insisted, "she want to see some woman's face that she know, not some man in a *uniform*."

"You a relative?" one of the men asked.

"That's right," interpolated Crook. "The kind that sticks closer than a brother. And it 'ud be a waste of breath tryin' to prove otherwise."

When Crook went back to the storeroom in the cellar he found Miss Phyllis seated on the bottom step, looking as though at any minute she might be the next candidate for a stretcher. It occurred to him they'd completely forgotten Miss Alice, who was missing all the bun-fight, as Crook would have put it, much as she'd missed it during her lifetime. But that was the way the system worked—nothing happens for weeks and weeks and then everything comes down like bombs from a raiding plane, so that you hardly know if you're standing on your head or your heels. He put his hand tentatively against the side of the aluminum coffee pot. It was still warm, so he poured out a cup and fitted it into the stricken woman's hand.

Obediently Miss Phyllis lifted it to her lips. "I can't believe it, Mr. Crook," she said at last. "It would be dreadful whoever it was, but my own nephew!"

"I wouldn't be too sure of that," murmured Crook. And he added gently, "The object of the exercise is to get the coffee down your larynx, not dye your smicket."

Like an automaton Miss Phyllis straightened the cup.

"But he did it, Mr. Crook. The key was in his pocket, we all saw you take it out."

"Sure you did. Question is—whose pocket? Now, your nephew. Never set eyes on him till he turned up a few weeks back and announced he'd come to look after his dear aunties' affairs, and call on him, and no trouble too great, and he'd reap his reward? Right."

"Yes. Yes, I think so," agreed Miss Phyllis, looking rather dazed as well she might.

"Ever had any photos of him?"

"Not since he was a small boy. Mr. Crook, what are you trying to tell me? That Jack Hardy wasn't my nephew?"

"Well, of course Jack Hardy's your nephew," responded Crook. "Point is, was this chap Jack Hardy?"

"But—where would be the sense of him pretending. I mean, it's not as though we were rich people, and Jack, the real Jack, only gets on in quite a modest way, so we've always been given to understand."

"You can inherit other things besides money," Crook pointed out. "Like a name, f'r instance, that ain't on the police record. I begin to wonder if the Canadian police would recognize a picture of our Jack Hardy, only in that case they wouldn't know him under that name."

"But—he knew about us, things he couldn't have known if he hadn't been one of the family."

"Oh, come to that, you served him butter in a lordly dish, so to speak. Didn't you say your sister got him to read all the old family letters—and I daresay she added a comment or two. It wouldn't be difficult for him to play ball, and if he said he was your nephew and had all the right papers, why wouldn't you believe him?"

"But Jack—our real nephew—that is, if you are right, Mr. Crook . . ."

"Well, I don't think he'd have taken the chance of the genuine article turning up or even starting inquiries, knowing, you see, just where to look. No, I think he saw his chance . . ."

"You can't mean that he—killed—Jack?"

"I mean, I think Jack's joined the great majority, though we've no reason to suppose it was anything to do with your impostor. He might just have come upon the situation, and seen his opportunity and jumped for it. After all, that's the way most chaps become millionaires. And, like I said, it might have been convenient for him to swap identities."

"But, Mr. Crook, no one's ever suggested—I mean, this is just an idea . . . why should anyone suppose . . ."

"I rather think two people did," said Crook slowly, "and that's why one of them died and we don't know yet about the other, though if I had Mrs. Politi at my bedside I wouldn't dare hand in my checks, I know she'd be after me for the rest of eternity. Look," he went on quickly, "you don't want to stay down in this charnel house, and I daresay the police 'ull be back. Why don't we go upstairs and continue the conversation nice and cozy in that telephone room, say."

As Miss Phyllis came rather giddily to her feet she saw May's neat plastic handbag and umbrella on the steps. "We ought to take those up. It was a good idea, wasn't it, to hang them under one of my father's coats?"

"Better idea to have chucked into the black hole along with their owner," demurred Mr. Crook crudely. "He must have forgotten about them, and even he hadn't got the nerve to open the door again. Hullo!" His quick ear had caught a sound. "Someone calling?"

"It'll be Mr.—oh dear, I never can remember names nowadays—the man from the undertaker. I really don't think I can attend to those details before tomorrow."

"I'll push him off, shall I?" Mr. Crook suggested, helping her up the steep stairs.

But it wasn't the undertaker, after all, but a man from the plainclothes squad who produced his warrant and asked if Miss Robinson felt up to answering a few questions. He looked rather balefully at Crook, but Crook said he was representing the lady, and anyway, he might be able to help.

"If you have any information, Mr. Crook, you should have told us," said the plainclothes man forbiddingly.

"Give me a chance," pleaded Mr. Crook. "I can do a

lot of things—granted—but I can't be in two places at once. Miss Phyllis and me have only just worked it out . . ."

"Mr. Crook thinks the young man may have been an impostor," Miss Phyllis explained gently.

"I'm sure Mr. Crook has a good reason for saying so."

"Tell me something," said Crook. "When they got Sugar—Miss Forbes—to the hospital, had she got anything in her hand? It was clenched tight, and in the circs, I didn't think I should try and prise it open. But if there was anything, you'd know, wouldn't you?"

"What sort of thing did you have in mind?" asked the officer, who knew something about Crook and the manner in which he persuaded the other chap to give him information which he then proceeded to turn to his own use.

"I thought maybe you found some torn-up scraps of paper," said Crook, and saw at once that he'd registered a hit, a palpable hit.

"Very true, Mr. Crook. What gave you the idea?"

"What no one's asked yet is why Sugar was down in the cellar. Jack—we'd better go on calling him that, anything else would be so confusing—had taken down the rubbish, including a lot of letters he'd torn up, according to him because your sister asked him. But there could be another motive. You see, right up till midday today everything was sweetness and light. Sugar told me herself you said how much you both appreciated having a young chap around, beam of sunshine to the old lady and always ready to give a hand. And then suddenly—whoosh! Chaps who haven't come straight out of the bin generally have reason for trying to polish off a neighbor. And you know the answer, it's what that writing chap said: It is Fear, little Hunter, it is Fear."

Miss Phyllis was still toiling down in the shadows. "But why on earth should Jack be afraid of Miss Forbes?"

"Because she knew something he couldn't afford to have known. And she'd only just learnt it. And the only thing that could have given her a clue was the notice that young buckaroo gave her. Now look!" He put the notice he'd torn off the door on the table. "Recognize the handwriting? No? I didn't think you would."

"It isn't like the letters he sent us," faltered Miss Phyllis.

"And that's what Sugar noticed. And that's why she went down to the cellar. Because Master Jack had carefully destroyed all the letters, *including his own,* so if aspersions were cast, there'd be no proof."

"I don't believe I'd ever seen Jack's handwriting before—at least, the one we've been calling Jack," acknowledged Miss Phyllis slowly. "Naturally, he wouldn't write to me . . ."

"But maybe he wrote to Linda Myers, and she being pretty quick on the uptake, saw right off just what Miss Forbes saw."

"And that was the nature of her hold over him? Is that why—you mean, you think Jack Hardy killed her?"

"Well, I don't think it was Mr. Polly, any more than I think it was Mr. Polly put her in the family way. Well, there was nothing in that for Linda. I mean, she was a pretty girl, so they tell me, she wouldn't be likely to embark on an affair with a chap more than twice her age, who wouldn't be able to marry her in any case. And if Mr. Polly hasn't been able to give his wife a child, it's quite probable he couldn't give anyone else one either. No, I think she realized Master Jack's situation and played merry hell with him."

"And—was he the father of her child?"

"Well, if she wouldn't throw herself away on Polly, I doubt if she'd risk her all for a man she knew was a fake. I'd be inclined to hold Coppernob responsible, but that's something we'll never be able to prove. Anyway, Coppernob couldn't have been responsible for trying to put out Sugar's light, and me, I doubt if Master Jack ever saw him go past here. I was up at the house this morning, saw him and his lady-mother, and I don't think he'd be anxious to show his face hereabouts right away. No, Sugar saw the notice, realized the difference in the handwriting, and as soon as Hardy went upstairs she went down to the cellar to collect your nephew's signature from the torn papers. *And he heard her.*"

"He said he heard the shop door close."

"And that's all he heard. I asked him particularly, twice. But when that door shuts, a bell rings, it rings loud and long. And he never heard any bell, ergo, he never heard the door shut. So—it follows that, not being a witch or any power of darkness, she's still on the premises. She ain't on the shop floor, she ain't upstairs, so what's left to you but the cellar?"

"And he heard her go down—and guessed?"

"I don't say he guessed right away, but a chap with a guilty conscience is always on the *qui vive*. And he found her with bits of one of the letters in her hand. He must have known it was all up with him then. Linda was in it for what she could get, not just the money, because I daresay there wasn't much of that, but she liked the feeling of power. Look how she played poor Polly up. He wasn't a criminal, but she could have made things very awkward for him."

"I suppose you mean she'd found out about this woman he used to meet on Thursdays?" hazarded Miss Phyllis.

Crook's mouth fell open. "Well, you consume your own smoke," he exclaimed. "How long . . ."

"I knew he didn't spend every Thursday evening at the salon as he liked people to think. I go past there that evening—or did before dear Alice had her final attack—to my women's meetings—they're held on Thursdays—and I used to notice there was no light on the premises. And then one evening, just by chance, I caught sight of the pair of them. I don't mean I'd have recognized *her* again, but I saw enough to know it wasn't Mrs. Polly. Anyway, she has a standing engagement that night, too."

"I suppose I should have known," murmured Crook, reflecting it was always the mousy ones who gave you the biggest shocks. "And, of course, it's hard to see what choice Jack Hardy had, unless like the wandering Arabs he decided to melt away, and that didn't suit his book. Girls like Linda Myers nearly always make the same mistake—they push their luck too hard."

"So if Jack had only thought of *printing* the first notice he would have been in the clear," marveled Miss Phyllis.

"If ifs and ans," Crook quoted. "One of the smallest words in the language—if, I mean—and one of the most powerful. I take it Jack had the run of the house, he'd know where the key of the cellar door was."

"Well, he must have done, mustn't he? Or he may have opened the drawer one day when he was telephoning and asked May. Naturally, she'd tell him—why not? Oh, Mr. Crook, I do so blame myself for not throwing out that old brazier long ago."

"Maybe it's lucky for Sugar you didn't," Crook reassured her. "If he hadn't thought of that way of putting paid to her affairs, he might have been a bit rougher. Must have been a shock to him when he noticed the bag and brolly, because, like Mrs. Politi said, she'd have left the premises by the back way. I suppose he thought no one would think of looking for her there, and he could get rid of them in his own time. You hadn't made a will in his favor, I suppose?"

"Now that dear Alice has gone I should certainly have executed a fresh will myself, and he would have been the eventual beneficiary." Another point occurred to her. "That letter trying to throw the blame on Mr. Polly—or anyway, distract your attention, was that Jack, too?"

"Who else?" inquired Crook. "Sugar was havering with a customer, you were up in the sickroom, easy enough to shove an envelope through the flap and then come breezing in with his nosegay . . . I daresay you weren't the only one who realized that Linda had a string round Polly's neck. Like I say, he didn't have much choice. Once Sugar had uncovered his mystery, it was her or him. Five thousand pounds wouldn't have bought her off, even if he'd had it to offer."

"I see you've got it all worked out, Mr. Crook," said the police officer, feeling it was time for him to stick his oar in. "Right down to the paternity of the dead girl's baby."

"Well," acknowledged Crook, "I never met the young lady but from what I'd heard it seems highly unlikely she'd have cast herself away on a shopman—because that's how she regarded him."

"It's what he was," said Miss Phyllis simply. "He told

MR. CROOK LIFTS THE MASK

us he had a little store in Canada, and someone waiting for him."

"And you thought he meant a young lady, whereas it wouldn't surprise me to learn it was someone in uniform. Like I say, we'll never prove it now, but my guess would be Willy Stephenson."

"But she couldn't have expected to do herself any good if she *could* have got him to marry her," Miss Phyllis argued. "He hasn't any money of his own. And she'd be much too sharp not to know that."

"It never does to play hanky-panky with nature," Crook reminded her. "I don't think the baby was any part of the plan; like you said, if he can't provide for himself how's he going to carry a wife and child? But he was in a right jam once he knew—point is there's no proof he ever did know. According to him, he'd fought shy of her lately, since his golden bride came back from her cruise. Anyway, I don't think Sugar saw the Honorable Willy's car in the wood that night. She may not know a lot about cars, but she'd know a racing model from a jalopy. And it 'ud be a mighty small corpse could get into that boot."

"It's a very neat story, Mr. Crook," said the officer in a chilly tone. "It would help, of course, if there was some proof."

"You've got proof he tried to finish off Miss Forbes, ain't that enough to be going along with? I mean, he wouldn't do that just to break the monotony, he had to have some motive. And I wouldn't want you to think I was tryin' to muscle in all over your show, you'll get any credit that's goin' anyway. Feeling better?" he added solicitously, turning to Miss Phyllis.

"I shall be perfectly all right," said Miss Phyllis steadily. "And Mr. Erskine will be here at any minute. I know you'll understand I would prefer to see him alone, and I don't want any mention of what's just occurred until after I have made the arrangements with him. First things first," she added.

A moment later the front doorbell rang, a discreet note, as if it, too, wore mourning.

The way women could effect quick changes was always something that flummoxed Crook. It wasn't a quarter of
an hour since Miss Phyllis had sat on the bottom step, looking
more like a ghost than a woman, watching her closest friend
being rescued from the death pit. Since then she'd had one
shock after another. But as she moved toward the door she said
quite firmly, "I will not have 'Now the Laborer's Task Is O'er'
at the funeral. Even if it were true, and we have no reason to
suppose it is, it has such a—such a supine sound."

"How about 'Fight the Good Fight'?" suggested
Crook. "A nice rousing tune. I never had the honor to meet
Miss Alice, but if she's anything like her sister she'd appreciate
it."

"Dear Father!" said Miss Forbes regretfully.

She was sitting up in bed, with Mr. Crook on one side
and a police officer on the other. Of course, the authorities
would much rather he hadn't been there, but apart from the
difficulty of dislodging him, he'd laid so much of the foundation of their case they felt they owed him something, and in
any case Miss Forbes had said firmly, "I should like my lawyer
to be present."

"You're lucky Mrs. Politi hasn't taken it into her head
to come, too," Crook assured the police officer. "She'd gobble
up even that Dracula of a Sister in her stride."

"Dear Father!" repeated May. "He always said women
had no logical intelligence. They had knowledge of a sort, but
they didn't know how to make it—make it cohere. A sort of
mental intelligence arithmetic, he meant."

"I was never much of a hand at foreign lingos," admitted Mr. Crook frankly. "Can't you get your tongue round a
few words of plain English that Robert here and me can understand?"

"I mean, that young man gave me the clue and I was
so stupid I didn't notice. It was one day when we were talking
about nothing in particular, and he said I reminded him of his
mother, always on the go. You should have been born a
Greek, he said, or something like that. Then you'd have been

a marathon runner. But, Mr. Crook, she had a clubfoot. However insensitive you were, you'd never say a thing like that about a woman who was even a little crippled. And then, she died before he was ten, and his father married again, but he never mentioned a stepmother."

"Because he didn't know the real Jack Hardy had one," said Crook.

"And the day he brought the flowers, I said thank goodness he'd remembered her birthday, but I'm sure he thought I meant Miss Phyllis not Miss Alice. Only—I never put the pieces together. I daresay there were a lot of other small things that I don't recall, but until I saw the handwriting, that notice to go on the door—well, it was like a flash of light, because I actually saw him writing it, and I'd seen the real Jack Hardy's handwriting quite often, and this wasn't even a bad copy. Of course, I told myself I must be crazy, so when I thought he'd gone I slipped down to the cellar and opened the back door and pulled in the rubbish bin. Miss Phyllis has the plastic kind that anyone can lift, she says it's not fair to expect men who're as human as we are to carry those big dirty metal bins up the steps. But he must have seen me go down or heard me, because suddenly there he was and I had the papers in my hand.

" 'Looking for something?' he said, and I told him I wanted to find Percy's letters. I was sure Miss Alice never meant him to throw them away. And he laughed, because of course he could see the scraps I was holding hadn't been written by Percy. And—oh, I can scarcely think of him as a human being—and he said, 'Don't you remember what happened to Bluebeard's wife? The story has a moral, you know,' and suddenly I was sure he was the one I'd seen on the Common that night, the night I lost the little cat. And it was as if he read my mind. I mean, he knew what I was thinking."

"Did he say anything, miss?" asked the policeman, who after a reasonably good start now felt himself an Also Ran in the Execution Stakes.

"I don't think so; that is, I don't absolutely remember, only when you're quite sure of a thing yourself it's very difficult to realize other people don't know, which is why, I suppose, it needs so much practice to become a good liar. I was never any good, I couldn't even deceive Father, not in quite small ways which seemed a good idea at the time. I started to say something—to Jack Hardy, I mean—but his hand came over my mouth. 'We don't want to disturb Aunt Phyl, do we?' he said. 'She's got trouble enough.' And I remembered that's probably how Linda died. It was surprising what a big hand he seemed to have. I think he must have knocked me out or something. I don't remember too clearly, I think his arm came round my neck . . ."

"Best and quietest way to stop anyone talking," murmured Crook.

"I don't remember his gagging me," added May in a wondering tone, "but presently I found myself all tied up, most uncomfortable—like, like a tortoise or something—and everything was very hot. Stiflingly hot. Then I saw the brazier and I wondered why he should particularly want to keep me warm. I thought of the most absurd things, like those stories one used to read where you light a fuse or something and it's attached to a homemede bomb—I wasn't really myself."

"He counted on no one looking for you there," Crook commented grimly. "He had his story all pat. Must have had a bit of a shock when he found your bag and brolly in the shop —he had to put 'em somewhere and even he seems to have been a bit delicate about opening that door again, or maybe he was afraid the draught would put the fire out. Anyway, he hid them very nice and thoughtful, and seeing no one goes to the cellar except to put the rubbish through the back door, no reason why they should be found either. A case of the little toy dog is covered with rust—my Mum used to recite that at chapel reunions, not a dry eye in the place, and she wasn't what you might call a sentimental dame."

"I suppose he was the one who telephoned Mrs. Politi, pretending to be you. What luck you should have come looking for me."

"All things work together for them as follows the right," intoned Crook rapidly. "You look as if you could do with a good meal, Sugar, and as soon as you're out on your owney-oh again, that's what you're going to have."

"But," persisted May, "if he wasn't—isn't—Jack Hardy, who is he?"

But Crook said let patience have her perfect work and they were waiting for information from overseas.

12

The Canadian police proved extremely helpful. They identified the fingerprints of the man who had been passing himself as Jack Hardy as a certain George Jardine, also known as Harrison, Blunt and Ocher. Jardine was wanted for grievous bodily harm, having attacked and seriously injured an old woman. They had traced his trail to a motel beside a lake, where the proprietor recognized his photograph. He had come for a night, saying his car had broken down and he had left it at a nearby garage. The records showed that a man called J. Hardy had also stayed there that evening. Hardy had told the man in charge that he was flying to England to see some relatives in connection with a pressing family business matter. The two men had gone off together the following morning. Subsequently, some clothes, together with a wallet and pocketbook marked George Jardine, were found on the beach. Of the owner there was no sign, nor was there any trace of his companion. The police were satisfied that Jardine had stayed at the motel that night, and presumed that he had gone bathing and been caught by a cramp and been drowned. The body was never recovered, the lake being very deep in parts, and there was strong reason to suppose it had eventually drifted seaward. In any case, by the time it had been recovered, it would probably be unrecognizable. According to the proprietor of the motel, the two men had been alike in height and of similar coloring. The only difference, he recalled, was that Hardy wore heavy-rimmed glasses.

"Hey!" said Crook when he heard that. "Any mention of glasses being found with the rest of the gear—the passport, the wallet and so forth—on the beach? Chaps don't normally go bathing in their specs."

But, of course, no such item had been included. "And for why?" said Crook. "Because Mr. Murdering Jardine needed them to put one over on the Customs officials when he presented himself at their shed. Oh, it was taking a chance, but he'd reached the stage where one chance more or less wasn't going to matter so much, and it's my experience that these wallahs" (he meant the Customs officials, passport section, as his audience appreciated) "don't look for differences, only the things that tally, and if they see a chap of approximately the right height and coloring and wearing glasses—besides, these passport photographers have genius on their side, they have really. Make the Fat Boy of Peckham, whoever he may have been when he was at home, look like he'd just escaped from a concentration camp."

"So what did you do with the real Jack Hardy?" the authorities demanded grimly of his stand-in. "And don't tell us you never set eyes on him because we can fly witnesses over if we have to."

Though it looked as if the Canadian government was claiming him, too, in respect of the old woman he'd banged up and who'd been tactless enough to die three days later.

"The stupid fool!" exploded Jardine. He didn't pretend to regret this victim. "If she hadn't created such a shindy she wouldn't have got hurt. At that age what use were a few rings and a necklace to her?"

His story, tricked up for the authorities, was that he and the real Jack Hardy had left the motel together and had decided to stop off for a swim. Hardy, who was the confiding type that asks for trouble, had prattled about his plans, his old aunts, the shop, even showed him his air ticket.

"Seems silly to think my only living relatives are two

aunts I've never set eyes on," he'd said. The older of the pair had recently had a stroke, and the other one had written to him. There was a snug little business, from what he could understand, and he was going over to help keep the flag flying. He had added that you couldn't but admire the spirit of the two elderly women, and if he didn't go now, it might be too late.

"Fools like that ask for whatever they get," Jardine added. According to him, the suggestion about swimming had come from Hardy. The morning was warm, they had time in plenty—the ticket was for a night flight—and Hardy's car was to be picked up at the airport by a man to whom he'd sold it. He'd get himself another jalopy when he got back from England.

"Hardy was a lot more experienced in the water than I was," he acknowledged. "He went out so far I shouted after him was he trying to swim to England—then suddenly he seemed to disappear. I thought at first he was doing a bit of underwater swimming, but he never surfaced."

"So what did you do then?"

"What any man of sense would do. I couldn't call the police, and I couldn't report to the motel, and it seemed to me here was my chance. I could do nothing for the dead man, the old ladies were expecting him, I might take over where he left off and do a bit of good all round."

"You were so sure you could throw dust in their eyes?"

"Well, why not? They'd never set eyes on him. There were letters in his wallet. I reckoned I could play it by ear."

Anyway, leading gullible old women up the garden was his living. He'd call at the houses of solitary females, representing himself as a buyer of precious stones, and mostly he could talk his way inside and seldom came out empty-handed. The last old woman he'd visited had had more spirit than the rest, and a lot of good it had done her. He'd had to be a bit rough with her, but he insisted—and would insist with his last breath—that she'd only herself to blame.

"Once they've asked me inside, it's up to them to take the consequences," he said.

"You can't argue with men like that, Sugar," Crook was to tell May later. "They've got a sense lacking, like chaps that are born deaf or blind."

If he'd been satisfied with his original plan, Jardine might never have been identified. The Misses Robinson accepted him as the prophet accepted his meat from the Biblical raven. Nobody in England was interested in a chap called Jardine who'd socked an old lady a bit too enthusiastically; nobody in that country had ever set eyes on Jack Hardy; and, of course, if the elder sister died, the second might be persuaded to sell the business, which would help to line the pockets of the self-styled nephew.

"You were the fox in the roost," Crook assured May. "He hadn't allowed for you, and that's one thing he can't be blamed for."

"But Miss Phyllis is in very good health, all things considered," protested May. "He might have had to wait years, and in the meantime the law could have caught up with him."

"The trouble with second-rate sharpies, which is the way I'd describe him, is they don't know the meaning of patience. I don't want to chill your blood, Sugar, but if it had gone the way that chap planned, I fancy Miss Alice would have had a companion in her solitary grave a lot sooner than she anticipated. Now you can get all these pills and what-have-you on the National Health, it shouldn't be difficult for a chap who's got his heart, to say nothing of the financial interest, in the job, to do a bit of switching. You know the sort of thing—I've got a chronic head, give me my aspirin, there's a dear boy—and heaven knows, half these tablets are as alike to the layman as a pair of Siamese twins. Still," he added quickly, "that's just my surmise. Not bein' a criminal myself, and even the police have never tried to pin that label on me, I couldn't be expected to know precisely how they tick. Well, there it is, Sugar. Anything I've left out?"

May considered. "I don't think . . . I suppose he

bought the mask at a toy shop or somewhere. That and the balaclava—did you know, Mr. Crook, those helmets are called after the Battle of Balaclava? I should think they needed them there—those Russian trenches must have been icy."

"We didn't say no to them in the trenches in Flanders," Crook assured her. "One thing, we ain't ever likely to set eyes on *that* helmet or *that* mask again. Maybe he made that himself, the mask, I mean. He seems to have been quite useful with his hands—and I don't mean just Linda Myers," he elaborated quickly. "There was my car."

"You think Jack Hardy disabled her that night?"

"It had to be one of those three, and I was pretty sure that whichever one was responsible was the one who left Linda on Broomstick Common. Y'see, he'd be the only one who had any real reason for wanting me out of the picture. I never really thought it was Polly. I don't fancy that chap could mend a fuse, let alone fiddle with a car like the Superb, which left me with the two others."

"What made you choose Jack?"

"I didn't, not right off. My trouble was motive. Mind you, I didn't think in what's called our permissive age any chap in his senses would have to strangle a girl because he'd got her in the family way. All these societies and a waiting list for adoption—no, it had to be something more than that, and that's what I didn't know. Only Mr. Polly gave me a lead. If she was putting pressure on him, she might be putting it on one or both of the others."

"If it was Willy Stephenson's baby," offered May rather diffidently, "that could be a motive. I'm sure I've heard he's engaged to a very rich woman and he hasn't anything of his own; I don't think Linda could have thought he would marry her or that it would do her much good if he did . . ."

"And if she could prove the kid was his," added Mr. Crook. "She seems to have racketed around more than some-what—of course, in nine months' time it could be a different story, kids do have a way of taking after their dads . . . No, all I could do was wait for X to show his hand. Trouble in cases like these is you can't guarantee control of the situation.

I mean, he'd had a shot at Linda and that came off, he had a shot at me and that didn't, and the next in line of fire . . ."

"Was me," May whispered.

"I never thought of him trying anything on the premises," confessed Crook, in a voice she'd never heard before.

"It wasn't your fault," May assured him earnestly. "Even you can't expect to be in three places at the same time. And though, of course, it's awful, that poor girl, and poor Miss Phyllis, it's been a great shock to her coming at the same time as Miss Alice's death, I can't help feeling that when the dust's settled—I mean, Mr. Crook, it will be something to remember, won't it? Nothing so dramatic has ever happened to me before."

"That's the spirit," said Mr. Crook heartily. "Take it by and large, Sugar, you come out of this the best of the lot. I hope young Lochinvar's grateful."

"You mean Mr. Wayland? How dreadful of me, I'd quite forgotten about him. And I'm the one to be grateful. If it hadn't been for you . . ."

"And Mrs. Politi. By the way, any notion what Miss Phyllis is planning for the future?"

May looked surprised. "She'll carry on with the shop, of course, and I shall help her; that'll suit us both. You see, Mr. Crook, when you're getting on, and if you don't keep house for anyone, and don't work for your living, you must feel you're a charge on the community."

Crook looked at her with respectful admiration. "That's something you'll never have to worry about, Sugar," he said. "Now, don't let's have any more of who owes what to who. All this talk of debts would get an astronaut down. Open the newspaper and it's stocks down, exports down, credit down, value of the pound—let's not you and me add to the general gloom. You remember I said we'd have a nice cut off the joint together when you felt like it—well, no time like the present, so . . ."

"Oh, Mr. Crook," cried May, "you wouldn't mind if we made it a threesome, would you?"

"If you mean Miss Phyllis, she's got a date."

"Oh, I didn't mean her, I meant Lilli Politi."

215

Mr. Crook actually paled. "That woman! Honest, Sugar, she makes me shake in me number nines."

"Of course she doesn't," said May comfortably. "She may look a little fierce, but underneath she's the kindest creature."

"Too bad I wasn't born with a spade in my hand," mourned Crook, but he knew when he was defeated. May Forbes, he reflected, always assuming her description of Mrs. Politi was accurate, was just the reverse. Soft as butter on the surface and pure cement below. No wonder even a villain like George Jardine hadn't been able to dispose of her.

"I hope I'm always ready to learn," said Mr. Crook resignedly.

"You see," explained May eagerly, "it would be such *fun* for her, and she doesn't have a lot of fun these days. Hearing you tell it, I mean."

"You could tell it as good as me," pleaded Mr. Crook, aware that he was on a losing wicket.

"Oh, I expect I could," agreed May modestly, "only it would be more exciting for her coming from you. I mean, she can talk to me any time."

So they took Lilli with them.

As soon as he was released from durance vile Chris Wayland recovered his car and drove to Hornby. It was another Sunday morning and enough had happened in the interim to fill a book. He stopped outside the news agent's and went in. Jennifer was behind the counter as before. He looked around him in some surprise that everything should seem so unchanged.

"What can I get you?" Jennifer said, and he came back to earth.

"I called in to know if you were free to have dinner with me tonight," he told her. "I said I'd be back."

"You've got a long memory," said Jennifer.

"What else have I had to think about? I mean, Mr. Crook had matters in hand . . ."

The door behind the counter flashed open and Mrs. Hart appeared.

"You?" she exclaimed unbelievingly.

"I said I'd be back. I've come to invite your daughter out to dinner."

"And I don't care for her to go," retorted Mrs. Hart bluntly. "Girls who get mixed up with you find themselves murdered."

"Only one," demurred Chris.

"Isn't one enough?"

"Others get offers of marriage," pleaded Chris.

"Only one?" asked Jennifer demurely.

"Jenny," said her mother sharply, "we've got customers." Two men had come in and were waiting expectantly further down the counter.

"It's astonishing," Chris marveled. "You haven't changed a bit." Mrs. Hart might have been not only invisible but inaudible.

"In a week?"

"It seemed like a lifetime."

"You, too?"

"No sense waiting here, mate," said one of the men. "Lummy, some chaps seem to enjoy hard labor seven days a week."

"Should get on to the union about it," the other agreed.

"He's the one," exclaimed the first. "Just like his pictures."

Chris turned his head slightly. "If I'd had time I might have grown a beard."

"Could be the young lady doesn't fancy beards."

"What did you want?" snapped Mrs. Hart.

She came back from serving them in time to hear Chris say, "And I thought we might ask Mr. Crook to be our best man."

"Mother was saying only the other day she'd like to meet that man—weren't you, Mother?"

"It's quite an experience," Chris agreed. "Lucky, really, he's not the marrying kind. I wouldn't like to be cut out on my own wedding day. We ought to ask Miss Forbes, though . . ."

"Don't mind me," said Mrs. Hart icily.

So they didn't.